PINK PANTHER™

The Ultimate Guide to the Coolest Cat in Town

LONDON, NEW YORK, MUNICH,
MELBOURNE, AND DELHI

Senior Editor Alastair Dougall
Senior Designer Guy Harvey
Designers Jill Bunyan, Anne Sharples
Design Assistant Mika Kean-Hammerson
Publisher Alexandra Allan
Art Director Mark Richards
Production Claire Pearson
DTP Designer Lauren Egan

First American Edition, 2005

05 06 07 10 9 8 7 6 5 4 3 2 1

Published in the United States by DK Publishing, Inc.
375 Hudson Street, New York, New York 10014

2240063

ISBN 0-7566-1033-8

A catalog record is available from the Library of Congress

DK Publishing, Inc. offers special discounts for bulk purchases for sales promotions or premiums.
Specific, large-quantity needs can be met with special editions, including personalized covers, excerpts
of existing guides, and corporate imprints. For more information, contact Special Markets Department,
DK Publishing, Inc., 375 Hudson Street, New York, NY 10014 Fax: 800-600-9098.

Published in Great Britain by Dorling Kindersley Limited.

Color reproduction by Media Development and printing Ltd., UK
Printed and bound in China by Leo Paper Products

www.pinkpanther.com.

discover more at
www.dk.com

PINK PANTHER™

The Ultimate Guide to the Coolest Cat in Town

by Jerry Beck

DK

CONTENTS

FOREWORD by Blake Edwards

THE PINK PANTHER PERSONIFIES STYLE AND ELEGANCE. He sees the world through a pink diamond with prismatic clarity and from many perspectives and since his debut in 1964, he has introduced all the Pink Panther films.

Serendipity has always found a way into my life and I learned to welcome the unexpected. Peter Ustinov was set to play the role of the Inspector, but he deserted the film just before we were to begin shooting. Ava Gardner was cast as Simone Clouseau, but she too jumped ship at the last minute. In the end Capucine and Sellers were brilliant together. And so the comedy of manners that preceded the filming, where actors and actresses came and went, set the scene for the unveiling of one of the most valuable jewels: a final cast so in sync that we were able to collaboratively fulfill my wildest notion. The film pulled together like a fairytale should. Its larger-than-life characters and budding talent drove the picture through creation and imbued it with a sense of improvisation and polish.

Just as production got underway, I asked DePatie-Freleng to create a Pink Panther, who would open the film with an animated sequence composed by Henry Mancini.

The music engages the audience from the first beat in the Pink Panther animated sequence to the last beat in the film. Music and art have been an inspiration in my personal life and my films. In comedy, timing a character's actions to music, or vice versa, is paramount. If music is the soul of movement, then art is the eye's guide.

By nature detective films involve the audience in unraveling a good mystery, but in the Pink Panther's debut film, there's no mystery except the density of Clouseau's mind as he earnestly sets out to discover the Phantom and his female accomplice…love is blind and our knight doth love too much. In the first film, it was all about removing Clouseau's mask and opening his eyes—the audience is in on the joke and enjoys an omniscient diamond-pink vision of the whole farce from the beginning, so my intention was to make the audience love a bumbling, naïve, buffoonish Inspector, one that they could simultaneously root for and warmheartedly laugh at.

Clouseau took on traits of an animated character. Peter Sellers was a master of improvisation and able to draw the character from the page in unexpected ways—the mutilation of the English language, the inevitable misunderstandings that followed. His cartoonishness allowed him to rebound quickly from explosions, midnight attacks by Cato and multiple assassination attempts. As Clouseau could rebound from all physical and mental traumas, Chief Inspector Dreyfus wasn't so fortunate. A perfect foil for Clouseau, Herbert Lom acted brilliantly opposite Sellers—two determined fools continually colliding with each other, yet moving in opposite directions.

There were bumps, "beumps", and more than a few bruises throughout the many years of filming the Panthers, but like our characters, I recovered, and in the words of Jacques Clouseau, famous world-renowned French Detective, "It wasn't easy."

Maybe not, but "It was worth it!"

Blake Edwards

INTRODUCTION by DAVID DEPATIE

IN ORDER TO CHRONICLE the creation of the Pink Panther character, we must first turn the clock back to 1963. My partner Friz Freleng and I had formed a new animation studio with the arresting name of DePatie-Freleng Ent. Inc. We were mainly subsisting on a diet of animated TV commercials and stewing over how to make next week's payroll, when one day the phone rang. On the other end of the line was producer-director Blake Edwards. I had previously met Blake through my association with his producer uncle, Owen Crump. Blake came right to the point—"Come over to my office, I want to talk to you." Over I went and Blake handed me a script with the curious title *The Pink Panther.* "Read it and get back to me," Blake said. I read it and thought to myself Blake has a real blockbuster here, loaded with great slapstick comedy, sex, suspense, and sophistication. On my return visit, Blake indicated to me that, although this was indeed to be a live-action movie, the script somehow conjured up the idea of an animated panther character. "Draw some examples of what a Pink Panther looks like and let me see them." I headed back to the studio and Friz and I summoned several of our best character designers together and presented them with the formidable task of solving the dilemma of what a Pink Panther looks like. In our opinion, the best models were drawn by our top layout artist Hawley Pratt. We made an appointment with Blake and took about 75 to 100 different Panther poses to his office. We set them out on the floor and Blake studied them carefully. He finally walked over to one of the drawings and decisively said, "This is it." And the Pink Panther character was born.

Blake went off to Italy to begin filming and the only use he made of the character was to adorn his production letterheads and business cards. Friz and I continued our television commercial making. At that point in time neither of us had any great expectations regarding the future of the Panther. Six months or so went by and then unexpectedly Blake called and requested a meeting. We hurried to his office where he told us, "The film is in post-production and I now know exactly what I want to do with the character—I want you to create an animated main title sequence with the Panther hamming it up with the various credits—it can run five or six minutes, if necessary. Back to the drawing board I went, with Friz and me collaborating with Blake and our head writer John Dunn and illustrator Arthur Leonardi on a proposed storyboard for the title. In the movie sequence prior to the main title, the camera moves in on the royal diamond and discovers a flaw which looks like "a leaping panther—a Pink Panther." To begin the title sequence, we decided to cross-dissolve from this panther to our animated version. It worked very well as a transition to introduce the Pink Panther character. We took the completed storyboard to Blake, who thought it was hilarious; however he had to get the approval of the production company, Mirisch Films. In those days, an animated title was somewhat of a novelty—the producer Saul Bass had used some animation for the titles for the movie *Around the World In Eighty Days,* but not the full character animation which we envisioned for *The Pink Panther.* Also, the process was going to be rather expensive. Well, Blake, Friz, and I went to a meeting with the three wise men—the Brothers Mirisch—Harold, Marvin, and Walter. After our presentation, the troika thought the project was great and approved the expenditure for its production on the spot.

Now we had to get serious and produce the piece. The animation process took us about two months. During this period, Blake wanted us to meet with

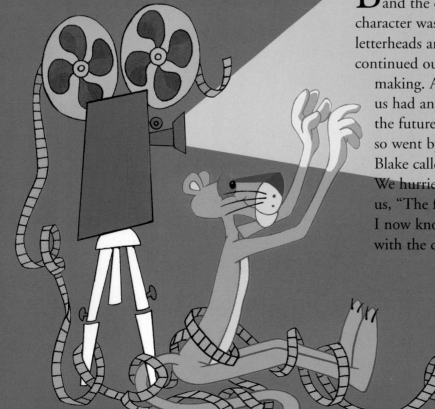

the film's composer, Henry Mancini, in order to coordinate our work with the music score for the main title. It turned out to be a most interesting meeting. Mancini, or "Hank", as he was known in the business, was used to scoring to a completed picture, while us animators needed a music track to animate to. Which came first—the chicken or the egg, or, in this case, the Panther or the egg? After some bickering Hank finally gave us a tempo to work with, namely: da da da, da da da da da da, and we were able to continue with our animation. It wasn't until Friz and I attended the scoring session for the title that I realized what a magnificent job Hank had done with "The Pink Panther Theme." It became one of his most famous and recognizable pieces. To this day, I give as much credit to Mancini for the success of The Pink Panther as I do to our own studio.

The moment of truth was fast approaching. A sneak preview of the film was scheduled for the village theater in Westwood Village, California. The memories of that night will remain with me forever. The projector started to roll and as the Panther first appeared there was a ripple of laughter from the audience which quickly became whistles and roars of approval as the Panther toyed with the various titles. At the conclusion of the main title the crowd went bananas.

The question now became: was there life for the character after the title. I thought so and immediately scheduled a meeting with Harold Mirisch. I asked Harold what he thought about our producing a five or six-minute theatrical short (in the 1960s the cartoon short, like the newsreel, was still very much in vogue with theater owners). Harold thought this was an excellent idea and agreed to present the proposition to United Artists. In my wildest imagination I could not have believed what happened next. Because UA was so pleased with the Panther—they thought that the title added as much as $1,500,000 to the film's gross—we were given an order to make 156 cartoon shorts, to be produced at the rate of one per month over the next several years. Also, the copyright ownership in the Pink Panther character belonged to our joint venture, Mirisch-Geoffrey-DePatie-Freleng. The first of the cartoons was entitled *The Pink Phink* and it won for Friz and me the Academy Award® for the Best Cartoon of 1964. The next four were *Pink Pajamas*, *We Give Pink Stamps*, *Dial "P" For Pink*, and *Sink Pink*, in which the Panther is denied entrance to Noah's Ark because there is only one of him. We decided, after an aborted attempt to give him a voice, to stick with the pantomime format (however in the 1990s we were persuaded to voice him due to the demands of a TV-syndicated series). Although pantomime is much more difficult to create because all the little nuances of action must be rendered in animation without the luxury of a voice track, we thought the Panther could sustain and he most certainly did. He went on to star in the main titles of six additional Panther movies and to Saturday morning network TV, where he enjoyed more than ten seasons on NBC and ABC. More recently, Panther cartoons have appeared on TCM and the Cartoon Network, as well as in syndication throughout the world. Merchandising has been a bonanza spearheaded by the license agreement with Owens Corning, where the Panther is the spokesperson for their product line. Presently, he is set to appear in the titles of the new MGM Pink Panther film, starring Steve Martin as Inspector Clouseau.

As we celebrated the 40th Anniversary of the Pink Panther in 2004, I realized that he has joined the ranks of the classic characters of all time. He has a place among the greats and he has earned it with distinction. To have been there, alongside my partner Friz Freleng, at his conception has been one of life's great blessings. I have tried to express my feelings herewith for our beloved character and it is my hope that after your have had the opportunity to read this book, you will gain a truer understanding of his history and of those people who have been instrumental in his creation. Think Pink.

David H. De Patie

**David H. DePatie
Sisters, Oregon
November, 2004**

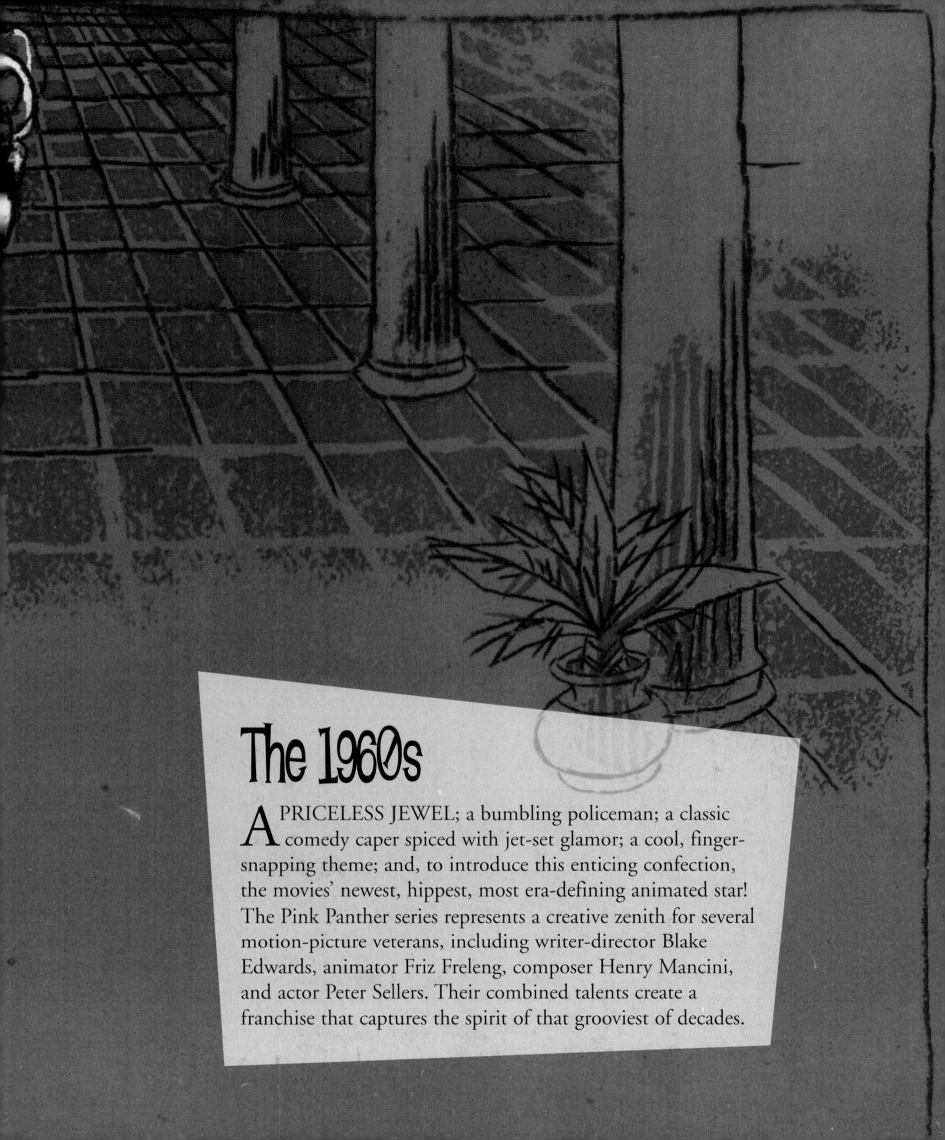

The 1960s

A PRICELESS JEWEL; a bumbling policeman; a classic comedy caper spiced with jet-set glamor; a cool, finger-snapping theme; and, to introduce this enticing confection, the movies' newest, hippest, most era-defining animated star! The Pink Panther series represents a creative zenith for several motion-picture veterans, including writer-director Blake Edwards, animator Friz Freleng, composer Henry Mancini, and actor Peter Sellers. Their combined talents create a franchise that captures the spirit of that grooviest of decades.

The earliest images of the Panther often showed him smoking, indicating the adult audience the character was originally conceived for.

INTO THE PINK

ONCE UPON A TIME, in 1962, Blake Edwards and Maurice Richlin wrote a screenplay called *The Pink Panther* and the Mirisch Company agreed to produce it. Ava Gardner was cast as Simone Clouseau and Peter Ustinov as her husband, Chief Inspector Jacques Clouseau.

Then things began to change. Gardner and Ustinov backed out of the film at the last moment, and it looked as though the film would have to be cancelled for the lack of a cast. Fortunately, Edwards was able to make a deal with the rising English star Peter Sellers and shooting began two days later. Edwards reunited with composer Henry Mancini, with whom he had worked on the successful TV series *Peter Gunn* and the smash hit romantic comedy *Breakfast at Tiffany's*.

Harold, Walter, and Marvin Mirisch formed the Mirisch Company in 1957 and gained a reputation for producing high-quality movies.

Born Pink

Roughly 100 designs for a "pink panther" were submitted by DePatie-Freleng to Blake Edwards, to select for the movie's main title sequence. This design, by Hawley Pratt, was chosen and a model sheet (above) showing the character in various poses was created for the animators to follow.

This classic image dates from 1965, by which time The Pink Panther had rocketed to superstardom.

David DePatie and Friz Freleng

In May 1963, Warner Bros. producer David DePatie and Oscar®-winning cartoon director Friz Freleng started a new animation studio to make commercials, movie titles and cartoons. A few months later, they received a phone call from Blake Edwards asking them to create a character to personify the title of a new film. The photo above shows, left to right, Pink Panther partners Friz Freleng, David DePatie, Harold Mirisch, and Blake Edwards.

David Niven

British actor David Niven was a rarity: a leading man who could play comedy and drama with equal skill. An Oscar® winner for *Separate Tables* (1958), Niven had starred in numerous movie classics, including *Wuthering Heights* (1939) and *Around the World in 80 Days* (1956). Cast in *The Pink Panther* as the debonair Sir Charles Litton—alias notorious jewel thief The Phantom—Niven brought instant international class to the production.

Peter Sellers

When Peter Ustinov pulled out of *The Pink Panther*, a frantic search for his replacement began. Peter Sellers was secured a week before filming began. Sellers had begun his career in BBC radio comedy with *The Goon Show* and moved into motion pictures with *The Ladykillers* (1955). His comic genius had flowered in *The Mouse That Roared* (1959) and *Lolita* (1962). Inspector Clouseau would become his most famous role, earning him a Golden Globe nomination.

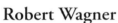

Robert Wagner

The Pink Panther's triumverate of male stars was completed by the casting of Robert Wagner as George Litton, Sir Charles' charmingly rakish nephew. Wagner had made his movie debut in 1950 with *The Happy Years*, and established his appeal with starring roles in such movies as *With a Song in My Heart* (1952) and *Prince Valiant* (1954).

Opening Night

Released on April 11 1964, *The Pink Panther* played its first run New York engagement at Radio City Music Hall. The movie won rave reviews and was a box-office smash. David Niven continued his sequence of successful films, Blake Edwards had another comedy hit, Peter Sellers created a classic character, and a cartoon star was born.

THE PINK PANTHER THEME

The COMPOSER, CONDUCTOR, and arranger Henry Mancini (1924-1994) was the musical heartbeat of the Pink Panther films. His sound helped bring the character to life, and make him the hippest cat on the screen. Mancini's jaunty theme is The Pink Panther's voice—at once sleek, sweet, and sophisticated.

Mancini often had a particular musician in mind when composing. For the final recording of "The Pink Panther Theme," he chose the tenor sax player Plas Johnson, who had exactly the cool, smoky style he wanted.

Of all the many accolades awarded Henry Mancini for his music, none were more prized by him than the approval of his colleagues and the enthusiastic appreciation of his audiences.

Movie Tunes

Nominated for 18 Academy Awards, and winner of four, Mancini scored many memorable films, including 1961's *Hatari* ("Baby Elephant Walk") and *Breakfast at Tiffany's* ("Moon River"), *Days of Wine and Roses* (1962), *Charade* (1963) *"10"* (1979), and *The Glass Menagerie* (1987). "The Pink Panther Theme" remains his most famous, instantly evoking the image of the cartoon character or of Inspector Clouseau.

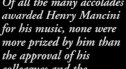

The Score

"The Pink Panther Theme" was originally written to underscore the stealthy actions of The Phantom, the suave jewel thief played by David Niven. "I had no idea what the little Pink Panther character would look like, until [DePatie and Freleng] showed me a cel, one frame, that they had done." Mancini then realized that his preliminary "tippy toe jewel thief" music would fit the character perfectly.

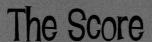

LSP-2795 STEREO

the **PINK PANTHER**

Music from the Film Score Composed and Conducted by **HENRY MANCINI**

BLAKE EDWARDS' **THE RETURN OF THE PINK PANTHER**
MUSIC COMPOSED AND CONDUCTED BY **HENRY MANCINI**

Original Motion Picture Soundtrack
PETER SELLERS in **THE PINK PANTHER STRIKES AGAIN**
Music Composed And Conducted By HENRY MANCINI
BLAKE EDWARDS
Includes the song "Come To Me" sung by TOM JONES Lyric by Don Black

ORIGINAL MOTION PICTURE SOUNDTRACK
REVENGE OF THE PINK PANTHER

TV Tunes

Mancini created memorable music for the small screen as well. He wrote scores for a number of television films including *The Thorn Birds* and *The Shadow Box,* as well as themes for the series *Peter Gunn, Mr. Lucky* (both for Blake Edwards), *Newhart, Remington Steele,* and *Hotel.*

For the Record

Henry Mancini received 72 Grammy nominations, and was honored with 20 Grammy Awards. Nine of those nominations were Panther related. "The Pink Panther Theme" won Best Instrumental Composition, Best Arrangement and Best Performance.

In 1984 Mancini conducted the National Philharmonic Orchestra in a successful collaboration with the flautist James Galway.

GALWAY MANCINI IN THE PINK

In 1978, Revenge of the Pink Panther *was Grammy nominated for Best Album of an Original Score Written for a Motion Picture.*

Pink, Plunk, Plink

In this 1966 cartoon, The Pink Panther battles The Little Man for the chance to conduct the Hollywood Bowl orchestra. The Panther wants to play "The Pink Panther Theme." In the end he gets his chance—and Mancini himself is shown, leading the applause.

RESERVED HENRY MANCINI

You only live once...so see the Pink Panther twice!!

THE MIRISCH COMPANY presents
A BLAKE EDWARDS PRODUCTION
DAVID NIVEN · PETER SELLERS
ROBERT WAGNER · CAPUCINE
and introducing
BRENDA DE BANZIE · COLIN GORDON · FRAN JEFFRIES
and also
CLAUDIA CARDINALE as the Princess

THE PINK PANTHER

TECHNICOLOR® TECHNIRAMA®
Released thru UNITED ARTISTS

Directed by
BLAKE EDWARDS · MAURICE RICHLIN and BLAKE EDWARDS · MARTIN JUROW · HENRY MANCINI

THE PINK PANTHER (1964)

THIS WAS THE MOVIE that introduced the world to The Pink Panther—both the fabulous jewel and the animated character, and to Inspector Jacques Clouseau, the unforgettably incompetent French detective. Combining "Swinging Sixties" elegance with frantic farce and slapstick, Peter Sellers and director Blake Edwards created a comedy classic.

Director Blake Edwards

Born in 1922, the son of an assistant director and production manager, and grandson of a famous director, G. Gordon Edwards, Blake Edwards broke into show business as an actor. He became a screenwriter and director, achieving successes with both comedy (*Breakfast at Tiffany's*, 1961) and drama (*Days of Wine and Roses*, 1962).

The original Pink Panther poster featured artwork by Jack Rickard of Mad *Magazine.*

The Pink Panther *set out to dazzle audiences with a new kind of jet-set sophistication.*

Edwards love of silent movie comedy influenced many sequences that combined action and laughs.

Yves St. Laurent's costume sketches confirmed his reputation as the hottest Paris fashion designer of the time.

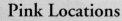

Pink Fashion

Yves St. Laurent created the screen wardrobe for Capucine and Claudia Cardinale. This was the designer's first Hollywood film project.

Pink Locations

Cortina in the Italian Alps was chosen for the skiing sequences. The resort was 650 miles north of Cinecittà Studios, where the movie's interior scenes were shot.

Movie Credits

DIRECTOR . . . Blake Edwards
PRODUCER . . . Martin Jurow
SCREENPLAY . . . Maurice Richlin and Blake Edwards
PHOTOGRAPHY . . . Philip H. Lathrop
FILM EDITOR . . . Ralph E. Winters
ART DIRECTOR . . . Fernando Carrère
MUSIC . . . Henry Mancini

CAST
David Niven . . . . Sir Charles Litton
Peter Sellers . . . . Inspector Jacques Clouseau
Robert Wagner . . . . George Litton
Capucine . . . . Simone Clouseau
Claudia Cardinale . . . . Princess Dala
Brenda De Banzie . . . . Angela Dunning
Fran Jeffries . . . . Greek 'cousin'

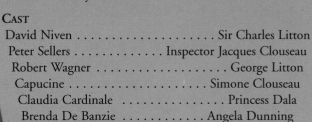

The Main Titles

"As in every stone of this size, there is a flaw. If you look deep into this stone you'll notice the tiniest discoloration. It resembles an animal. A leaping panther." "Yes, a pink panther!" With these lines, the main titles began and a cartoon star was born. DePatie-Freleng Enterprises created the unforgettable opening sequence with only Henry Mancini's theme music and Blake Edwards to guide them.

The sophisticated Pink Panther uses a diamond as a monocle.

The first appearance of The Inspector.

The minimalist backgrounds were inspired by the jewel's interior.

A pink ink line gives the character a softer feeling.

The Pink Panther paints his own name into the credits.

The Pink Panther's moment of glory is cut short.

The Pink Panther is only too happy to pose for the camera.

The Pink Panther tries to finagle a script credit.

Tricked by The Phantom's glove!

THE WORLD OF THE MOVIE

BLAKE EDWARDS filmed the story of Inspector Clouseau's pursuit of the mysterious jewel thief "The Phantom" from November 1962 through February 1963. Shooting took place in various Italian locations, including Rocca di Papa, a village dating back to 1181, and a ski lodge at Cortina D'Ampezzo in the Alps.

Little does Clouseau suspect that his glamorous wife Simone is a crucial member of The Phantom's gang. She is fond of Clouseau—but she loves Sir Charles.

"No matter. Once you've seen one Stradivarius you've seen them all."

The Plot

Inspector Jacques Clouseau, a bumbling police detective who can hardly move without smashing a vase, has been chasing a jewel thief known as "The Phantom" for 15 years. The trail leads to an Italian ski resort, where playboy Sir Charles Litton, his American nephew George, and Clouseau's beautiful wife conspire to relieve an Indian princess of a fabled treasure, The Pink Panther diamond.

Blake Edwards had the idea of creating a fabulous pink diamond. A close look reveals a flaw that resembles a leaping pink panther.

Alpine Paradise

A ski lodge in the millionaire's playground of Cortina made a suitably luxurious setting for much of the action. In the early 1960s, skiing holidays tended to be a preserve of the wealthy. Most cinemagoers could only have dreamed of emulating the champagne lifestyle depicted in the movie—adding to the movie's box-office appeal.

"At times like these I wish I were a simple peasant!"

Clouseau on the Case

Called away for police work, Inspector Clouseau must leave his wife in their hotel room alone—or so he thinks! Sir Charles joins her for a rendezvous; then his nephew George drops by. Clouseau returns unexpectedly, and a farcical game of hide and seek ensues as Sir Charles hides under the bed and George hides in the bathroom.

Under the bed, Sir Charles can do nothing as Simone tries to humor her husband, and get rid of George.

Three Men and a Lady

Simone does her best to keep track of her suitors: George hides in the shower, then the closet, and finally under the bed; Sir Charles goes from under the bed to out on the frozen terrace. Inspector Clouseau, despite some suspicions, ends up with his wife alone—and a surprise bottle of champagne, which pops its cork at the most inopportune moment!

The party scene required more than 100 extras.

George and Sir Charles both end up in gorilla suits, trying to outwit the other in pursuit of the Pink Panther gem.

Fancy Dress Ball

Angela Dunning (Brenda De Banzie), the hostess with the mostest, throws a masquerade party for Princess Dala and her fabulous jewel—a party that attracts the attention of Clouseau and The Phantom. Once The Phantom strikes, the fireworks begin (literally), and a wild car chase ensues with costumed characters zooming around a sleepy village square.

The Fall Guy

With the Littons in the dock, Clouseau takes the stand. The defense queries the lavish spending of Simone Clouseau, despite the Inspector's modest income. Clouseau, shame-faced, replies that her $10,000 mink and $30,000 wardrobe are the fruits of her frugal way with the housekeeping money!

Clouseau mops his fevered brow and his handkerchief snags on something in his pocket...The Pink Panther necklace! Could Clouseau himself be The Phantom?

Clouseau arrives back unexpectedly and his ever-resourceful wife Simone hides her admirer George in the bathtub.

The Pink Panther reappears to wave poor Clouseau off to jail.

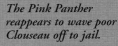

The Pink Phink's Oscar®

THE PINK PHINK

FRIZ FRELENG'S Academy Award®-winning cartoon, *The Pink Phink* (1964), was both a sequel to The Pink Panther's acclaimed main title appearance in *The Pink Panther* movie and the beginning of his new career as a cartoon superstar. A clever series of gags, a unique new visual style, and the establishment of The Little Man as his foil, secured The Pink Panther's place in animation history.

Cartoon Hero

The Pink Panther came across as an individualist making his own way, doing his own thing, and leaving his own mark—preferably pink—in an increasingly complex world. He quickly became an anti-establishment hero. United Artists spared no expense to promote the new series. Movie posters, newspaper advertising and special publicity worthy of a feature film were created to trumpet the arrival of the cartoons. The Pink Panther was ready to pounce!

Oscar® Winner

The Pink Phink won the Academy Award® for Best Animated Short Film of 1964. Competition came from Canada (Grant Munroe's *Christmas Cracker*) and Prague (*How To Avoid Friendship* and *Nudnick #2*, both directed by Gene Deitch). The win not only established The Pink Panther cartoons, but transformed DePatie-Freleng Enterprises into a major Hollywood player.

David DePatie (left) and Friz Freleng (right) after winning their Oscars® on April 5, 1965.

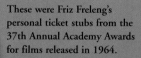

These were Friz Freleng's personal ticket stubs from the 37th Annual Academy Awards for films released in 1964.

Pratt and Dunn

Much of The Pink Panther's visual charm was devised by Hawley Pratt. Co-director Pratt was Freleng's lead character designer and art director. Pratt started working with Friz in 1944, and was instrumental in the success of Freleng's previous Oscar® winners with Bugs Bunny, Tweety, and Speedy Gonzales. Storyman John Dunn, a veteran story sketch artist from Disney and Warner Bros., had written gags for The Pink Panther feature titles and was familiar with Friz Freleng's comic style. The Panther's distinctive humor owes a great deal to his contributions—which included the punning cartoon titles.

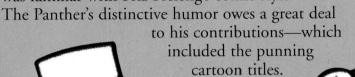

A 1990s collectors' cel which pays tribute to The Pink Panther's classic debut.

The Little Man

Also known as "Friz" among animators at DePatie-Freleng, The Little Man made a perfect fall guy for the Panther's pranks. At the end of *The Pink Phink*, the Panther moves into his new pink pad in a pink world—signalling the start of the duo's relationship.

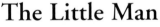

In Tom O'Loughlin's backgrounds, walls, doors, and stairs appear only when necessary; everything else is black line on white, to allow the pink and blue colors to read most effectively.

THE LITTLE MAN

IRRITATED, IMPATIENT and irate, The Little Man is the perfect all-purpose opponent for the cool Pink Panther. This pint-sized person's stubborn stand against the forces of all things pink guarantees some outrageous Pink Panther retaliation—and a whole lot of fun.

Prehistoric Man

The earliest historical guise of The Little Man is as a caveman in *Prehistoric Pink* (1968). In this cartoon, he and the Pink Panther are partners, vainly attempting to transport a large stone across the landscape.

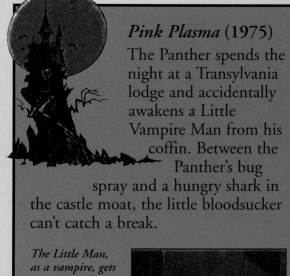

Pink Plasma (1975)

The Panther spends the night at a Transylvania lodge and accidentally awakens a Little Vampire Man from his coffin. Between the Panther's bug spray and a hungry shark in the castle moat, the little bloodsucker can't catch a break.

The Little Man, as a vampire, gets a surprise when the Panther pulls down the window shades, creating an instant sunrise.

The Little Man was known around the studio as "the Friz guy" because he was a caricature of Friz Freleng.

Pink Paints

Hawley Pratt designed The Little Man to be the Panther's exact opposite. The Panther is tall, the Man is squat; the Panther is cool, the Man is flustered; the Panther is solid pink, the Man is solid white. The solid color characters (Ant, Aardvark, Blue Racer, and Tijuana Toads) gave the 1960s-era DePatie-Freleng cartoons a distinctive look.

This original cel from Pink Streaker *(1975) shows the Panther giving The Little Man a helping hand to become a champion skier. But, typical of the Man, he gives the Panther the cold shoulder!*

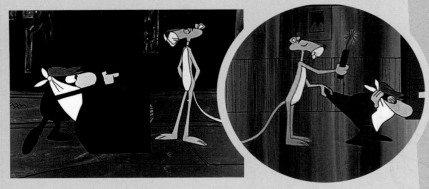

Dial "P" For Pink (1965)

The Little Man is a masked thief trying to crack open a safe. Unfortunately for him, the Panther himself is the contents! Our pink hero changes the locks, douses the dynamite, and ultimately tricks the bandit into stealing away with the unsafe safe—which blows up in his face!

Pink Adversary

The Panther never lets The Little Man stand in his way for long. The Panther has big ideas and a pink agenda—and he likes to mark out his territory in broad strokes.

A rootin'-tootin' Little Man story sketch by John Dunn for Little Beaux Pink *(1968).*

The Universal Man

Doctor, lawyer, Native American chief—The Little Man's occupation may change, the time may be the present or the distant past, but the face remains the same. Here's a rundown of some of his finest moments.

Laying Down the Law

The Little Man is a policeman in *Pink Of The Litter* (1967). He orders a certain pink litterbug to clean up the town, but soon regrets it!

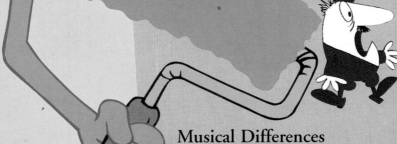

Army dramas: in G.I. Pink *(1968), The Little Man is an army sergeant who has to endure his worst nightmare— a pink private.*

Musical Differences

In *Pink, Plunk, Plink* (1966) the Little Orchestra Conductor confronts the Panther, who hijacks the concert to play his theme song. In the end, the Panther wins out—and is applauded by the theme's composer, Henry Mancini.

It's yellow flowers versus a pink bouquet in a war of the roses with The Little Man in Pink Posies *(1967).*

Crazy Stargazer

An astronomer, in *Twinkle, Twinkle, Little Pink* (1968), The Little Man finds a pink life form invading his space, and ends up in a mental ward!

Exit Stage Right

Mad at the Panther, The Little Man packs his bags in this original production drawing from *Gong With The Pink* (1971).

Trouble in Paradise

Even a desert island isn't Panther-proof! Like Robinson Crusoe, The Little Man enjoys a quiet life with his faithful dog in *Pink Paradise* (1967)—until a certain pink castaway is marooned on the same isle.

SO WHO IS THE PINK PANTHER?

Sometimes he's the person that we would like to be—cool, calm, and collected. At other times he's the average Joe we know we are—lovelorn, accident-prone, misunderstood, a bit of a dreamer. Overall he's someone we can *all* identify with—a character filled with good intentions and unique talents, personified as a pink pussycat.

Role Player

The Panther is an optimist and a dreamer who makes his dreams come true. In *Pink-A-Rella* (1969) he finds a magic wand and helps a poor girl become a princess. In *Genie With The Light Pink Fur* (1966) he takes over for a genie in a magic lamp, and tries his best to grant proper wishes. The Panther only wants to please—and he does so with ease.

The Pink Superhero
The Pink Panther sometimes imagines himself righting wrongs as a super-strong comic book hero.

Pink Dreams

The Pink Panther tries his hand at bodybuilding.

To achieve his dreams, the resourceful Pink Panther will take on various roles, don many disguises, or go undercover. But no matter how difficult the task seems to be, the Panther keeps supremely calm, cool, and confident. Whether disguised as a lamp or serving chop suey in a Chinese restaurant, he always uses his debonair, charismatic charms to best advantage.

Artistic Appreciation

The Pink Panther has an opinion whenever paint and a paintbrush are near. His pink color sense irritates The Little Man in *The Pink Phink* (1964), and his sign-painting skills are challenged in *Pink Punch* (1966), but his artistic choices make the Mona Lisa smile in *Pink Da Vinci* (1975).

Music Lover

The Pink Panther and music are synonymous and harmonious. When your theme is by Henry Mancini, you gotta like your jazz real cool. And that hep cat the Panther is at his coolest when he's playing a solo to astound that little square, The Little Man. The Pink Panther walks to the beat and plays from the heart. You dig?

In Pink, Plunk, Plink *(1966), the Panther makes music at the Hollywood Bowl, playing "The Pink Panther Theme" on violin—and rattling the nerves of The Little Man, who is trying to conduct a classical music concert. The Panther took the baton in the opening titles of* Son of the Pink Panther *(1993) leading jazz singer Bobby McFerrin in an a cappella version of "The Panther Theme."*

Animal Rescuer

In Pink Pranks *(1971) the Panther stops a seal hunter from doing his job.*

Being an animal himself, albeit a very special one, The Pink Panther is always keen to help less fortunate members of the animal kingdom. In *Bobolink Pink* (1975) he teaches a small bird to fly; in *Pink Elephant* (1975), he shares his room with a pachyderm; and in *Salmon Pink* (1975) he adopts a fish.

In Trail Of The Lonesome Pink *(1974), the Panther is crowned king of the forest after he defeats two hunters.*

Despite a reputation as a ladies' man and a swingin' bachelor, The Pink Panther is a hopeless romantic.

In and Out of Work

The Panther's jobs have included photographer, farmer, forest ranger, soldier, cook, secret agent and sports pro. When out of cash, he's been a stowaway, a castaway, and a hitch hiker.

The Pink Panther In Love

The 1981 TV special, *Pink At First Sight,* cast the Panther as an out of work, lovelorn messenger boy who imagines his dream girl everywhere he goes. He finally meets her in a park. She walks past a bench where he's sitting. She gives him a look. She drops her handkerchief. She wants to be his Valentine! The two hook up for a "happily ever after" ending, proving love conquers all—especially between Pink Panthers.

A SHOT IN THE DARK (1964)

THE SECOND Inspector Clouseau movie started out as a 1961 Broadway play by Harry Kurnitz that didn't feature Inspector Clouseau! When United Artists bought the rights, there were no plans to make it a sequel to *The Pink Panther*. However, transformed by the movie-making process, *A Shot in the Dark* would establish the Pink Panther franchise.

Film Credits

PRODUCER/DIRECTOR . . . Blake Edwards
SCREENPLAY . . . Blake Edwards and William Peter Blatty, based on the play *A Shot in the Dark* by Harry Kurnitz, adapted from the French play *L'Idiot* by Marcel Achard
MUSIC . . . Henry Mancini
PHOTOGRAPHY . . . Chris Challis, B.S.C.
FILM EDITOR . . . Bert Bates
PRODUCTION DESIGNER . . . Michael Stringer
CAST

Peter Sellers	Jacques Clouseau
Elke Sommer	Maria Gambrelli
George Sanders	Benjamin Ballon
Herbert Lom	Charles Dreyfus
Tracy Reed	Dominique Ballon
Graham Stark	Hercule Lajoy
Moira Redmond	Simone
Ann Lynn	Dudu
Burt Kwouk	Cato

The original poster made no mention of Inspector Clouseau or the Panther—but made much of Elke Sommer as the radiant, innocent Maria.

On Location

Several major scenes were played out in real Parisian settings, ranging from a splendid chateau to the bustling city streets. Both locations were, in their own ways, fascinating and exotic to audiences of the time.

Above: The Ballon mansion, the crime scene where much of the action unfolds.

Left: Consternation breaks out on the streets when passersby notice a mini containing a nude Maria and Clouseau.

An assassin waits for Clouseau and Maria—a Paris backstreet scene recreated in the studio.

Enter Clouseau

After the director Anton Litvak left the production due to illness, the Mirisch brothers asked Blake Edwards to take over. Edwards and Sellers agreed to transform the story into a comic vehicle for Inspector Clouseau.

The Main Titles

As a follow-up to *The Pink Panther*, Edwards commissioned the DePatie-Freleng studio to create another memorably humorous, animated opening credit sequence. This time, without the Panther for inspiration, they focused upon the Inspector's zany crime-fighting activities set to Henry Mancini's delicious mystery musical theme.

The Brothers Matzoriley, designed by John Dunn.

A "ransom note" lettering style was employed.

George Dunning directed the animated opening.

He later directed Yellow Submarine *(1968), starring The Beatles.*

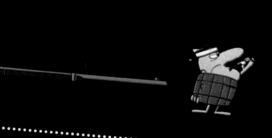

A brief moment of cartoon nakedness!

The nudist colony sequence inspired this portion of the titles.

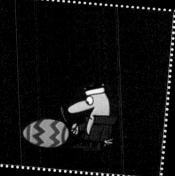

These animated titles suggested a series of Inspector cartoon shorts.

The Inspector was redesigned to look more like Clouseau in later animated appearances.

THE WORLD OF THE MOVIE

MANY OF THE TRADEMARKS of the Pink Panther series were established by *A Shot in the Dark*. Chief Inspector Dreyfus and his crazy Clouseau complex; Cato, Clouseau's long-suffering manservant; and Clouseau's love of eccentric disguises were all introduced here.

The bodies soon pile up—all incriminating the maid, Maria Gambrelli.

The Plot

Maria, a maid at the home of wealthy Benjamin Ballon, is accused of murder, but Inspector Clouseau, influenced by her beauty, is sure she is innocent. He has her released from prison in order to follow her. When they find a dead body at a nudist camp, the pair escape—nude—and their car gets stuck in a Paris traffic jam. People keep dying all around the pair and, in classic detective style, Clouseau finally gathers the Ballon household together to unmask the murderer. The lights go out, shots are fired, and the truth is revealed.

Maria Gambrelli

Beautiful German starlet Elke Sommer played Maria, after the part was turned down by established stars Sophia Loren (illness) and Romy Schneider (conflicting assignments). Elke Sommer brought great charm and comic flair to this key role.

Maria's beauty and wide-eyed air of innocence immediately wins Clouseau's susceptible heart.

"You'll find that it's great for curve shots!"

Hercule Lajoy

Clouseau's deadpan assistant Hercule was played by Graham Stark. A highly talented comic actor, Stark was a friend of Peter Sellers and had appeared with him on BBC radio's *The Goon Show*. Stark appeared in several Pink Panther films in various roles, including Prof. Auguste Balls in *Revenge of...* (1978) and *Son of...* (1993). He reprised the role of Hercule just once, in *Trail of...* (1982).

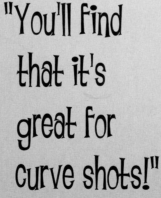

Disguised as a humble balloon seller, Clouseau waits outside the prison as Maria is released. What a wonderful, foolproof disguise!

Unfortunately, a nosy gendarme asks to see Clouseau's peddler's licence, and Clouseau hasn't got one!

Master of Disguise

To follow Maria Gambrelli effectively, the Inspector must blend in perfectly without arousing the slightest suspicion. Clouseau dons many disguises—balloon seller, artist, nudist camper—but always ends up under arrest.

Who can that be, under that hat, behind that beard? Could it be Clouseau, incognito as a street artist?

Unfortunately for the undercover maestro, Clouseau doesn't have an artist's licence either!

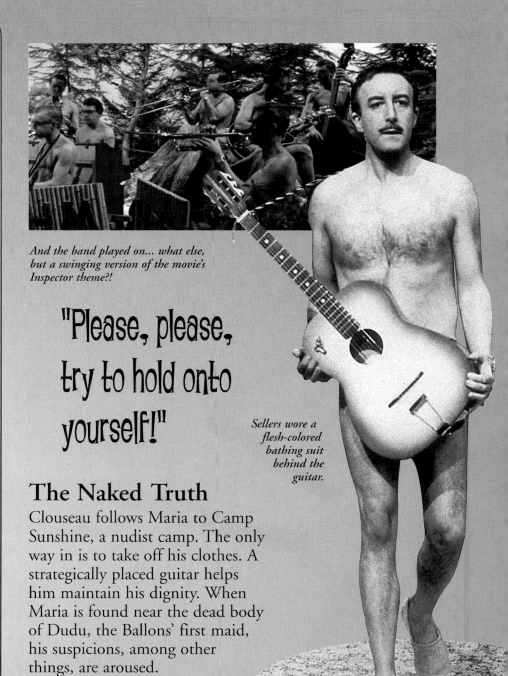

And the band played on... what else, but a swinging version of the movie's Inspector theme?!

"Please, please, try to hold onto yourself!"

Sellers wore a flesh-colored bathing suit behind the guitar.

The Naked Truth

Clouseau follows Maria to Camp Sunshine, a nudist camp. The only way in is to take off his clothes. A strategically placed guitar helps him maintain his dignity. When Maria is found near the dead body of Dudu, the Ballons' first maid, his suspicions, among other things, are aroused.

Shot at in the Dark

In the interest of the case, naturally, Clouseau takes Maria out for a romantic night on the town. The pair miraculously survive a series of mysterious assassination attempts.

Hercule counts down the seconds before throwing the main switch in the Ballons' house at the precise moment Clouseau claims to be about to reveal the killer's identity to the residents. Clouseau is sure the murderer will reveal himself in the chaos.

Explosive Finale

"One of you is a murderer!" Clouseau bluffs, having called together the Ballon household and demonstrated his unique repertoire of clumsiness. The lights go out. The guilty parties run for Clouseau's car—only to be blown up by a bomb meant for Clouseau!

ACTION SHOTS

CLOUSEAU'S FAITHFUL SERVANT, Cato, has two main jobs—to answer the Inspector's telephone and to attack him when he least expects it! As soon as Clouseau comes home, the workout begins. Cato will ambush his master anytime, anyplace, anywhere—and sometimes at the most inconvenient moments.

Fountain Fight

Hyaaah! The final shot in *A Shot in the Dark* belongs to Cato as he pounces on Clouseau and Maria as they leave the Ballon mansion. They all tumble into the fountain, splashing and kicking as they go under. Maria is soaked, Clouseau receives a watery workout and Cato gets the last laugh.

The director Blake Edwards employed a team of expert acrobatic stuntmen for rough and tumble scenes like this.

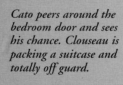

Cato peers around the bedroom door and sees his chance. Clouseau is packing a suitcase and totally off guard.

Clouseau is lost in thought—he has just been sent packing by Dreyfus!

Cato attacks, pushing Clouseau down into the suitcase he is packing. But the Inspector somehow wriggles free from Cato's grip, and the fun really begins...

Surprise, Surprise!

Acting on Clouseau's strict instructions to attack when least expected, Cato strikes from the shadows without warning. Bouts nearly always end suddenly with the ringing of the phone, in this case a call from police headquarters asking Clouseau to return to duty.

"Inspector Clouseau's residence."

Flying Visit

Suspecting Madame Ballon of murder, Clouseau trails her to a hotel apartment. He tells Hercule: "If I'm not down in ten minutes, call for reinforcements." Clouseau is down a few moments later—but not the way he intended.

Clouseau hears screams coming from inside the apartment.

He bursts in, just as a butler opens the door. An opera singer is giving a recital!

Cato's appearances are a "running gag" —a situation that recurs throughout the film with no ties to the basic plot.

Clouseau hurtles through the room, out the window, and into the moat.

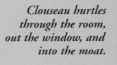

Clouseau, not above a little cheating to win, catches Cato with a surprise chop.

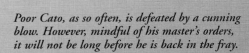

Poor Cato, as so often, is defeated by a cunning blow. However, mindful of his master's orders, it will not be long before he is back in the fray.

THE INSPECTOR

COOL, CALM, and calamitous, The Inspector is a police detective with a nose for clues, an eye for intrigue and a mind like a steel trap—one that won't open! Inspired by Peter Sellers' Inspector Clouseau and the animated titles from *A Shot in the Dark*, DePatie-Freleng launched this cartoon series as a companion to the Pink Panther theatrical shorts in 1966.

The Main Title

The opening titles featured a spyglass and an eyeball in the logo. The series also utilized Henry Mancini's stylish theme music from *A Shot in the Dark*.

"Don't say 'Si,' say 'Oui!'"

YOU'RE CHOKING ME, M'SIEUR!

The Inspector's habitually half-closed eyes reflect his peculiarly Gallic nonchalance.

Police Sketches

Writer John Dunn drew numerous storyboards (such as the one pictured above) to illustrate the comic capers of The Inspector and his sidekick Sergeant Deux-Deux. Gerry Chiniquy designed the final character models, employing non-symmetrical lines and angles. Adding to the series' special feel, background designer Tom Yakutis xeroxed layout drawings onto cels and placed them over color card—creating unique, stylish settings for the characters.

The Inspector

He is an expert in martial arts and has a genius for finding trouble. As voiced by comic actor Pat Harrington, The Inspector always remains relaxed and assured—even when confronting a villain's ticking time-bomb, facing The Commissioner's fiery wrath, or correcting Deux-Deux's latest boo-boo.

One leg is thick at the top, the other thin—designed to reflect The Inspector's offbeat personality.

The Office

Police headquarters, The Inspector's base, contains a gymnasium for practicing judo with Deux-Deux; The Inspector's costume collection and female disguise wardrobe; a science lab, mainly for mixing antidotes to Jekyll and Hyde potions; and a garage where The Inspector's latest police-car smash-up can be repaired.

Sergeant Deux-Deux

The Spanish-speaking French policeman, Sergeant Deux-Deux is The Inspector's crime-solving partner. He looks up to The Inspector as a mentor, a friend and a superior officer, and will follow him anywhere into danger—usually to pull him out of it.

Deux-Deux may seem dozy, but he is actually quite wise, and often comes up with a brilliant sleuthing solution.

Deux-Deux's look is based on a French gendarme's uniform.

The Inspector's frequent attempts to correct Deux-Deux's French—"Don't say 'Si,' say 'Oui' "—became a long-running gag of the series.

The Commissioner uses any tool to stamp out crime.

The Commissioner

The Commissioner is a tough crime fighter, keen to assign the best man to tackle each criminal case. He reserves the most bizarre, outrageous cases for The Inspector. The Commissioner's patience is thin, his manner brusque, and his presence is large—extra large. His gruff voice was originated by Larry Storch in the initial cartoons, and later provided by Paul Frees.

Ladies' Man

The Commissioner is hard on crime but he also has a softer side. In *That's No Lady—That's Notre Dame* (1966), The Inspector disguises himself as a woman to catch a purse-snatcher, but captures The Commissioner's heart instead.

The Commissioner confronts the toughest criminals without fear, but becomes a quivering jelly when his wife is around. She does a lot of the cooking and in the stories where the Inspector plays the dangerous parts.

Their Special Relationship

The Inspector and Sgt. Deux-Deux have a special bond. Wherever one goes, the other follows, with The Inspector always in charge. "I'll do the deducting, Deux-Deux!" The character of Deux-Deux was based on Inspector Clouseau's assistant Hercule in the movie *A Shot in the Dark*. The odd name came from another character in that film—a female murder victim named Dudu.

THE INSPECTOR'S CASEBOOK

In Sicque! Sicque! Sicque! (1966) Deux-Deux drinks a Jekyll and Hyde potion to cure an attack of hiccups.

MAD BOMBERS, jewel thieves, vampires, insurance salesmen... all manner of bizarre bad guys and their weird and wicked plans can be found within the pages of The Inspector's legendary casebook. The Inspector's hilarious adventures prove that crime may not pay—but it can make great material for comedy!

When The Inspector is on patrol, thieving chickens better beware!

Cock-A-Doodle Deux-Deux (1966)

The world's largest diamond, the Plymouth Rock, has been snatched. The jewel's owner, Madame Poule Bon, made her fortune in chicken plucking. All her servants are hens, so The Inspector goes undercover as a chicken.

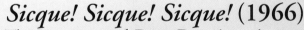

An original background painting of Madame Poule Bon's ballroom, the scene of the crime, in Cock-A-Doodle Deux- Deux.

Deux-Deux finds the diamond hidden in a chicken egg.

Deux-Deux gets an important lead.

The Inspector, that master of disguise, has a costume for every eventuality.

Sicque! Sicque! Sicque! (1966)

The Inspector and Deux-Deux investigate a mad scientist's house for evidence. In the course of their investigation Sgt. Deux-Deux drinks what he thinks is seltzer. The potion turns Deux-Deux into a monster who only wants to pound The Inspector.

Mild-mannered Sgt. Deux- Deux is transformed into a horrible Mr. Hyde.

The Inspector thinks he's safe in a room with the door nailed shut—but mere doors cannot keep out the raging creature that is Deux-Deux!

The Villains

The Inspector's rogues' gallery includes some spectacularly weird foes, including a near-invisible thief, a mad bomber, a multi-armed pickpocket, and a grinning trio of master criminals!

Case Notes

Plastered In Paris (1966)

Ordered to go after a man called "X," The Inspector and Deux-Deux chase the mystery man through the streets of Paris, the deserts of Egypt, the jungles of Nairobi, and up and down the snowy slopes of Kilimanjaro. "X" turns out to be the police department's new physical trainer!

The Blotch

Pronounced "The Bleutch" by The Inspector, this shadowy criminal can change shape from a splatter of paint, helping him to blend into any colored background. The Blotch usually targets the artistic treasures of Paris' famous Louvre Museum.

THE BLOTCH
FILE NO. 69961

Captain Clamity

The clammy pearl smuggler is so irritated by The Inspector and Deux-Deux in *Reaux, Reaux, Reaux Your Boat* (1966) that he breaks out in a shower of pearls: "They may be pearls to you, but they're ulcers to me!"

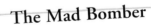

WANTED BY THE SURETE NATIONALE
Captain Clamity
notorious smuggler

Spider Pierre

Alias "The Pique Poquette of Paris," Spider Pierre uses his four arms to snatch people's wallets. Sgt. Deux-Deux finally apprehends him with a spray can of DDT.

The Mad Bomber

In *Napoleon Blown-Aparte* (1966), this maniac escapes prison to get revenge on The Commissioner. The Inspector, The Commissioner's bodyguard, literally makes The Bomber explode with laughter!

The Brothers Matzoriley

Weft, Wong, and White debuted in the titles for *A Shot in the Dark*, and starred in The Inspector's first cartoon—trying to steal the DeGaulle diamond in their Matzo-mobile!

INSPECTOR CLOUSEAU (1968)

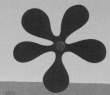

ON THE LOOSE in London, as clueless as ever, Clouseau bumbles into action, mystery, and romance. Alan Arkin brought a fresh sense of nonsense to the main role, but reaction was mixed. Clouseau, in the film, says it best: "There is a time for laughing and a time for not laughing—this is not one of them!"

Film Credits

DIRECTOR . . . Bud Yorkin
PRODUCER . . . Lewis J. Rachmil
SCREENPLAY . . . Frank Waldman and Tom Waldman
PHOTOGRAPHY . . . Arthur Ibbetson
FILM EDITOR . . . John Victor Smith
ART DIRECTOR . . . Norman Dorme
MUSIC . . . Ken Thorne

CAST

Alan Arkin	Jacques Clouseau
Frank Finlay	Supt. Weaver
Delia Boccardo	Lisa Morrel
Patrick Cargill	Sir Charles Braithwaite
Barry Foster	Addison Steele
Beryl Reid	Mrs. Weaver
Clive Francis	Clyde Hargreaves
Richard Pearson	Shockley
Michael Ripper	Frey

The crooks go behind bars—chocolate bars—in the climax of the film, as the stolen money is disguised, and shipped off as Swiss chocolate.

The Plot

A spy has infiltrated Scotland Yard. Only one man can be trusted to find him and prevent a new outrage by the gang who pulled off The Great Train Robbery: Inspector Clouseau, France's greatest detective! At the home of Superintendent Weaver, Clouseau finds an ally in sexy undercover Interpol agent Lisa, and also receives unwanted and persistent attention from Mrs. Weaver. The plot involves a gang of criminals, all wearing Clouseau masks, robbing the 13 largest Swiss banks—and framing the Inspector for the crime. The trail leads to a Swiss chocolate factory, where the loot is hidden in candy bar wrappers. The Inspector subsequently unmasks the crooked policeman behind the plot.

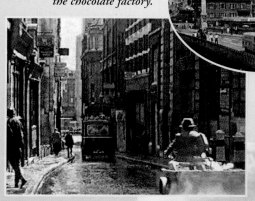

Riding a fishmonger's three-wheeler, Clouseau follows a lead in Paris (below). In Zurich (right), Clouseau's sweet tooth leads him to a crooked scheme at the chocolate factory.

Welcome to London: a shot of Big Ben opens the film as Clouseau disembarks at London airport in his socks, having left his shoes on the aircraft.

Groovy Time Trip

Location filming in three countries gave director Bud Yorkin an opportunity to have Clouseau bungle international law in two different time zones. *Inspector Clouseau* remains the only Pink Panther picture to have a genuine 1960s setting, with mini-skirted fashions and long hairstyles.

The Main Titles

Inspector Clouseau stars, without The Pink Panther, in titles created and designed by DePatie-Freleng Enterprises. John Coates' TVC studios in London, animated the sequence using the design of Clouseau from the popular Inspector short subjects.

Clouseau enters, the picture of vigilance, in front of a tricolor backdrop.

Despite Clouseau's watchfulness, the snatch is made... and the chase is on!　　*Clouseau grabs his gun and fires—but too late!*

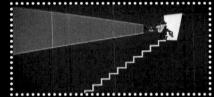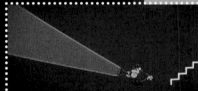

Clouseau follows the thief into a darkened basement—his flashlight beam picks out the first credits.

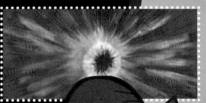

Hiding behind the name Clouseau, the thief hands the Inspector a "b-u-rmb"—with the inevitable result!

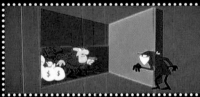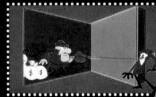

The next time the thief strikes, the Inspector is waiting, hiding inside the bank vault.

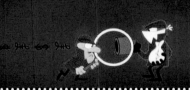

Clouseau's detective work leads him straight to the criminal!

The Clouseau versus Clouseau showdown hints at the movie's eventual denouement.

The Aardvark's voice was patterned after that of New York comedian Jackie Mason.

The Aardvark's solid blue color allowed him to stand out clearly against multi-colored backgrounds.

THE ANT AND THE AARDVARK

A HUNGRY BLUE Aardvark and a savvy red Ant matched wits in 17 classic cartoons that proved that the bigger and bluer they are, the harder they fall. Whenever it's time for The Aardvark to eat, the chase is on.

Mr. Blue

The Aardvark is so determined in his quest for an ant dinner that we never learn his real name. At various times, The Ant calls him Claude, Pal, Sam, Buddy, Daddy-O and Old Blue. The Aardvark just wants to have The Ant over for a meal.

Original Sketches

The success of the Pink Panther shorts allowed DePatie-Freleng to expand their universe with subsequent cartoon characters for United Artists. Friz Freleng directed the first cartoon—one of the last shorts he personally directed. Artist Corny Cole designed the characters and initial look of the cartoons.

Comedian, actor and impersonator John Byner performed all the voices featured in The ANT and the AARDVARK cartoon series.

The Aardvark's only clothes were a pair of blue shorts and a matching T-shirt.

Storyboard and Design

Storyman John Dunn kept the gags plentiful and fast-paced. But his initial concepts for the characters (left and on opposite page) were quite abstract. Animator and designer Corny Cole refined the look of both characters and their environment. He created landscapes and ant hills, usually placed over a color card streaked and smeared with paint.

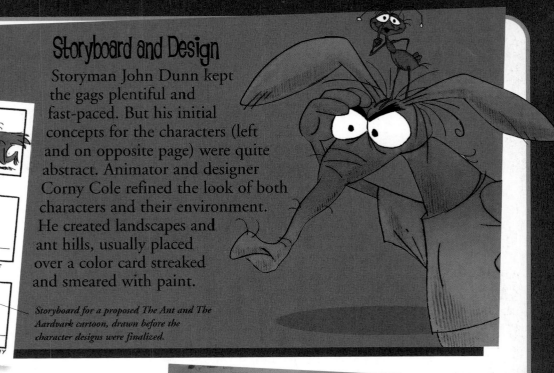

Storyboard for a proposed The Ant and The Aardvark cartoon, drawn before the character designs were finalized.

Paper Tear Titles

Art Leonardi was in charge of DePatie-Freleng's main title graphics. For *The ANT and the AARDVARK* series he expanded on a technique he introduced on 1964's *The Pink Phink*, tearing paper into the forms of objects and characters, to form unique and appropriate stylized images.

Aardvark Jazz

Musical director Doug Goodwin assembled a superb jazz group for *The ANT and the AARDVARK* series. Bassist Ray Brown, trumpeter Pete Candoli, pianist Jimmy Rowles, trombonist Billy Byers, drummer Shelly Manne, and guitarist Tommy Tedesco, all received on-screen credit—a first for animated cartoons—for the great theme music and lively musical cues.

"It takes over 200,000 ants just to make a decent sandwich, and I'm having trouble with just one, and the day's half over!"—The Aardvark.

The Ant has the half-closed eyes of a typical bon viveur.

The Ant was named "Charlie" in several cartoons.

The Ant

This little wise guy never lets The Aardvark's dinner plans interfere with his lifestyle. Sounding remarkably like suave singing star Dean Martin, he's got a cool attitude, a quick mind and a pair of fast legs. He also has the extraordinary strength of an ant, being able to lift 100,000 times his body weight—especially useful in getting Aardvarks off his back!

ROLAND & RATTFINK

GOOD GUY versus bad guy. Hero versus villain. Roland versus Rattfink. The eternal conflict between good and evil distilled to its purest form. Dashing, debonair Roland was beset by sneaky, malevolent Rattfink in 17 hilarious adventures with settings that criss-crossed the globe and spanned across time.

Hard-hitting pacifist Roland adopts a classic "teapot" pose.

As the proverbial good guy, Roland dresses in white.

In the Beginning

Hawks And Doves (1968) introduced peace-loving Roland of "Doveland" to hate-thriving Rattfink from "Hawkland" ("the only warmonger who ever drafted his mother"). John Dunn's stylish, innovative character designs helped sell the series to United Artists as a companion to the Pink Panther theatrical cartoons.

Roland

A peacenik, a flower child, a boy scout, Roland (voiced by Lennie Weinrib) is a well-meaning, jut-jawed, upstanding, all-around good guy. He is polite, yet firm—and when challenged, he readily takes on the fight against evil. Roland loves flowers and is dedicated to his mother, Mumsy (voiced by June Foray). He is the personification of pure goodness—he is everything that Rattfink hates most!

Cartoon Hero

Roland evokes heroic idols such as Tom Mix, Flash Gordon, and Jack Armstrong, the All-American Boy. He challenges Rattfink to war after the fiend shoots down a dove.

The end of Hawks And Doves *features a rare example of social commentary. Roland is taxed out of his reward money—which is handed to a destitute Rattfink as "rehabilitation aid for defeated nations."*

Hurts And Flowers (1969)

Everything that flower child Roland does—playing music, protest marching, picking flowers—is disturbed by evil "weed" Rattfink. Each time Roland thwarts one of Rattfink's schemes, he presents him with a flower.

Hippie flower child Roland later turns violent when Rattfink sprays his daisies with "hate gas."

The Roland And Rattfink cartoons were inspired by 1960s political activism and the peace movement against the war in Vietnam.

Sweet And Sourdough (1969)

Yukon Territory, 1897: bandit Rattfink robs the bank and Northwest Mounted Policeman Roland is on his trail—usually one step ahead of him. Pursuing him to his hideout, or up a tree, or across the border, Roland of the Mounties gets his man!

Accompanying dialogue appears beneath the relevant panels.

A present for Roland.

Storyboards

These original storyboards for the first *Roland And Rattfink* cartoon were created by storyman John Dunn. Storyboards are drawn out in sequential panels like a comic strip and explain the story visually. This board for *Hawks And Doves* includes intertitles explaining some of the action, in the manner of an old silent movie.

Black garb for the archetypal bad guy.

In Flying Feet (1969), chain-smoking Rattfink tries to outrun "that dirty clean-living so and so," Roland. He tries sled dogs, motorcycles, pogo sticks, catapults and rocket packs to beat his opponent in the Cross Country Race. Rattfink comes in last—as usual!

THE TIJUANA TOADS

*"Frijoles" is Spanish for "beans."

"Holy frijoles!"

TWO CRAZY CROAKERS from south of the border, El Toro and Pancho are forever on the lookout for fresh food and cool shelter. However, they spend most of their free time avoiding kooky cranes, fat cats, and hungry gators who'd *love* to have them for dinner. The Toads' antics kept everyone and everything hopping for 17 theatrical cartoons released between 1969 and 1972.

Pancho keeps his brains under his sombrero.

Pair Of Greenbacks (1969)

El Toro and Pancho test their friendship when they catch "La Cucaracha" and decide to share him at breakfast time. That night, each tries to have a cucharacha midnight snack and realizes the other cannot be trusted. At dawn, they find their cucharacha gone and beat themselves silly accusing each other. Says Pancho, "I think I'm gonna croak!"

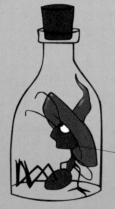

A Toad delicacy: La Cucaracha under glass.

El Toro

"The fastest tongue in the west," El Toro is the brains of the duo. Fat, pompous, always hungry, his schemes may backfire, but his muscular legs help him leap from danger and his muscular arms help him keep sidekick Pancho in his place. El Toro can flip a fly at 20 paces, lasso a locust in mid-flight, and grab a grasshopper before it leaves the ground.

Hole on the Range

The Toads' adventures often begin in a waterhole like this one, created by veteran background artist Richard H. Thomas.

Two tasty frog's legs.

This model sheet shows the proper way to make a Tijuana Toad hop. Skilled animation combined with comical voices (Tom Holland as Pancho, Don Diamond as El Toro) created two classic cartoon characters.

Pancho

Skinny, hungry, and slow, Pancho wants nothing more than peace, quiet, and a big fat insect to eat. He is a loyal amigo to El Toro, whom he looks up to as a brother, a partner, and a personal hero. Pancho remains devoted to his froggy friend, despite the occasional smack in the face or bang on the head. Says Pancho, "That El Toro is my best friend! He gives till it hurts!"

The Froggy Froggy Duo (1970)

Directed by Hawley Pratt, this cartoon finds the Tijuana Toads relaxing poolside at the Acapulco Hotel. The hotel cook, with orders to serve frog's legs, starts chasing the Toads around the resort. At the same time a notorious bandit checks in for some peace and quiet. But with the Toads in a wild chase, peace and quiet hasn't got a chance!

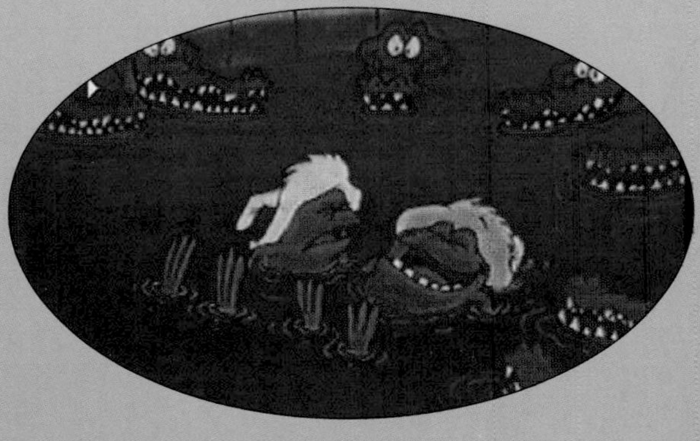

Never On Thirsty (1970)

During a drought, the Toads seek water anywhere they can find it. After cleverly distracting a vicious guard dog, the Toads make it into a private swimming pool—only to be joined by a half-dozen hungry alligators!

Fatso & Banjo?

When The Tijuana Toads came to television in 1976, as part of *The Pink Panther Laugh And A Half Hour And A Half Show*, they were rechristened "The Texas Toads" and given Texan accents. Their names were changed to "Fatso" (El Toro) and "Banjo" (Pancho), and the settings were altered accordingly. The good news: the characters were just as funny.

Panther Pink Panther

THINK OF ALL THE ANIMALS YOU'VE EVER HEARD ABOUT
LIKE RHINOC'RUSES AND TIGERS CATS AND MINK
THERE ARE LOTS OF FUNNY ANIMALS IN ALL THIS WORLD
BUT HAVE YOU EVER SEEN A PANTHER THAT IS PINK?

THINK!

A PANTHER THAT IS POSITIVELY PINK,

WELL HERE HE IS, THE PINK PANTHER,
THE RINKY-DINK PANTHER,
ISN'T HE A PANTHER EVER SO PINK?

HE REALLY IS A GROOVY CAT,
AND WHAT A GENTLEMAN, A SCHOLAR, WHAT AN ACROBAT !

HE'S IN THE PINK - THE PINK PANTHER
THE RINKY-DINK PANTHER,
AND IT'S AS PLAIN AS YOUR NOSE,
THAT HE'S THE ONE AND ONLY, TRULY ORIGINAL,
PANTHER-PINK (PANTHER) FROM HEAD TO TOE!

Lyrics © 2005 Warner/Chappell Music

The show's title song "Panther Pink Panther" by Doug Goodwin (lyrics above) was heard over the opening titles on the first season of The Pink Panther Show. The title sequence also featured shots of the custom Toranado-powered Pink Panthermobile (pictured below).

THE PINK PANTHER SHOW

IN SEPTEMBER 1969, NBC expanded its Saturday morning children's programming to include a block of new shows. *The Pink Panther Show* was the centerpiece of this new programming plan, telecast each week at 9:30am. Preceded by DePatie-Freleng's *Here Comes The Grump*, the show was a solid pink success!

The Call of Television

The show featured the best of the Pink Panther theatrical cartoons, combined with live-action host segments, with zany comic Lenny Schultz and skits featuring the Paul and Mary Ritts' puppets. The hosts were later dropped in favor of more Pink Panther cartoons.

Child-friendly Changes

For children's TV, the NBC network edited or altered sequences in several Pink Panther cartoons to remove gags aimed at adult audiences. A laugh track was added to the cartoons and some featured a narrator explaining The Pink Panther's actions and thoughts.

"Gull wing" passenger door on right side.

The Pink Panthermobile

The Pink Panther's futuristic automobile featured in the opening credits and was created by renowned car stylist Bob Resiner. The body is 26 feet long, and steering is controlled with twin-lever push buttons. A lift-up door opens to a lounge area, which contained a television, stereo, phone, AM/FM radio, digital clock, and lots of soft pink fur.

Pink leather driver's seat.

The Pink Panther and The Inspector make a grand entrance at the start of the show.

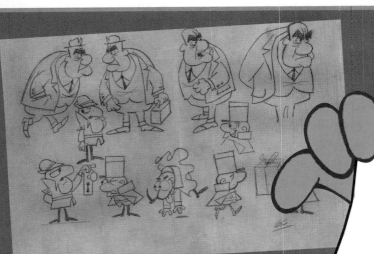

New Characters

Co-starring with the Panther were The Inspector, Sgt. Deux-Deux and The Commissioner (shown on model sheet, above). These cartoons, painted and prepared for theater showings, were probably the best looking, most lavishly designed cartoons on Saturday morning television.

Cartoon Hero

The Inspector and Deux-Deux were voiced by actor Pat Harrington, who was well known for his comic appearances on *The Steve Allen Show*. In addition to The Inspector, Harrington voiced The Atom on *The Superman/Aquaman Hour of Adventure*, and later became famous for his role as building superintendent Schneider on the hit 1975 TV series *One Day At A Time*.

Known for his razor-sharp mind, the Inspector has cracked cases involving the most notorious fiends in the annals of crime. But one character has somehow always eluded him: The Pink Panther.

Pickled Pink (1965)

When an intoxicated man notices the lonely Pink Panther sitting on a park bench, he offers to take him home. However, his grumpy wife is sick of her husband's habit of bringing strangers home and throws them both out.

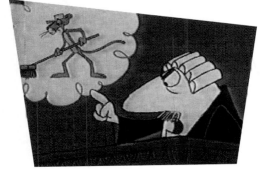

Pink Of The Litter (1967)

Arrested for littering in Litterburg, the dirtiest town in America, The Pink Panther is sentenced to clean it up. Doing this, he is stuck with a mountain of trash—and nowhere to put it!

Pinto Pink (1967)

A footsore Pink Panther tries to tame a wild horse—who, at first, won't allow himself to be saddled, and then won't budge. The Panther finally gets him going—but now he won't stop!

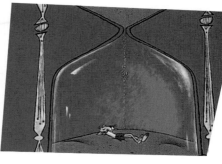
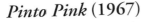
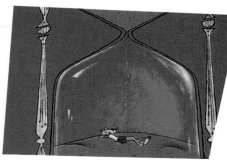

Pink Outs (1967)

This cartoon contains a series of skits, each ending when the screen "pinks out." In one, The Panther is sunbathing at the beach, when he starts to sink in the sand. We discover he is in a giant hourglass—cue Pink Out!

An Ounce Of Pink (1965)

The Pink Panther encounters a weight and fortune machine that seems able to forecast the future. The Pink Panther decides to take the machine home—but its predictions get him into several dangerous and hair-raising scrapes.

MEMORABILIA 1960s

THE PINK PANTHER cartoons and movies were originally aimed at adults, but the Panther's appeal to children was obvious. So early memorabilia tended to be both sophisticated and fun. Merchandise was based mainly around the character himself or Henry Mancini's popular musical theme. Today, these first pieces are highly prized collectibles.

Early books
In 1968, The Pink Panther Press (a subsidiary of Lion Press) published a series of illustrated books aimed at adults.

Soft Toys

Plush, pink, and perfect—everyone wanted their own Pink Panther, which soon became one of the most popular soft toys since the teddy bear. Panthers like these added a touch of pink mischief to your Swinging Sixties lifestyle.

This Pink Panther doll marked the beginning of Mighty Star Inc.'s long relationship with the character.

Famous doll maker Gund produced this hand puppet.

The Panther's snazzy pink roadster outclasses the Inspector!

Block Puzzle

The Pink Panther's international fame was just beginning: Clem Toys of Italy made this block puzzle, one of the first games aimed at children.

This book was based on the 1966 DePatie-Freleng cartoon Super Pink.

The Collection

Julia Tapia's Pink Panther love affair began in 1964 with the release of the first movie. Whenever she saw something with The Pink Panther on it, she had to have it. Today, she has one of the largest collections of memorabilia in the world. Her husband Paul encouraged her to turn their California home into a Pink Panther Museum.

Julia Tapia with a small part of her Pink Panther collection.

Record Player

What better way to hear "The Pink Panther Theme," than on this portable record player in the shape of the Panther's head? It was produced in 1968 by Coliet Toys.

An extended-play record with picture sleeve of "The Pink Panther Theme," on RCA Victor #RCX-7136 (1964).

Pink Panther Music

This 45 rpm EP features Henry Mancini's "The Pink Panther Theme" along with other music and songs from the first movie. The back of the sleeve boasts amusing notes by Peter Sellers.

The Pink Panther's cigarette holder was prominent in early publicity art, emphasizing his air of humorous affectation.

Cartoon Poster

Theatrical cartoon shorts were getting scarce in the 1960s, and movie posters to promote them were even scarcer. However when *The Pink Phink* (1964) won an Oscar®, helping to cement the Panther's movie-star status, the first few Pink Panther cartoons were promoted with dedicated one-sheet posters.

Though traditionally a mute character, the poster depicts The Pink Panther speaking directly to movie fans.

The 1970s

THE PINK PANTHER continues to prowl as he shoots to the highest heights of superstardom on Saturday morning television, the big screen, and on numerous toys, books and merchandise. Inspector Clouseau returns, strikes again and gets revenge in his continuing classic comedies. It's a dy-no-mite decade to be the world's pinkest pussycat!

THE BLUE RACER

The Blue Racer's appearance alters slightly in each film. In Support Your Local Serpent *(1973), director Art Davis provided the character with a hat, collar, and tie!*

SPEED, QUICK WITS, and a fast comeback: these are the trademarks of the Blue Racer, "the fastest little serpent this side of San Simeon." His forked snake's tongue gave him a lisp, and his empty stomach led him into trouble, as he slithered through one hilarious adventure after another. Birds, bees, bears, and beetles beware— The Blue Racer is slinking into a garden party near you!

The Blue Racer usually talks directly to the audience in each cartoon ("Hello, Snake Lovers!"), explaining his actions, and letting us in on his sneaky plans.

A Racing Start

The Blue Racer made his first appearance in a Tijuana Toads cartoon, *A Snake In The Gracias* (1971), in which the Toads persuade an amnesiac Crane that he's a frog to gain his protection from the Racer. Audience reaction to the speedy blue villain was very positive, and within a year, an entire series of theatrical cartoons were devised around him.

Freeze A Jolly Good Fellow (1973)

This cartoon introduced a small but overbearing bear, whose personality resembled that of the irascible comic W. C. Fields. This bear, thrown out of a bruin flophouse, competes with the Racer for a warm cabin in the frozen north. "Mischievous macaroni!" and "Prehistoric pipsqueak!" are two of the names he calls The Blue Racer.

"I'm the fastest snake alive!"

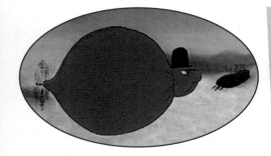

Scheming Snake

The Racer may be fast, but he's also blue. He's blue over trying catch his dinner, finding a place to live, and avoiding two-legged characters larger than he is. In *Support Your Local Serpent* (1972), the blue-hued reptile inflates himself with helium to fly after The Japanese Beetle (above).

"Kid"

This little chick, who appears in *Fowl Play* (1973), decides to adopt The Blue Racer as a playmate. When papa rooster, a musclebound bird with an eye patch and a "John Wayne" Texas accent, forces The Blue Racer to play with his boy, the snake tries every way he can think of to chicken out.

Changing Skin

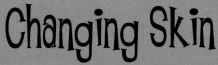

The character of the Blue Racer wasn't set in stone and, like all great cartoon stars, he evolved over the course of the series, with each director having his own take on his look and personality. Looney Tunes veteran animators Gerry Chiniquy, Art Davis, Sid Marcus, and Robert McKimson directed most of The Blue Racer's cartoons, and each provided the blue snake with a bit of style all their own.

To each his own Racer: director McKimson drafted a straggly snake in the grass (left), and Marcus drew a slippery serpent (center), while Chiniquy preferred an asp with a lisp (right).

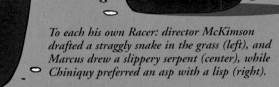

Antenna receives NHK, a U.S. sports station broadcasting in Japanese.

The Japanese Beetle

He's the latest buzz from Japan! The Racer's most elusive foe is The Japanese Beetle—a flower-munching menace with a black belt in karate. This Asian insect packs quite a punch, and could easily upset a blue snake's stomach—especially if swallowed during mealtime. Don't let his polite manner fool you. He's one sharp killer beetle!

In Wham And Eggs *(1973), the Racer hatches a Chinese egg. The egg contains a dragon, who thinks the Racer is his mom!*

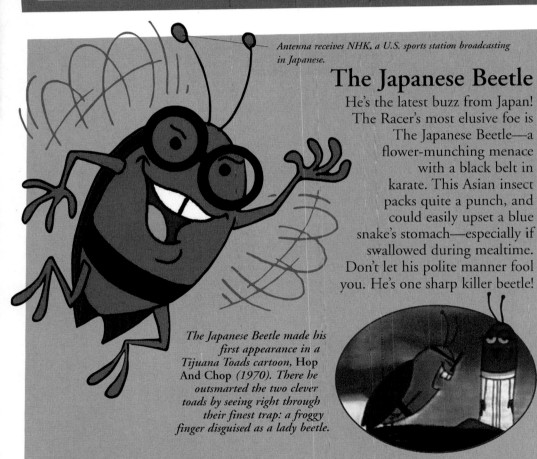

The Japanese Beetle made his first appearance in a Tijuana Toads *cartoon,* Hop And Chop *(1970). There he outsmarted the two clever toads by seeing right through their finest trap: a froggy finger disguised as a lady beetle.*

Bugging Out

The Japanese Beetle's broken English often leads him into trouble. While introducing himself to a bumble bee, he remarks, "I am son of a Japanese Beetle, you are son of a bee!" He loves to sing while flying. Some of his favorite tunes: "I Wish I Was In Dixie (Tokyo)", and "Won't You Come Home Bill Bailey (Beetle)." He ends each appearance by bidding adversaries a fond "Sayonara!"

Aches And Snakes (1973)

This was one of several cartoons in which Crazy Legs Crane matched wits with The Blue Racer. The Crane tries to catch a honey bee to quell the cravings of his wife who is expecting a little crane. After numerous wild chases, The Blue Racer ends up with the bee and Crazy Legs becomes a father—of a dozen bee-craving chicks!

A huge Stetson hat, big green shades, and cowboy boots are the key elements of Kloot's look.

Kloot sets out full of dogged determination to track down and capture the bad guys.

HOOT KLOOT

SHORT AND SHORT-TEMPERED, stout and stout-hearted, Sheriff Hoot Kloot is a modern-day western lawman with a ten-gallon hat and an even bigger ego. Kloot's way is the law of the land, but in a county containing crazy cowboys, goofy gunslingers, and wacky wolves, calamity waits around every corner.

"Get off my back!"

Hoot Kloot's steed Fester is an honest and faithful four-legged friend. He enjoys giving Hoot Kloot the benefit of his homespun wisdom.

Kloot's County

In his first cartoon, *Kloot's County* (1973), Sheriff Kloot helps Miss Bo Peep retrieve her sheep from outlaw Crazywolf. Kloot was inspired by character actor Joe Higgins, who appeared in several popular 1970s-era car commercials for Dodge Challenger. Higgins, as a portly Southern sheriff, pulled motorists off the road and informed them, "You in a heap o' trouble, boy!"

Fester waddles along, more like an old man than a fiery steed.

This 1973 model sheet neatly captures Kloot and Fester's turbulent relationship.

Fester

This "poor ol' hobblin' horse" took his name from Festus, Marshal Matt Dillon's hillbilly sidekick in the popular TV western series *Gunsmoke*. Fester is Kloot's loyal buddy—he just doesn't like to be sat on. "Why are you, all the time, ridin' me?" is his regular complaint. Bob Holt voiced both Fester and Hoot Kloot.

Fester has a nose for trouble.

Kloot never calls Fester by name. He simply calls him "Horse."

Storyboards

The storyboards above, by Art Leonardi, were for a proposed opening to a Hoot Kloot cartoon. The idea is reminiscent of Tex Avery's "breaking the fourth wall" approach, with Kloot directly addressing the audience. Various ideas were suggested and rejected. In Leonardi's final version, used in the actual Kloot cartoons, the credits were spelled out on swinging saloon doors.

Large paws—all the better to tickle the audience's funnybone!

The masked Lone Stranger rides into town and Kloot is immediately suspicious. When the Stranger shouts "Hi-ho Silverman!" he's not calling for his horse—he's calling for his lawyer!

Crazywolf

"The shadiest, shoddiest, side-door slinkiest, sheep-stealing, shifty-eyed shyster in the county!" This zany canine heckled Kloot in several off-the-wall adventures. Larry Mann voiced Crazywolf in an appropriately loony manner.

Long lanky legs keep the cackling hillbilly "varmint" racing ahead of Hoot Kloot.

THE DOGFATHER

THIS CANINE crime boss marked his toon territory in 17 theatrical shorts produced in the mid-1970s. The Dogfather and his kennel of criminals muscled their way through a series of comic misadventures—ambushing all cartoon competition and offering moviegoers a large reward of laughs.

Pug

The Dogfather's right-hand (or "right-paw") man is a lummox known as Pug. This simple-minded mutt is a mix of bloodhound and bulldog. His first priority is obeying his boss and his second is filling his stomach.

Boss Dog

His friends respect him, his foes fear his bite, the law wants him on a leash. Inspired by Marlon Brando as Don Corleone in *The Godfather*, voice actor Bob Holt barked instructions to the mob in a humorous, semi-audible mumble as The Dogfather (alias Cocker the Spaniel, alias convict #397-1863).

"D'uh... Gee Boss!"

The Dogfather shows he's all heart in M-O-N-E-Y Spells Love *(1975) when he decides to wed a widow worth $20 million. "When she falls for my charms, I'll grab the old bag's loot, buy up an orphanage, kick out the kids, and turn it into a retirement tenement for my boys!" he declares. The Dogfather selects his favorite hench-hound to be his Best Man. "He used to say I was his worst!" says Pug.*

The short, shaggy arm of the lawless.

ROCKY 3209 DEE

Model Design
Art leonardi

Dogfather

Rocky

Rocky was an all-purpose hood in the Dogfather universe. This model sheet by Art Leonardi shows him in *M-O-N-E-Y Spells Love*, in which he vies with the Dogfather for the hand of a rich widow. In *Heist & Seek* (1974), Rocky is a loyal gang member hiding out with Pug from Sam Spaniel, private eye.

Louie

Voiced by Daws Butler, Louie is a pint-sized hit man in a ten-gallon hat. Louie looks on Pug as a hero, yet he often pulls his pals out of danger with his quick wit, loud bark, and big bite.

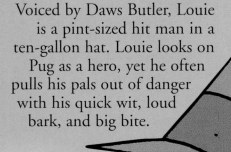

The Dogfather always holds all the aces, no matter what his boys tell him!

The Wheels

The Dogfather makes his getaway in a snazzy roadster that dates back to the height of gangland activity. The Dogfather cartoons had a 1920s-1930s feel due to the retro art-deco look of the opening titles, the formal dress of the lead characters, and the automobiles designed for the series.

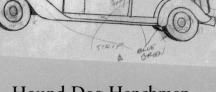

The Dogfather's car, based on a vintage Rolls, as seen in an original animation drawing and color guide (right).

DUH BIG-BB CA-CAT!

LOUIE RUNS THRU SC

B.G. 32

Hound Dog Henchmen

They may look threatening, but the Dogfather mob never uses guns. Pug and Louie are the greatest of friends. In the first cartoon, *The Dogfather* (1974), Louie bravely steps in when Pug is frightened by an escaped wildcat. This original layout sketch (left) by Hawley Pratt captures their personalities and their relationship.

Haunting Dog (1975)

Machine Gun Kolly, a rival gangster, is rubbed out by the Dogfather. In his will, Machine Gun leaves his classy Twelve Cylinder Hound-Mobile to the boss. The Dogfather and Pug use it as a getaway car—but Kolly's ghost returns to haunt the car and drive them crazy, leading them directly to the front steps of police headquarters.

Saltwater Tuffy (1975)

The Dogfather puts a contract out on Lucky McClaw (right), a cat who won his yacht *Mary Belle* in a crooked card game. Pug and Louie try everything to reclaim the yacht and grab the cat, but in vain.

Misterjaw was an affectionate parody of the terrifying shark in the 1975 movie Jaws.

Misterjaw was voiced by comic actor Arte Johnson, a star of the hit TV show Rowan and Martin's Laugh-In.

MISTERJAW

JUST WHEN you thought it was safe to go back in the water... "Gotcha!" Misterjaw, the ever-hungry shark, is on your tail and after your funnybone. The character made his debut on TV's *The Pink Panther Laugh And A Half Hour And A Half Show* in 1976.

Big Mouth

Besides his top hat, Misterjaw only has one thing on his mind: eating! He spends all his time hunting his next meal, coming up with zany food-finding schemes and trading wisecracks with his loyal sidekick, Catfish. With his vest, collar, and bowtie, this man-eater is always dressed for dinner!

5030   72A

Happy Snapper

Shouting "Gotcha!" in a faux-German accent, Misterjaw loves scaring swimmers silly!

Crash Landing

By land, by sea or in the air, Misterjaw is determined to get his fill of fast food—no matter how fast it is! However, his ingenious methods have their ups and their downs. In *Flying Fool* (1976, above) he learned how to fly—but was mistaken for an enemy aircraft and shot down!

Misterjaw's tail fins double as feet when he is on dry land.

Misterjaw's biggest fear: crabs. Why? They tickle!

Shark Tales

This is just a sample of Misterjaw's biggest bites, championship chomps and greatest "Gotchas." He starred in 33 undersea epics, all produced in 1976, and each one the acme of animated aquatics!

Showbiz Shark

Wanting to be in showbiz, Misterjaw auditions for a starring slot at the seaside marina. His competition is a superstar porpoise who plays piano, does a high-wire act, and dives 40 feet into a bucket of water!

Catfish

A streetwise, whiskered feline fish, Catfish is Misterjaw's trusty first mate (whom he calls "Pally"). Catfish calls Misterjaw "Boss" and "Chief." He's never on Misterjaw's menu—he's too valuable as a confidant and conspirator.

Cool Shark

When Misterjaw gives an octopus a "Gotcha," the eight-legged trouble-maker sprays him with paint—and leads him on a chase to the North Pole. Misterjaw tries skis, skating, and a snowmobile but all of these leave him cold. And a polar bear leaves him flat.

Harry Halibut

Misterjaw's tastiest target, little Harry Halibut is always the one that gets away. Minding his own business, Harry wanders the deep keeping one step ahead of the biggest mouth in the sea.

To Catch A Halibut

In the interests of healthier eating, Catfish suggests a halibut diet, but catching Harry Halibut isn't easy—even equipped with rocket power. Misterjaw eventually goes out of control, and swallows the rocket motor.

Hard to Swallow

Catfish's book recommends the "buckshot and electro-magnet bit" for catching Harry Halibut in *To Catch A Halibut* (1976) The fish mistakes buckshot for caviar and is caught by the magnet.

Merry Sharkman, Merry Sharkman

Fearless Freddie the shark hunter is called in when an oil-rig crew spots Misterjaw circling around. When Freddie throws him a hook, the clever shark ties the fisherman's line to a torpedo and blows him sky high.

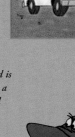

Escape

Pursuing Harry Halibut has its price—and Misterjaw pays it every time he chases him through a small porthole or has to squeeze under a rock.

Shopping Spree

Catfish tells Misterjaw about the food to be had in grocery stores. They head for the nearest supermarket but fall foul of the police.

CRAZY LEGS CRANE

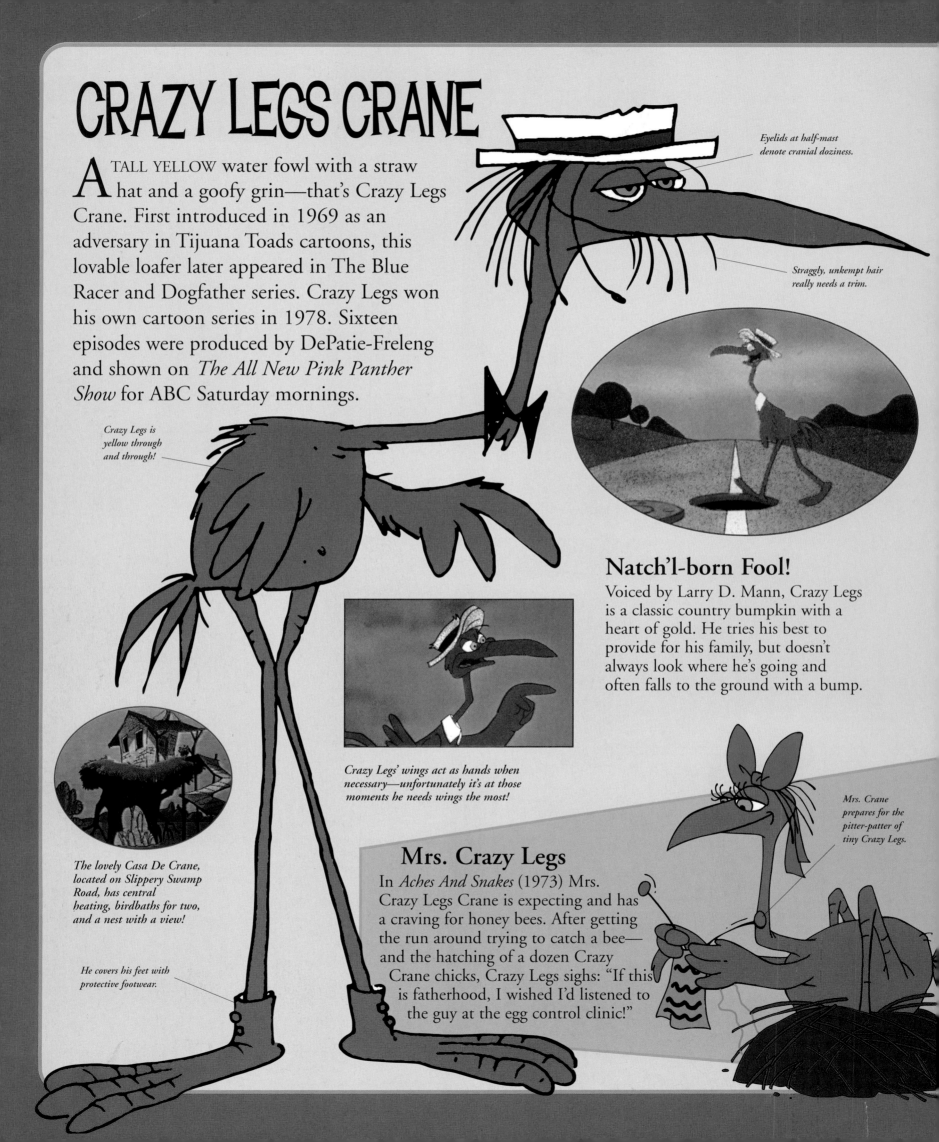

A TALL YELLOW water fowl with a straw hat and a goofy grin—that's Crazy Legs Crane. First introduced in 1969 as an adversary in Tijuana Toads cartoons, this lovable loafer later appeared in The Blue Racer and Dogfather series. Crazy Legs won his own cartoon series in 1978. Sixteen episodes were produced by DePatie-Freleng and shown on *The All New Pink Panther Show* for ABC Saturday mornings.

Eyelids at half-mast denote cranial doziness.

Straggly, unkempt hair really needs a trim.

Crazy Legs is yellow through and through!

Natch'l-born Fool!

Voiced by Larry D. Mann, Crazy Legs is a classic country bumpkin with a heart of gold. He tries his best to provide for his family, but doesn't always look where he's going and often falls to the ground with a bump.

Crazy Legs' wings act as hands when necessary—unfortunately it's at those moments he needs wings the most!

The lovely Casa De Crane, located on Slippery Swamp Road, has central heating, birdbaths for two, and a nest with a view!

He covers his feet with protective footwear.

Mrs. Crazy Legs

In *Aches And Snakes* (1973) Mrs. Crazy Legs Crane is expecting and has a craving for honey bees. After getting the run around trying to catch a bee—and the hatching of a dozen Crazy Crane chicks, Crazy Legs sighs: "If this is fatherhood, I wished I'd listened to the guy at the egg control clinic!"

Mrs. Crane prepares for the pitter-patter of tiny Crazy Legs.

Crazy Legs' favorite hot meal is a fire-breathing, happy-go-lucky dragonfly, but the elusive firebug teases his feather-brained head. Crazy Legs calls him a "flyin' fire hazard" and a "future tenant of my tum-tum." Veteran voice actor Frank Welker supplied The Dragonfly's voice.

In the Dogfather cartoons, Crazy Legs sometimes transported loot for the Dogfather mob.

Part-time Job

Crazy Legs was also sometimes shown filling in for the stork—bringing bundles of joy to happy couples everywhere.

The Shame of It

Crazy Legs' son loves his father, but when dad gets whupped by Dragonfly time and again, he prefers not to show his face in public. "Father, why do you try over and over again to humiliate me?" he asks. "It's the only way I'll ever get it right!" replies dad. Frank Welker voiced Crazy Legs' reproachful offspring.

Crazy Crane Stories

The following are just a few of the storylines and scenes from the adventures of Crazy Legs Crane. The directors for the series were Sid Marcus, Gerry Chiniquy, Bob Richardson, Dave Detiege, Art Davis, and Brad Case.

This female dragonfly decoy was one of Crazy Legs' better ideas.

Crane Brained

Crazy Legs' son asks dad to bring something home for dinner. After ruling out a huge alligator and a bull, Crazy Legs chases after the Dragonfly—who leaves him in stitches, and in bandages, and on crutches...

Life With Feather

Crazy Legs gives his son a crash course on Dragonfly catching. Crazy Legs' female decoy finally does the trick, and Crazy Legs prepares the combustible bug for dinner. He adds a pinch of pepper, the Dragonfly sneezes... and explodes, destroying the Crane residence!

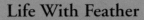

King Of The Swamp

Crazy Legs considers himself King of the Swamp—until he runs into tough alligators and tangles with an even tougher rival crane. Even the tiny Dragonfly puts him in his place—to the embarrassment of Crazy Legs' son.

Sonic Broom

Blasting off on "Operation Dragonfly," Crazy Legs renews his attempts to catch the little winged pest and bring him home for dinner. He competes with a witch, who needs the fire bug to brew some dragonfly shampoo.

Winter Blunderland

After vainly chasing the Dragonfly in the snow, Crazy Legs gives up and goes south for the winter. The Dragonfly misses his playmate and follows him to Miami!

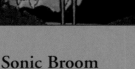

IN THE STUDIO

FROM 1964 TO 1984, before computers were used to assist cartoonists, every part of creating a Pink Panther cartoon was done by hand. Fortunately, the DePatie-Freleng studio possessed the top talent in Hollywood, veterans of Disney films and Looney Tunes, with the skills and expertise to put together the coolest theatrical cartoons of the time.

The Layout Man

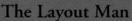

Dick Ung (that's his desk at left) started at Disney in the 1950s, and went on to become DePatie-Freleng's most prolific layout man. His job was to translate the action on the storyboard and set the shots for the film. His drawings would go to the background painter—who would render a full color background based on his design—and the animator.

Storyboard Conference

Ace story man John Dunn (left) confers with director Friz Freleng (right) during the 1960s. The story is the most important part of any film. The director and his story man create a scenario that is funny and visually pleasing. At this point the character designs can be very rough—but if the plot and gags are solid, a cartoon is on its way to being produced.

Character Designs

After a story is approved, character designers come up with ideas for any new characters required. Once a character sketch is selected, a model sheet showing that character in different poses is then drawn up.

Character sketches by Hawley Pratt.

These individual cels from String Along In Pink *(1979) show the meticulous care each frame of artwork receives—these five images represent just half a second of actual screen time.*

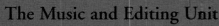

Cutting out letters and pasting them onto a clear cel made it easier to fix typos or change billing. This technique was a DePatie-Freleng invention.

Direction

The animation director times the visual action using an "exposure sheet" (above) which indicates to the animator and cameraman the action that has to happen on a frame by frame basis. It also indicates when dialogue will be spoken by which character, effects notations, and the animator assigned to draw that scene.

The Music and Editing Unit

Henry Mancini's great theme music is used throughout The Pink Panther and The Inspector cartoons. However, the musical directors William Lava, Walter Greene, and Doug Goodwin also contributed music to DePatie-Freleng's cartoons over the years. Sound effects are also a crucial part of a cartoon's impact and DFE film editor Joe Siracusa (left), who started as a drummer with Spike Jones and his City Slickers, remains one of the top effects editors in the business.

Beyond the Panther

The success of the Pink Panther caused DePatie-Freleng, United Artists and Mirisch Corporation to be courted by the TV networks to supply programming for their busy Saturday morning cartoon schedules. *Super President* (1966), created in response to the 1960s super-hero craze was the first; other popular DePatie Freleng Saturday morning cartoons included: *The Further Adventures Of Dr. Doolittle* (1970), *The Barkleys* (1972), *The Houndcats* (1972) and *Bailey's Comets* (1973).

A model sheet for Here Comes The Grump (1969), a zany fairy tale.

A model-sheet drawing of Super Bwoing, one of The Super Six (1966). The other five were Granite Man, Elevator Man, Super Scuba, Magneto Man, and Captain Zammo.

This scene of Crazy Legs skating with ice blocks on his feet was later cut.

From Script to Screen

The storyboard is the cartoon script that all directors, artists and producers follow. In the storyboard phase, all the creative principals make notes, edit, and fine tune the story, visual gags and dialogue. When the final board is approved, the film goes into production. Compare the storyboard above with the final frames from the film.

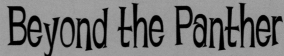

Friz Freleng's original storyboard for Pinkfinger (1965). Friz wrote or co-wrote many of the early Pink Panther theatrical shorts himself.

THE ANIMATION DIRECTORS

A N ANIMATED CARTOON is a collaborative effort, and several dozen talents behind the scenes contribute to the final production. However the most important member of the team is the director, whose unifying vision shapes each production. Here are some of The Pink Panther's favorite leading men—the directors who put him through his paces.

Friz Freleng

It all started with Friz. He set the pace with his supervision of the original Pink Panther titles and the first dozen theatrical shorts. His specialty was timing comic action to music, while establishing the personality of The Pink Panther and The Little Man. Both talents shone in *The Pink Phink* (1964), pictured left.

Robert McKimson

The hallmarks of McKimson's cartoons were good storytelling, clear layouts, and funny gags, as in *Pink DaVinci* (1975), pictured above. Like Friz Freleng, he had established his name as one of the great Warner Bros.' Looney Tunes' directors. At DePatie-Freleng, McKimson's comic instincts made him one of Freleng's most trusted collaborators. One of the best artists and animators in the business, McKimson was also one of the *fastest* cartoonists!

Hawley Pratt

A master layout artist and character designer, Hawley Pratt co-directed the earliest Panther shorts with Friz Freleng. Pratt's unique color palette and sparse backdrops helped set the tone for the entire series. His great design sense can best be seen in such visually stylish cartoons as *Pink Punch* (1966) and *Psychedelic Pink* (1968), pictured right.

Changing Styles

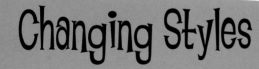

The Pink Panther's cool remains timeless. He's pink and he's a panther—a perfect combination. However his look has undergone subtle changes over the decades.

The 1970s

Now a TV and movie star, The Pink Panther no longer walks on four legs, but has become more humanoid in appearance and behavior.

The 1980s

As merchandising and home video propel the Panther to even greater fame, the "Me" decade becomes the "Pink" decade, as The Pink Panther dresses for success.

The 1960s

His 1964 debut, complete with sophisticated cigarette holder, was The Pink Panther's most feline incarnation.

Gerry Chiniquy

Chiniquy specialized in making the most out of simple situations. Cartoons like *Jet Pink* (1967, left) with its uncluttered backdrops, allowed The Pink Panther to stand out against a stark field of color.

Art Davis

Davis enjoyed using a wide repertoire of filmmaker's techniques—rapid cutting, dissolves, montage—as in *In The Pink Of The Night* (1968, right), where a simple setting, The Pink Panther's bedroom, is staged from several different angles.

Sid Marcus

Veteran director Marcus had gained invaluable experience with Max Fleischer, Charles Mintz, Warner Bros., and Walter Lantz studios. His cartoons, such as *Pinky Doodle* (1976, left), had tight gag timing, appealing characters, and clever stories.

Art Leonardi

The youngest member of the DePatie-Freleng team, Leonardi's cartoons display his strong drawing style and his direction brought a brisk pace to later theatrical shorts such as *Pink Campaign* (1975, right).

The 1990s

A black outline now defines The Pink Panther. The suave sophistication, however, remains.

The 2000s

The designer Shag's retro look redefined The Pink Panther for the 21st century. This new interpretation is a reminder of the character's continuing relevance to popular culture.

Other Artists

Bold, innovative use of flat colors, empty space, and ornate props typify the design style of DePatie- Freleng cartoons. Nowhere is this more apparent than in the sensational layouts and backgrounds of Tom Yakutis, most notably on The Inspector cartoons (above).

Animator Don Williams was one of The Pink Panther specialists. Williams made the Panther appear more cat-like, showing him twitching his whiskers and adding bits of business with his tail—little traits that added depth to the character's personality.

Layouts

The layout artist takes the storyboards and sets up the scenes for the animators and background artists to work with. Roy Morita's work (above) stands out for its sharp style and strong poses.

BACKGROUND ART

A S HILARIOUS as the antics of The Pink Panther characters are, the distinctive backdrops behind the animated stars often have a humor all their own. Hand painted in a matter of hours by some of DePatie-Freleng's top artists, backgrounds such as those shown on these pages played a vital role in setting the scene and atmosphere in the studio's theatrical shorts.

Layout Drawing

A background begins as a layout drawing, usually done by a layout artist or the director. The idea for the image comes from the storyboard. A completed layout drawing is used as a guide for the finished color version, which is usually handled by another artist. This background drawing was made by studio veteran Hawley Pratt.

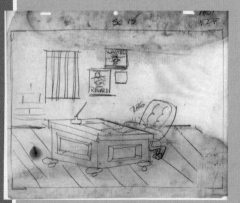

Hoot Kloot's Desk

This layout drawing for *Apache On The County Seat* (1973) by Dick Ung is designed to allow the main character to command our eye. The low, off-kilter desk also reflects Hoot Kloot's stature and mindset.

Establishing the Environment

This painting by Richard Thomas from *Snake In The Gracias* (1971), a Tijuana Toads cartoon, uses simple brushstrokes to indicate high grounds, with a cel overlay of rocks and plants.

Scratch Technique

The background and layout artist must be adept at drawing simple, everyday items to fit the style of the film. This scene, from the end of *Les Miserobots*, 1968 (layout by Dick Ung, background by Tom O'Loughlin) uses a technique that has become identified with DePatie-Freleng's animation—a scratch effect. Paint is applied with a sponge then scratched off with a blade to get the required look. This technique helped to give The Inspector cartoons a unique feel, and was quite sophisticated for the time.

520 BG-1

Chateau Crime Scene

This background from the beginning of The Inspector cartoon *Crow De Guerre* (1967) by Tom O'Laughlin used the original layout drawing by Dick Ung xeroxed onto a cel as an overlay. This resulted in a flatter, two-dimensional feel—a reversal of decades of classic, Disney-style animation that attempted to duplicate reality. In the 1960s, DePatie-Freleng's innovative approach gave the studio an artistic edge over the competition.

A final cel set up, with the characters—The Ant and The Aardvark—in the center foreground over the final background painting, makes a complete scene ready for filming. The registration holes at the top are used to align the cel in the correct position over the background.

THE PINK PANTHER STRIKES AGAIN (1976)

A WEAPON of mass destruction! A maniac on the loose! Clouseau is back on the case—in fact, this time he *is* the case! A great script, hilarious set-pieces, and dynamic performances ensured that the fifth Pink Panther movie struck gold at the box-office.

The original movie poster was designed with artwork on the back, featuring The Pink Panther and The Inspector playing cards. Inevitably, the Panther is winning!

The Main Titles

Created by the Richard Williams studio, the credits celebrated classic Hollywood movies—with The Pink Panther popping up in each one. Included in Blake Edwards' witty parody of some of the Silver Screen's most famous scenes was his wife, Julie Andrews, as Maria in The Sound of Music.

Clouseau is always in the dark!

He enters the lobby of a classic theater.

Classic Clouseau: not looking where he's supposed to.

There's a Panther in the projection booth!

A monstrous head fills the screen...

...and out pops The Pink Panther!

Suddenly the Hills Are Alive...

Whatever the role, The Pink Panther....

...always makes a splash!

The Pink Panther plays a classic Buster Keaton scene.

66

Behind the Scenes

The Pink Panther Strikes Again was shot at Shepperton Studios, near London, and on location in Bavaria and in France. At Shepperton, four full sound stages were required for 70 separate sets.

Above: Director Blake Edwards lines up a shot for the Oktoberfest sequence.

Left: Filming a close-up of a stuffed dummy of Clouseau. In the movie, the doll is part of Inspector Dreyfus' therapy.

Over the main title, his shadow takes on a familiar shape.

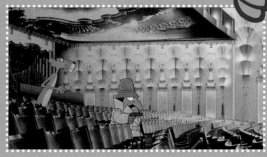

The backgrounds are photos of a real London theater.

Clouseau's got pink on the brain!

First The Pink Panther assays an Alfred Hitchcock cameo.

The Panther then tries on a super-hero costume for size.

Lo and behold...it's Bat-Panther!

...With The Pink Panther!

Next up–Pink Dracula!

"Singin' in the rain," while Clouseau looks on.

Clouseau is trapped on the Silver Screen!

The Pink Panther has vanished and Clouseau fades out.

THE WORLD OF THE MOVIE

CLOUSEAU must save the world—but as the target of the top assassins from 12 different European countries, how will he save *himself*? In his wildest adventure yet, Clouseau's methods defy not only international conventions and international law, but international sanity as well!

Dreyfus snatches Tournier, one of the world's greatest criminal minds, out of police custody. Step one in Dreyfus' plan to rid the world of Clouseau.

A Reunion of Sorts

Charles Dreyfus has spent the last three years in a mental hospital trying to conquer his obsession to kill Clouseau. On the home's tranquil grounds, Dreyfus and Clouseau once again renew their special relationship.

"Out with the bad air, in with the good!"

A dummy Inspector Clouseau rests in the office of Dr. Duval, the psychiatrist. His patient, Dreyfus, has used it to resolve his violent impulses numerous times over the past three years.

The Plot

Former Police Chief Inspector Charles Dreyfus escapes from a mental asylum and kidnaps a weapons scientist, whom he orders to build a Doomsday machine. Dreyfus threatens to destroy the planet unless Clouseau is killed. Assassins from all over the world hunt Clouseau, who trails Dreyfus to his castle hideout. Their final showdown involves ray guns, laughing gas, a rusty suit of armor, and an old catapult.

Clouseau's Many Faces

The wardrobe department and costume designs by Tiny Nicholls and Bridget Sellers (no relation; she had worked with Peter Sellers for 17 years), and the expertise of makeup artist Harry Frampton, allowed the Inspector to investigate everywhere virtually undetected—until he fell out of a window or tripped up on the stairs.

M. Balls' costume shop in a Paris backstreet is Clouseau's secret weapon in his fight against crime.

Clouseau as "Dr. Shurtz," the dentist who pulls Dreyfus' tooth. Naturally, Clouseau takes out the wrong one.

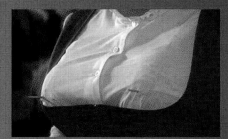

As Quasimodo with an over-inflated hump, Clouseau gets a bird's-eye view of Notre Dame cathedral.

Lesley-Anne Down as the sultry Russian agent Olga.

Booby Traps

Clouseau's knack for being in the wrong place at the right time helps him remain blissfully unaware of assassins at his back, bombs beneath his feet, or knives coming his way. The only thing more dangerous than being Clouseau is being the assassin trying to kill him!

In the Lowenbrau Hall at the Oktoberfest, Clouseau thwarts this deadly pair of weapons with a large pretzel!

Love From Russia

Beautiful Soviet assassin Olga lies in wait in Clouseau's hotel bedroom, planning to use all her wiles to do him in. Instead, she decides to run away with the Inspector, believing she has found the man of her dreams.

Now You See Him...

After getting into Dreyfus' castle lair, Clouseau accidentally zaps Dreyfus with the mysterious ray. First the lower half of Dreyfus disappears, then the rest of him, until just a single twitching eye is left, floating in midair. Finally that, too, vanishes.

Clumsy Does It!

Catapulted onto the barrel of Dreyfus' secret weapon, Clouseau unintentionally swings the ray gun toward Dreyfus—and destroys his plans for world domination.

Zapped by the ray, Dreyfus' Bavarian mountain hideout fittingly glows a bright shade of pink, before disappearing off the map!

ACTION SHOTS

CRASH! BANG! Boom! Wherever Clouseau goes, trouble of all kinds naturally follows—national disasters, bizarre accidents, pratfalls, bangs on the head, or sudden, unexpected immersions in cold water.

Permanent Vacancy

"Do you have a *reum*?" Clouseau asks the hotel clerk (Graham Stark). "I do not know what a *reum* is," he replies. Clouseau finds the proper translation in his guide book: "Zimmer!" The clerk nods. "Ahh... a *reum*!"

"No."

"I thought you said

"Does your dog bite?"

your dog did not bite!"

"That is not my dog!"

Castle Calamities

This sequence is the closest the Pink Panther movies ever came to matching the cartoon sensibility of Chuck Jones and Friz Freleng. Here, Clouseau (Peter Sellers, doubled in long shot by stuntman Dick Crockett) attempts to enter Mondschien Castle, where a power-mad Dreyfus has a secret headquarters, a death ray, two hostages—and a toothache.

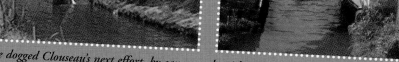
The ever-resourceful Clouseau attempts to scale the drawbridge over the castle moat—only to be let down at the crucial mom

The dogged Clouseau's next effort, by canoe, ends with another ducking.

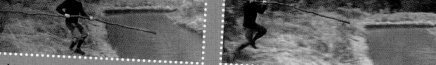
Nothing ventured... Clouseau demonstrates his pole-vaulting prowess.

In Quasimodo mode, Clouseau over-inflates his hunchback hump and floats out the window—just as Dreyfus blows up his apartment.

Cato pounces while Clouseau and Olga are making love. The bed smashes through the wall, and all three occupants plunge into the River Seine.

Going With a Bang

Massive explosions added greatly to the visual spectacle of *The Pink Panther Strikes Again*. Special-effects chief Kit West (later to work on the movies *Raiders of the Lost Ark*, 1981, and *Return of the Jedi*, 1983) destroyed Clouseau's apartment not once but twice!

Monster of the Deep

The movie ends with a piece of animation that dovetails brilliantly with the last live-action scene. Hurled into the water due to Cato's impetuosity, the Inspector swims off. Little does he know he is being stalked by a man-eating Pink Panther—a parody of the movie *Jaws* (1975), released the previous year.

This scene lampoons Jaws' famous movie poster. The cartoon chase continues under the end titles, until the final fade-out.

No assignment is too low for Inspector Clouseau!

PINK PANTHER COMICS

DURING THE 1960S, The Pink Panther became the star of a long-running series of American comic books, which also became hugely popular with international audiences. The comics featured The Pink Panther in new adventures with The Little Man, and gave him a new ability—the power of speech!

Due to printing techniques, the Panther's pink-ink outline had to be black in the comics.

Pulp Fiction

Western Publishing's Gold Key comic books featured Pink Panther and Inspector stories by Pete Hansen and Mark Evanier with artwork by Pete Alvarado. Warren Tufts drew most of the artwork from 1974 through 1982. Western published 87 issues from 1971 to 1984.

Warren Tufts

The Pink Panther's main comic book artist, Warren Tufts was best known for realistic western comic strips, such as Casey Ruggles and Lance, as well as Disney's Zorro comic books.

Outrageous action and funny facial expressions were Tuft's trademark.

GULP!

WHOOSH!!

MAN, NOW THAT'S CHILI!!

International Comics

"La Pantera Rosa" in Spain, "Rosa Pantern" in Sweden, "Vaaleanpunainen Pantteri" in Finland—The Pink Panther's comic book exploits gained him legions of new fans. In some countries, the comics were written and drawn locally, in others, publishers simply translated the original American comic books.

History's Best Kept Secrets

INVENTION OF THE WHEEL   HIGH-PRICED MODEL

The Panther gets the top-of-the-range model once again.

Newspapers

A comic strip by Eric and Bill Teitelbaum, syndicated by Tribune Media Services, will debut in 2005 (above). DePatie-Freleng tried to sell a Pink Panther newspaper strip in the 1960s. These rare drawings (right) are samples.

THUMP THUMP

Comic Annuals

Hardcover Pink Panther Comic Annuals were published once a year in England by various publishers. Each edition measured 8 x 10.75 in. (120 x 270 mm.), had between 70 and 80 pages, and was printed in color. The Annual at left and one of its pages at right are from the 1980 Annual from Polystyle Publications Ltd. These annuals contained the best comic book stories of the year and sometimes featured activity pages, such as crossword puzzles and animal quizzes.

MEMORABILIA 1970S

Puppets, playthings, and paint sets are prized in pink, especially if The Pink Panther and his friends are involved...! The Panther's popularity, fueled by the success of his Saturday morning animated series, is reflected in the wealth of merchandise available during this decade.

"I'm the Pink Panther; don't wrinkle my fur."

The Panther Speaks

This Mattel Chatter Chum from 1976 speaks one of nine phrases when a ring is pulled.

Panther Art

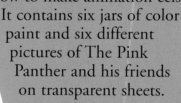

Become an ace animator! The Cartoonarama set (above) showed children how to make animation cels. It contains six jars of color paint and six different pictures of The Pink Panther and his friends on transparent sheets.

This pencil kit comes with a supply of pink pencils.

Pencil Box

Made by Freelance, Inc. in 1979, this box was perfect for carrying your crayons to the beach!

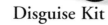

Disguise Kit

This rare Clouseau kit from Pressman in 1979 allows you to become a "master of disguise" like the great detective himself!

String Puppet

This classic marionette, from Pelham Puppets, England, was a popular item in Europe.

Board Games

Roll the dice! No one could be bored playing these classic board games, which also featured exciting Pink Panther box art. Left to right: Whitman, 1974; Warren, 1977; Milton Bradley, 1969.

Sinking the Pink: this box art shows The Pink Panther being pestered by seagulls and sharks.

the PINK PANTHER game

AGES 7 TO 15

MILTON BRADLEY COMPANY

SPRINGFIELD MASSACHUSETTS

4011

MADE IN USA

MB KEY TO FUN and learning

The Inspector and Deux-Deux are hot on the trail.

for 2 to 4 players
The PINK PANTHER
CHASE GAME

PINK PANTHER Game

A dicey game of chance.

The Aardvark and Misterjaw join in the fun.

Panther Talc

Stay as cool as The Pink Panther, and smell sweet, too! Cover yourself in Pink Panther Talc! This was one of the few Panther products designed for both children and adults during the decade.

ROSEDALE
Pink Panther talc

This talc tin is now a highly sought-after collectible.

Pink Panther Car
REQUIRES NO BATTERIES
A MARX PUSH AND GO TOY

The Pink Panther's vehicles reinforced his cool image

Pink Panther Wheels

The Panther motorcycle (above) is part of a highly collectible Corgi series from 1979. The Pink Panther Car, by Marx Toys, is one of the first in a long line of vehicles associated with the feline hipster.

Homemade Panther

This crocheted, 24-inch Pink Panther soft toy is typical of the cuddly toys one could create from licensed patterns then available.

REVENGE OF THE PINK PANTHER (1978)

REVENGE IS SWEET—and funny, especially when Inspector Clouseau is looking for it! While finding his own killer, unmasking the "French Connection," and toppling the "Godfather," Clouseau finds love, dons various disguises, confounds Chief Inspector Dreyfus, and blows up half of Hong Kong!

Leading Lady

Dyan Cannon plays Simone Legree, mistress and secretary to powerful crime boss Philippe Douvier. When she is dumped by her lover, she befriends Clouseau and aids in his scheme to catch the killers. Most of her scenes were filmed on stages in London and on location in Hong Kong, China.

The same year *Revenge of the Pink Panther* was released, Dyan Cannon appeared in another comedy smash, *Heaven Can Wait*, for which she received an Oscar® nomination for Best Supporting Actress.

The plot of *Revenge of the Pink Panther* allowed Clouseau to spend much of the movie in disguise. The original poster reflects his many masquerades.

Film Credits

DIRECTOR AND PRODUCER . . . . Blake Edwards
EXECUTIVE PRODUCER . . . . Tony Adams
SCREENPLAY . . . Frank Waldman, Ron Clark and Blake Edwards
PHOTOGRAPHY. . . . Ernie Day
FILM EDITOR . . . Alan Jones
PRODUCTION DESIGNER . . . . Peter Mullins
MUSIC . . . . Henry Mancini

CAST
Peter Sellers . . . . Inspector Jacques Clouseau
Herbert Lom . . . . Charles Dreyfus
Burt Kwouk . . . . Cato
Dyan Cannon . . . . Simone Legree
Robert Webber . . . . Philippe Douvier
Tony Beckley . . . . Algo
Robert Loggia . . . . Marchione
Paul Stewart . . . . Scallini
André Maranne . . . . François
Graham Stark . . . . Prof. Auguste Balls

Cato drives an ice-cream cart through the streets of Hong Kong on the way to meet with Clouseau.

The World's a Stage

Most of the elaborate stunts were shot at Shepperton Studios in London, and location photography in Paris and Hong Kong added realism and glamor. In Hong Kong, extensive shooting took place in the streets, in the lobby of the Hotel Excelsior, and on the Kowloon Peninsula, the waterfront harbor.

Clouseau's Paris apartment has an incredible view of the famed Arc de Triomphe on the Champs-Elysées.

The Main Titles

The title animation for *Revenge of the Pink Panther* was created by the DePatie-Freleng studio, the creators of the original Pink Panther animated character in 1964. Due to the success of the animated Pink Panther's debut, Depatie-Freleng went on to animate Pink Panther theatrical short subjects. Art Leonardi and John Dunn designed the gags and clever visuals.

Clouseau chases The Pink Panther into his own title.

The Panther confounds Clouseau with his long barreled gun.

 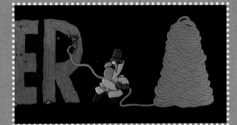  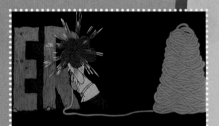

Clouseau pulls the Panther's tail, miles and miles of it...   *The tail turns out to be attached to a "b-u-rmb!"*

Chief Inspector Dreyfus gets his revenge, as the letters in Herbert Lom's name become an attack dog.

  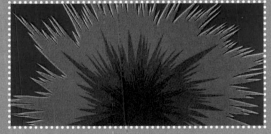 

The painterly Panther exits and leaves a bomb...   *The explosion melts the paint which splats Clouseau.*

Two rules of cartoon survival: double-check your zeppelin...   *...and never hug a flaming Panther.*

THE WORLD OF THE MOVIE

A HONG KONG fireworks warehouse, a Paris nightclub, a mental hospital and a downtown costume shop are just a few of the places where Clouseau's clues lead him. No wonder he's France's greatest detective—he'll go anywhere to crack the case and drive Dreyfus crazy!

The Plot

Drug baron Douvier decides to impress "The Godfather" by killing Inspector Clouseau. In a case of mistaken identity, Clouseau is pronounced dead and decides to use his "death" as a cover to seek out his killer. Meanwhile, Douvier decides to have his mistress Simone killed. When Clouseau saves her life, she becomes his accomplice. With Clouseau's servant Cato, the three fly to Hong Kong, tackle Douvier and capture "The Godfather."

Case Closed?

Seeking clues to his own murder, Clouseau makes an incognito appearance at his own funeral— revealing himself only to Inspector Dreyfus. Dreyfus faints with shock— and falls into Clouseau's grave.

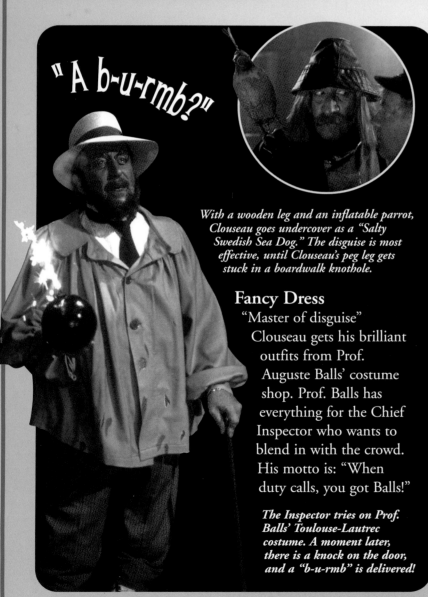

"A b-u-rmb?"

With a wooden leg and an inflatable parrot, Clouseau goes undercover as a "Salty Swedish Sea Dog." The disguise is most effective, until Clouseau's peg leg gets stuck in a boardwalk knothole.

Fancy Dress

"Master of disguise" Clouseau gets his brilliant outfits from Prof. Auguste Balls' costume shop. Prof. Balls has everything for the Chief Inspector who wants to blend in with the crowd. His motto is: "When duty calls, you got Balls!"

The Inspector tries on Prof. Balls' Toulouse-Lautrec costume. A moment later, there is a knock on the door, and a "b-u-rmb" is delivered!

Love on the Run

Simone thanks Clouseau for rescuing her from Douvier's hit men by inviting him to her apartment. Clouseau reveals his identity to her and she informs him of Douvier's plot. But the romantic mood is broken as gangsters attack again.

A Clouseau Complex

"Clouseau is gone and I am free, forever." Dreyfus' obsession with Clouseau disappears within minutes of hearing of the Inspector's murder. Seemingly cured, Dreyfus resumes his police career. "When I first heard he was dead, for a few moments, I was actually convinced I was in a state of grace," he declares.

Before he hears the news that Clouseau is dead, Dreyfus is in a terrible, twitching state, seeming to see Clouseau wherever he looks!

When he discovers that Clouseau is alive after all, Dreyfus goes gunning for him.

Cato accompanies Clouseau to Hong Kong. The Inspector has disguised himself as a gangster in an attempt to get close to Douvier.

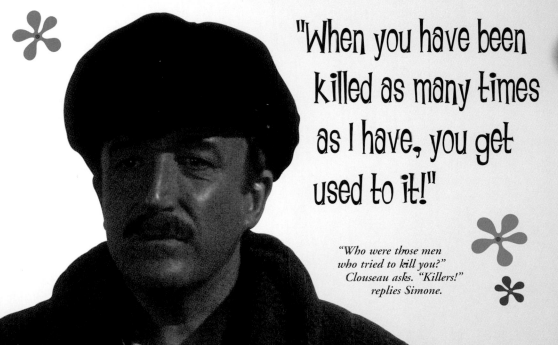

"When you have been killed as many times as I have, you get used to it!"

"Who were those men who tried to kill you?" Clouseau asks. "Killers!" replies Simone.

Car Chase

Clouseau and Cato try to outrun Douvier's gangsters —and the murderous Inspector Dreyfus—in a Hong Kong shipyard. Havoc soon erupts, with vehicles plunging off the docks, smashing into fishing boats, and crashing into each other.

Final Blast

A showdown between Douvier, Clouseau, Dreyfus, the Godfather, and the police explodes on the Hong Kong waterfront as a gunfight breaks out in a fireworks factory. Clouseau gets his men and the Medal of Honor— cementing his reputation as France's foremost detective!

The 1980s

THE WORLD of The Pink Panther expanded in new directions during this decade, maintaining the high profile of the coolest pink cat! In a prime-time TV special, The Pink Panther gained a lady love, and his two sons and a gang of their panther cub friends starred in a new Saturday morning cartoon series. Keeping the whole world tickled pink, the final live-action comedy starring Peter Sellers as Inspector Clouseau appeared, quickly followed by another movie without Clouseau altogether.

TRAIL OF THE PINK PANTHER (1982)

Part tribute, part memorial to Peter Sellers, who had passed away in 1980, *Trail of the Pink Panther* combined highlights from past movies with a few new scenes. The storyline, which featured Joanna Lumley's intrepid reporter interviewing some of Clouseau's best-known colleagues and adversaries, allowed cast members to bid a final farewell.

The newest and funniest 'Panther' of them all.

PETER SELLERS in BLAKE EDWARDS'
Trail of the Pink Panther

This one-sheet poster played up Inspector Clouseau and The Pink Panther without alluding to the all-star cast or plot details.

  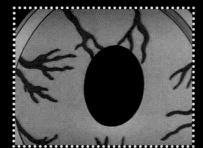

Hot on The Pink Panther's tail, the Inspector appears to be suffering from severe eye strain...

 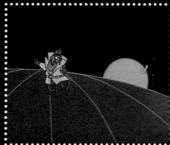 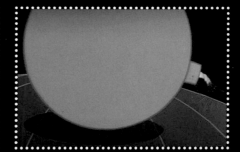 

A Pink Panther warning: there's a big pink surprise rolling Clouseau's way!

As a fitting tribute to the series' composer Henry Mancini, The Pink Panther sends Inspector Clouseau a note... in fact, several notes!

STORY by BLAKE EDWARDS

When you gotta go, you gotta go... Clouseau makes a splash celebrating director/screenwriter Blake Edwards' contribution.

Classic Memories

The film begins with a dedication—"To Peter... The one and only Inspector Clouseau"—and proceeds to honor him with unseen footage from *The Pink Panther Strikes Again* (1976) and *Revenge of the Pink Panther* (1978), plus a "greatest hits" selection of scenes from those films as well as *The Pink Panther* (1964) and *A Shot in the Dark* (1964).

To spread the word about Trail of the Pink Panther, *buildings at the former MGM movie studio in Culver City, California were adorned with pink footprints!*

Film Credits

DIRECTOR . . . Blake Edwards
PRODUCERS . . . Blake Edwards and Tony Adams
SCREENPLAY . . . Frank Waldman, Tom Waldman, Blake Edwards and Geoffrey Edwards
PHOTOGRAPHY . . . Dick Bush
FILM EDITOR . . . Alan Jones
ART DIRECTORS . . . Tim Hutchinson, John Siddall, Alan Tomkins
MUSIC . . . Henry Mancini

CAST
Peter Sellers . . . . Inspector Jacques Clouseau
David Niven . . . . Sir Charles Litton
Richard Little . . . . Sir Charles Litton (voice)
Herbert Lom . . . . Chief Inspector Dreyfus
Joanna Lumley . . . . Marie Jouvet
Capucine . . . . Lady Litton
Robert Loggia . . . . Bruno Langois
Harvey Korman . . . . Prof. Auguste Balls
Burt Kwouk . . . . Cato
Graham Stark . . . . Hercule Lajoy
Richard Mulligan . . . . Clouseau Sr.
André Maranne . . . . François
Ronald Fraser . . . . Dr. Longet
Harold Kasket . . . . President Haleesh
Harold Berens . . . . Hotel Clerk

The Main Titles

The titles were animated and directed by Arthur Leonardi at Marvel Productions. In a series of comic cartoon blackouts, The Pink Panther baffles, bothers, and bewilders the hapless Inspector Clouseau. These sequences represented the last time, to date, that these two characters have appeared together on screen.

The opening chase scene was influenced by Pacman, then the latest craze in video games.

The trail of the Pink Panther...

The Panther pulls a hair out of the projector gate—and with it makes a "cat's cradle."

For the Director of Photography credit—a flash photo!

The Pink Panther's ultimate Clouseau deterrent—a roller fully loaded with pink paint!

Inspector Clouseau's world suddenly turns pink!

THE WORLD OF THE MOVIE

CLOUSEAU IS SHOWN in several familiar locations in *Trail of the Pink Panther*, ranging from Professor Balls' costume shop and his own battleground apartment, to London and Lugash. Clouseau, Peter Sellers and Blake Edwards part company in this bittersweet film—a tribute to a man, a character and a legend.

The Plot

Dreyfus orders Clouseau to Lugash to investigate the theft of the Pink Panther diamond. Soon Clouseau's plane is reported missing. Is Clouseau dead? Hoping to learn more about France's greatest detective, television reporter Marie Jouvet interviews his friends and foes: Cato, Hercule LaJoy, Sir Charles and Lady Litton, mob boss Bruno Langlois, Prof. Balls and Clouseau's elderly father.

The fabulous jewel with the distinctive Pink Panther flaw is desired by criminals everywhere. This time Inspector Clouseau and the Pink Panther diamond both go missing.

Clouseau goes head over heels as soon as he lands at London's Heathrow airport.

Landing in London

Clouseau believes that Sir Charles Litton, alias The Phantom, has yet again stolen the Panther diamond. He flies incognito to London—which to Clouseau means wrapping himself in bandages from head to toe, crashing into every passenger on the flight, and knocking everyone off the aircraft steps when disembarking.

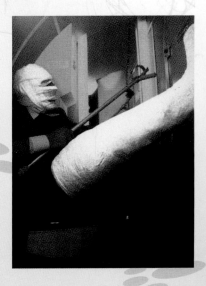

Even in the aircraft's lavatory, Clouseau maintains his disguise—no easy task with head bandaged, one leg in a cast, and no sense of balance.

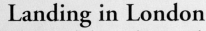

"Look, don't you try the tricks anglais with me, Monsieur!"

Missing in Action?

When Clouseau's plane disappears en route to Lugash, his disappearance is reported in the international press. The trail goes cold—until crusading reporter Marie Jouvet decides to look into the man, the myth, and the legend of Inspector Clouseau.

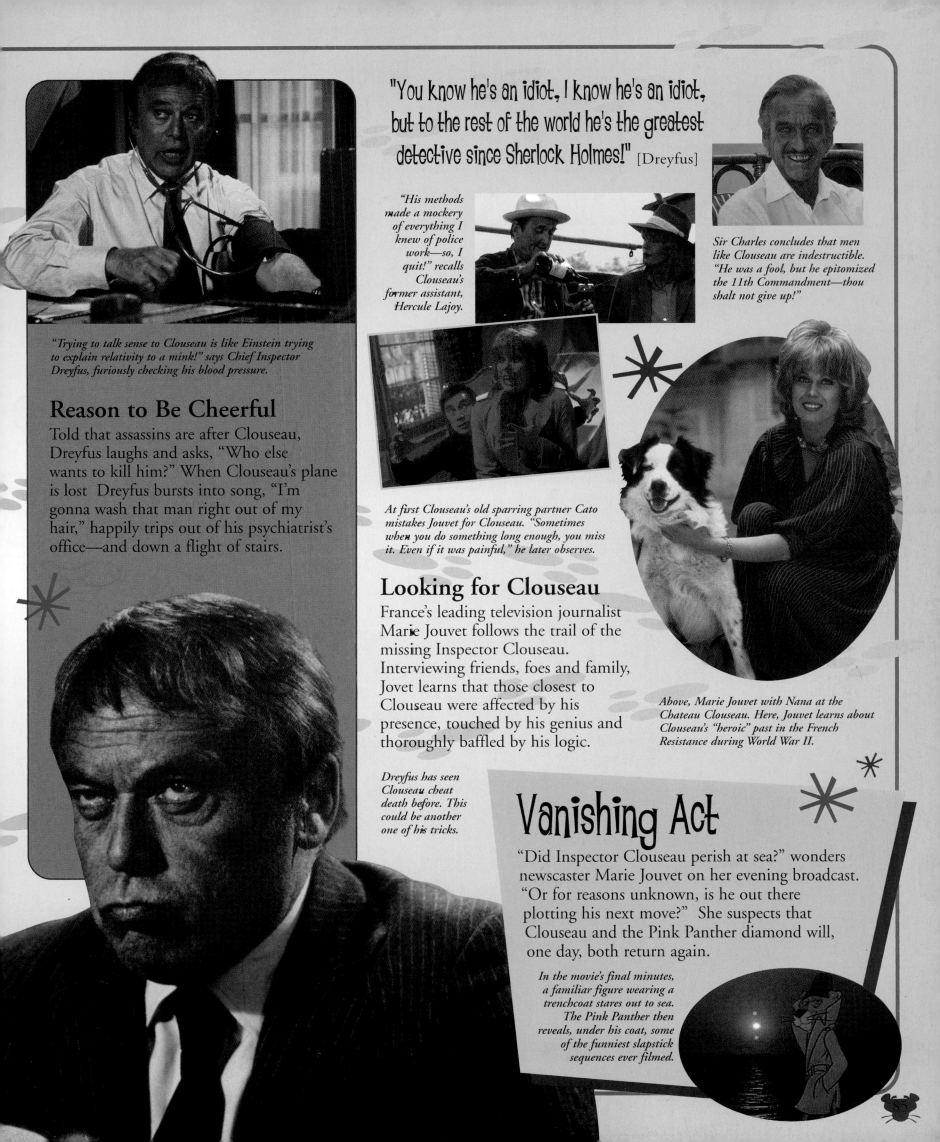

"Trying to talk sense to Clouseau is like Einstein trying to explain relativity to a mink!" says Chief Inspector Dreyfus, furiously checking his blood pressure.

Reason to Be Cheerful

Told that assassins are after Clouseau, Dreyfus laughs and asks, "Who else wants to kill him?" When Clouseau's plane is lost Dreyfus bursts into song, "I'm gonna wash that man right out of my hair," happily trips out of his psychiatrist's office—and down a flight of stairs.

"You know he's an idiot, I know he's an idiot, but to the rest of the world he's the greatest detective since Sherlock Holmes!" [Dreyfus]

"His methods made a mockery of everything I knew of police work—so, I quit!" recalls Clouseau's former assistant, Hercule Lajoy.

Sir Charles concludes that men like Clouseau are indestructible. "He was a fool, but he epitomized the 11th Commandment—thou shalt not give up!"

At first Clouseau's old sparring partner Cato mistakes Jouvet for Clouseau. "Sometimes when you do something long enough, you miss it. Even if it was painful," he later observes.

Looking for Clouseau

France's leading television journalist Marie Jouvet follows the trail of the missing Inspector Clouseau. Interviewing friends, foes and family, Jovet learns that those closest to Clouseau were affected by his presence, touched by his genius and thoroughly baffled by his logic.

Above, Marie Jouvet with Nana at the Chateau Clouseau. Here, Jouvet learns about Clouseau's "heroic" past in the French Resistance during World War II.

Dreyfus has seen Clouseau cheat death before. This could be another one of his tricks.

Vanishing Act

"Did Inspector Clouseau perish at sea?" wonders newscaster Marie Jouvet on her evening broadcast. "Or for reasons unknown, is he out there plotting his next move?" She suspects that Clouseau and the Pink Panther diamond will, one day, both return again.

In the movie's final minutes, a familiar figure wearing a trenchcoat stares out to sea. The Pink Panther then reveals, under his coat, some of the funniest slapstick sequences ever filmed.

SATURDAY MORNING PANTHER

THE PINK PANTHER has always been a swinger, but in 1984 it was decided that he should settle down and raise a couple of kids. The Panther's Saturday morning appearances that year were thus bolstered by the addition of two rose-colored cubs and a gang of their friends.

Pink Panther and Sons

Created by Friz Freleng, the *Pink Panther and Sons* series was produced by Mirisch-Geoffrey-DePatie-Freleng in association with Hanna-Barbera Productions. The stories center on Pinky and Panky and their friends, the Rainbow Panthers. The show places them in situations most children can relate to, including regular confrontations with a delinquent rival lion pack named Howl's Angels.

Original sketches of the multi-colored Panther progeny by Friz Freleng. These kids could also do something The Pink Panther rarely did—they spoke!

Unlike The Pink Panther, his sons are drawn with a black outline.

Pinky & Panky

Pinky (voiced by Billy Bowles) and Panky (voiced by B. J. Ward) are The Pink Panther's sons. Pinky is the leader of the Rainbow Panthers and he resolves all their problems with his inherited Pink Panther charm. Little Panky, the smallest of the group, communicates with baby-talk that only Pinky can understand.

Anney O'Gizmo

Like a junior secret agent, Anney has a gadget for every situation—unfortunately most of her inventions break or backfire!

Murfel

Mush-mouth Murfel mumbles so badly that Pinky has to interpret what he says for the gang.

Rocko

He's ready to rumble—though he usually stumbles! Two-fisted Rocko is the gang's resident fitness freak.

Punkin

Wherever his mind wanders, Punkin goes along for the ride. He mixes up his words, but at least he knows what he means.

Chatta

She has an opinion on everything. Chatta has a crush on Pinky and is always trying to make an impression.

Although Panky is instructed to follow his brother, it is he who usually leads the Rainbow Panthers into trouble.

The Lions

Finko (voiced by Frank Welker) and Howl (voiced by Marshall Efron) are the neighborhood bad boys. They and their gang ride around town, always looking for a good time—which usually means messing with the Panthers.

Finko the Fang, the town's punky lion.

Howl's Angels

The gang of four young bike-riding lions is led by Howl. They wear black leather jackets, and use pots and pans for safety helmets. Their sole purpose is to give the Rainbow Panthers a hard time.

Fastest member of the pack.

Howl, the leader of the gang.

The Angels' right hand man.

He's got their back.

Liona

The little lioness who hangs out with Howl's Angels, Liona has an independent attitude. She likes Pinky, despite the disapproval of the other lions, and of Chatta.

Despite Liona's romantic advances, Pinky has other matters on his mind—such as finding Panky!

The Cartoons

For *The Pink Panther and Sons*, DePatie-Freleng reinforced the Hanna-Barbera production team with Art Leonardi (who co-produced and directed the opening titles) and animator Jim Davis. Freleng had a strong hand in the show's design. Each half hour included two ten-minute stories and a Pink Panther solo vignette (directed by Leonardi). The stories were fresh and clever. Here are some of the best:

Take A Hike (1984)

The Rainbow Gang has a day in the woods—but spends most of it looking for Panky, who has wandered off to take a nap in an eagle's nest!

Pinky At The Bat (1984)

Real-life baseball star Tommy Lasorda coaches the Rainbow Panthers, who compete with Finko and the Angels over the use of the local playing field.

Haunted Howlers (1984)

Finko and Howl dress as ghosts and try to scare the Panthers as they run around a haunted house in search of Panky.

Pink Enemy # 1 (1984)

Pinky, Panky, and the Rainbow gang try to catch the crook who's been pulling heists dressed in a Pink Panther costume.

Meanwhile...

With the kids in control on Saturday mornings, The Pink Panther appealed to grown ups in TV specials: *Olym-Pinks* (1980), tied in with that year's Winter Olympics; and *Pink At First Sight* (1981), was broadcast on Valentine's Day.

The Panther found his true love in Pink At First Sight *(1981). Could she be the mother of Pinky and Panky?*

PINK PANTHER ADVERTISING

THE COOL, CALM demeanor of The Pink Panther and his air of resourceful intelligence has helped to make him the ideal pitchman for several major companies. In humorous commercials, in print ads and on billboards, the Panther comes across as trustworthy, likable, funny, smart, and assured.

The saintly Panther ensures satisfaction with Safeco Insurance.

Safeco Insurance

Safeco, in business since 1923, is a Fortune 500 company that sells auto, home and small-business insurance through independent agents and brokers nationwide. The Pink Panther was recruited in the late 1970s and early 1980s, assuring potential customers that buying insurance was easier with Safeco than with anyone else.

Concept color storyboards for an Owens Corning TV spot.

Owens Corning

The most famous association between The Pink Panther and a corporate sponsor began on August 15th 1980, when the Panther became Owens Corning's mascot, promoting the sales of pink fiberglass foam insulation. Art Leonardi boarded and directed the 30-second commercials.

TDK ◆TDK®

In the late 1980s, the Japanese electronics company TDK employed The Pink Panther for a television advertising campaign. The ad showed The Pink Panther and The Inspector eating their Christmas dinner, while TDK video cassettes videoed television programs.

These storyboards for the TDK ad campaign were sketched by animator Ted Hall.

Deutsche Telekom, Europe's largest communications company, used The Pink Panther to advertise its tariffs. Their corporate color is pink!

T··Com·   T··Com·

**Mit dem xxl Tarif
xxl telefonieren, xxs bezahlen!**
Die unverschämt günstigen Tarife von T-Com.

T··Com·   T··Com·

**Mit dem xxl Tarif
xxl telefonieren, xxs bezahlen!**
Die unverschämt günstigen Tarife von T-Com.

A Panther at Work

The Stuart Williams Paper Co. commissioned a series of Pink Panther occupational paintings (this one shows the Panther working for a fictitious pizza company) from DePatie-Freleng in the mid-1970s. The images were used on folders, calendars, and notebook covers.

DePatie-Freleng Studios in Los Angeles and Richard Williams Animation in London both produced TV commercials featuring The Pink Panther for Owens Corning. This is a rare original watercolor design.

On May 12, 1987, Owens Corning made legal history by becoming the first company to trademark a color: pink.

89

CURSE OF THE PINK PANTHER (1983)

FRANCE'S GREATEST detective is missing—"Get the world's greatest detective to find him," declares Chief Inspector Dreyfus. But finding Clouseau is the *last* thing Dreyfus has in mind... For this Pink Panther caper a new hopeless lawman, Detective Sgt. Clifton Sleigh, joins the party, and pushes Dreyfus over the edge—literally!

Film Credits

DIRECTOR . . . Blake Edwards
PRODUCERS . . . Blake Edwards and Tony Adams
SCREENPLAY . . . Blake Edwards and Geoffrey Edwards
PHOTOGRAPHY . . . Dick Bush
FILM EDITOR . . . Ralph E Winters
PRODUCTION DESIGNER . . . Peter Mullins
MUSIC . . . Henry Mancini

CAST

David Niven . . . . Sir Charles Litton
Robert Wagner . . . . George Litton
Herbert Lom . . . . Chief Insp. Dreyfus
Ted Wass . . . . Sgt. Clifton Sleigh
Capucine . . . . Lady Litton
Joanna Lumley . . . . Chandra
Robert Loggia . . . . Bruno
Harvey Korman . . . . Prof. Auguste Balls
Burt Kwouk . . . . Cato
Roger Moore . . . . Jacques Clouseau
(credited as Turk Thrust II)

BLAKE EDWARDS'
CURSE OF THE PINK PANTHER

He's been bombed, blasted and plugged in the parachute... Is this any way to welcome the Worlds Greatest Detective?

"Blake Edwards says that if Clouseau was Charlie Chaplin, then Sleigh is Harold Lloyd," explained actor Ted Wass in a studio publicity release.

Animation Director Art Leonardi drew model sheets, like the one pictured below, to enable the animators to maintain a consistent look to the film.

Double Decker

Both *Trail of the Pink Panther* and *Curse of the Pink Panther* were filmed simultaneously. Likewise the cartoon main titles for both were produced back to back at Marvel Productions.

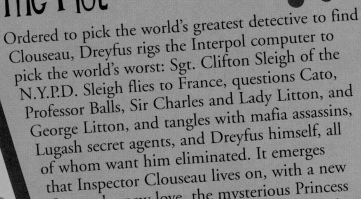

The Plot

Ordered to pick the world's greatest detective to find Clouseau, Dreyfus rigs the Interpol computer to pick the world's worst: Sgt. Clifton Sleigh of the N.Y.P.D. Sleigh flies to France, questions Cato, Professor Balls, Sir Charles and Lady Litton, and George Litton, and tangles with mafia assassins, Lugash secret agents, and Dreyfus himself, all of whom want him eliminated. It emerges that Inspector Clouseau lives on, with a new face and a new love, the mysterious Princess Chandra. The Panther diamond ends up in the hands of an old foe, The Phantom.

Part of the city of Nice (right), in the south of France, was cordoned off for a crazy car chase.

Locations, Locations, Locations!

Filmed in Europe during the spring of 1982, *Curse of the Pink Panther* revisited several places from the series' past. Nice in the south of France, the streets of Valencia, Spain, the Italian mountain resort of Cortina, and the island of Ibiza, off the Spanish coast, were among the many picturesque locations chosen. Interiors were shot at Pinewood Studios, near London.

The Main Titles

The cartoon main titles foreshadow key events in the movie. A surreal, gag-filled segment begins with The Pink Panther searching for Clouseau, shows the computer search for a new detective and the arrival of Sgt. Sleigh, and concludes with the Panther embracing a new kindred soul.

The Panther searches for Inspector Clouseau.

A tip of the hat to the great silent comedians that inspired Edwards and Sellers—the Panther evokes a classic Buster Keaton gag as a ladder falls over him.

The Panther programs a computer with Clouseau's trademark trenchcoat, hat, and a drawing of his legs...

... and then requires a 25 cent coin! As the Panther bends down, Clouseau's lower half kicks him into the computer's inner workings.

Trapped in an electronic world, the Panther is pranked in a booby-trapped photo booth.

A blinding flash returns the Panther to the real world, along with his new bespectacled friend.

PINK PANTHER PUBLISHING

AS WELL AS being a world-famous star of movies, television, and merchandising, The Pink Panther is no stranger to the literary world. He has been the subject of several dozen books, appealing not only to children but sometimes to adults—a natural move for a cool cat with plenty of tall "tails" to tell!

Storybook Adventures

The Western Publishing Company has been a Pink Panther favorite. He appeared in two Little Golden Books, *Pink Panther in the Haunted House* (1975) and *Pink Panther and Sons: Fun at The Picnic* (1985) as well as two Big Little Books published in 1980, *Pink Panther Adventures in Z-Land* and *The Pink Panther at Castle Kreep*.

"I've shrunk!" shrieked the ghost. He flitted about like a hummingbird with hiccups. "I'm ruined!" he moaned. "My haunting days are finished!"

"How true," the Pink Panther admitted. "But I have an idea! This house is big enough for both of us. Stay here and help me!"

This 1976 British annual also features the Pink Panther supporting characters The Inspector, Sergeant Deux-Deux, and The Little Man.

Novelty Books

In the 1960s, The Pink Panther Press (a subsidiary of Lion Press) published a series of satirical mini books aimed at adult readers.

Talking Books

In the 1980s, Kid Stuff Records released a series of read-along picture books to go with their audio adventures of The Pink Panther versus The Inspector. In comics, children's books, and recordings, The Pink Panther was required to vocalize.

The original TV voice cast was used on these recordings.

Annual Fun

From 1973 through 1986 the UK's World Distributors Limited published a comic annual, reprinting the best American and British Pink Panther and Inspector comic strips, games, and text stories. These annuals were linked to The Pink Panther's successful BBC television series, and are highly prized by collectors.

Cards and Calendars

Nothing brightens up the holidays or commemorates a birthday quite like a greeting card—especially if The Pink Panther is on the scene! The DePatie-Freleng studio itself created the images on these 1980s cards and calendars. The latter featured specially themed original artwork for each month of the year.

This Christmas card for DePatie-Freleng was specially created by top studio artist Arthur Leonardi.

The Inspector and Sgt. Deux-Deux were the only other characters to feature in these highly entertaining calendars.

DePatie-Freleng created their own corporate holiday cards every year. Since these were only sent to clients and friends of the studio, these cards are some of the rarest Pink Panther items.

Taking things easy with a good book fits in well with The Pink Panther lifestyle.

Activity Books

Coloring books, connect-the-dots, sticker albums, paper cut-outs, and activity books of all shapes and sizes were specially created to appeal to younger children. Kappa Graphics created a line of coloring and activity books in 2004.

MEMORABILIA 1980s

HERE, THERE, and everywhere—The Pink Panther appeared on toys for children, merchandise for adults—and on some items that only the most committed collector of Pantherabilia would desire. By the 1980s, The Pink Panther had truly become a household name.

Transfers

Colorform's Rub-n'-Play Transfers were one of many items licensed from *Pink Panther and Sons* Saturday morning TV show. Coloring books, lunch boxes, and school supplies all featured the young panthers and their friends.

Hold the Phone!

"Inspector Clouseau's residence!" That's the perfect way to answer this Panther-phone made in Japan by Greenhill Kato, 1980.

Pink Panther Lamps

Let the Panther light up your life, with this stylish Italian table lamp from Nuova Linea Zero (above). The Panther with a watermelon cart (right) is a much less expensive night-light, also from Italy.

Kinder Surprise

This salesman's sample kit of Pink Panther Kinder Egg Toys from 1989 demonstrates the wide variety of Panther toys hidden inside Ferrero chocolate eggs. These toys are highly collectible.

Royal Orleans Ceramics

Royal Orleans created an entire line of molded ceramics from 1982 through 1985, which included statuettes, holiday scenes, candle holders, trinket jars, bookends, mugs, and much, much more.

These figurines, with their high-gloss finish, are popular for their craftsmanship and humorous poses.

Toy Vehicles

The Pink Panther's worldwide reputation for fast wheels and for high-flying fun is reflected by the large selection of toy cars and planes that became available. The cartoons placed the Panther in all kinds of locales, costumes, and time periods; this gave toymakers the freedom to cast the cat in any playtime scenario that caught their fancy.

Airplane made by Bully, West Germany.

THE PINK PANTHER™
© 1982 UNITED ARTISTS
DIE CAST METAL CAR
PULL BACK ACTION • WOBBLY ENGINE

FOR AGES 3 AND UP

Die-cast Metal Car: Talbot Toys, 1982.

Pink Panther cars circa 1983–1985, by CB Toys, Italy.

Three-wheeler
This wind-up toy from Spain places the Panther on a tricycle. Shoelace legs make it look as if the Panther is pedaling as the wheels go round.

Hot Roddin'
The Pink Panther racer inspired model kits, slot cars, and toys based on its distinctive design.

HOT RODDING
FEATURES:
BOB REISNER'S CALIFORNIA SHOW CARS

ELDON
"the PINK PANTHER"

Musical Panthers
Children could create their own Pink Panther themes with this 1984 battery-powered organ by Antonelli.

Blow-up Panther
This inflatable Pink Panther was created for *Ringling Bros. and Barnum & Bailey® Circus* in 1983.

The 1990s

NEW PERSONALITIES, different voices,
changing times—but the same great color!
The Pink Panther gains a voice for his latest
television incarnation, but remains just as suave
and sophisticated as ever. Roberto Benigni brings
the Panther legacy to the big screen, combining
a fresh take with classic slapstick comedy.
The color of cool, this decade, is pink.

SON OF THE PINK PANTHER (1993)

WHEN OFFICER Jacques Gambrelli introduces himself to Chief Inspector Dreyfus as "an errfficer of ze lerr" in an accent painfully familiar—and when it turns out that Gambrelli is the son of the great detective Jacques Clouseau, the Chief Inspector's eye starts to twitch with a vengeance. Blake Edwards gathered his Panther players for one final Pink production in the 1990s—with a new Clouseau on board.

Roberto Benigni

Funny has a color all its own.

Blake Edwards'

SON OF THE PINK PANTHER

The Main Titles

The opening title sequence is a combination of live action, animation, and computer graphics. Bobby McFerrin performs the Pink Panther theme a cappella, and for the first time in a Pink Panther feature, Henry Mancini appears on screen. Geoffrey Edwards (Blake's son) directed the sequence for Desert Music Productions, and Bill Kroyer provided the character animation of the Panther.

The Pink Panther appears on the podium, like the famous conductor Leopold Stokowski.

Italian character actor and comedian Roberto Benigni invested the role of Clouseau's eccentric, opera-loving son with his own special brand of quirky charm and slapstick clowning.

He strolls onto a film scoring stage, where Bobby McFerrin and his backing singers are warming up. A pair of shades give the Panther the requisite cool.

Henry Mancini hands the Panther the baton, and he proceeds to lead the a cappella singer. However, something's amiss in the projection booth.

Film Credits

DIRECTOR . . . Blake Edwards
PRODUCER . . . Tony Adams
SCREENPLAY . . . Blake Edwards, Madeline Sunshine
and Steve Sunshine
PHOTOGRAPHY . . . Dick Bush
FILM EDITOR . . . Robert Pergament
PRODUCTION DESIGNER . . . Peter Mullins
MUSIC . . . Henry Mancini

CAST

Roberto Benigni . . . . Jacques Clouseau Jr.
Herbert Lom . . . . Charles Dreyfus
Claudia Cardinale . . . . Maria Gambrelli
Shabana Azmi . . . . The Queen
Jennifer Edwards . . . . Yussa
Robert Davi . . . . Hans
Burt Kwouk . . . . Cato
Graham Stark . . . . . . Prof. Auguste Balls

Setting the Scene

Blake Edwards brought his cast and crew to exotic locations in Europe and the Middle East, including Nice, Monte Carlo, London, Marseilles, and Petra and Amman in Jordan. The battle scene was filmed with the help of 50 Special Forces paratroopers and two large helicopters loaned by the Royal Jordanian Army.

Blake Edwards directs Cato (Burt Kwouk), who is hiding behind a statue erected in Clouseau's memory.

The Panther investigates the projection booth where Clouseau Jr. has made a mess of things. Frowning, the Panther then rewinds the film...

...but Clouseau Jr. hits the wrong lever, sending the Panther into the projector and out toward the screen!

Clouseau Jr.'s scooter suddenly backfires, sending the gormless gendarme flying right off the screen...

... and crashing into the instruments. A relieved Panther finds that his baton is still in one piece—until it suddenly droops!

THE WORLD OF THE MOVIE

THIS FINAL FILM of Blake Edwards' original group of Pink Panther comedies is filled with fresh faces and new places. Roberto Benigni's acrobatic antics bring an appropriate classic comedy sensibility to the movie, and exciting Middle Eastern locations and spectacular action sequences ramp up the danger, romance and humor.

Gambrelli wears the same Giorgio Armani hat and coat that Inspector Clouseau made famous.

Son of Clouseau

Roberto Benigni joined the Pink Panther universe as Jacques Clouseau Jr. Benigni is best known for his subsequent Academy Award winning film, *Life Is Beautiful* (1997), which he wrote, directed, and starred in. Benigni had made several hit films in Italy, including *Johnny Stecchino* (1991) when he met Blake Edwards to discuss a starring role in *Son of the Pink Panther*.

The Plot

Princess Yasmin of Lugash is kidnapped and Commissioner Dreyfus is put on the case by the President. Dreyfus is assigned a local gendarme. This officer is accident prone, mispronounces words, and his first name just happens to be Jacques. Jacques's mother, Maria Gambrelli, confirms Dreyfus's worst fears—the gendarme is Clouseau's illegitimate son! Now it's up to Clouseau Jr. to rescue the Princess and save Lugash from a military coup.

Like Father, Like Son

The son of France's greatest detective has inherited many of his father's most inept—and funniest—traits. A bumbler who mangles the language and fumbles assignments, Gambrelli has the spirit of Clouseau in his genes. When it came to culture, Senior liked to play violin; Junior, however, loves to sing opera and spout poetry. Both are romantics. Each has a way with the ladies. Both have the same effect on Dreyfus—utterly disastrous!

Just as he did with the father, Cato sneaks up on the son. Gambrelli meets the old family friend, and new ally, at the base of a statue honoring the late great Inspector.

To help Clouseau Jr. get into Lugash without being recognized, Professor Balls (Graham Stark) disguises him as a beggar.

Old Friends

Maintaining continuity with the previous Pink Panther films, Blake Edwards surrounded Clouseau Jr. with familiar faces. Returning for a final time were Burt Kwouk as Cato, Herbert Lom as Dreyfus, and Graham Stark as Professor Balls. Claudia Cardinale—who starred in the first Pink Panther film as the Princess—rejoined as Maria Gambrelli, mother of Jacques Clouseau Jr.

Clouseau Jr. visits Omar's Café, a nightclub, where he knocks over half the patrons and is immediately recognized by assassins.

Cato Incognito

Cato, Clouseau's faithful manservant, offers his services to Clouseau Jr. free of charge and joins him undercover in Lugash. Professor Balls outfits him in a perfect disguise, "his most original creation," a rabbi—in black robe, black hat, long hair and a Hitler mustache!

Hiding in an ancient jar, Cato surprises chief kidnapper Hans and lands the knockout blow that saves Clouseau Jr. and the Princess.

"Ah-ha! That Felt Good!"

Determined to rescue his beloved from the clutches of her evil kidnappers, Clouseau Jr. hitches a ride from a passing helicopter and swings into the fortress where the Princess is held captive.

Clouseau's Daughter

In the finale, Clouseau Jr. gets honored, Dreyfus and Maria Gambrelli get married and a family secret is revealed. To Dreyfus's horror it turns out Clouseau Sr. had twins with Maria! Jacques's sister Jacqueline is introduced. She catches the wedding bouquet, falls over tables, knocks Dreyfus off his feet, and whips the whole wedding party into a

Clouseau Jr. and the Princess embrace at a ceremony honoring him for his services to Lugash.

THE 1990s SHOW

Now the Panther can dance AND sing!

THE PINK PANTHER returned in 1993 in a TV series that allowed him to interact with The Inspector, The Ant and The Aardvark and The Dogfather. It returned him to the spotlight, revitalized the supporting characters and introduced several new players. More importantly, the show gave the Panther a new voice!

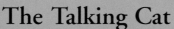

The Talking Cat

Actor Matt Frewer (Max Headroom) delivers the Pink Panther's wry and witty lines, adding a new dimension to the Panther's personality. The series was produced by an in-house MGM Animation unit led by Paul Sabella and Mark Young, and the cartoons were directed by Charles Grosvenor and Byron Vaughns.

David DePatie and Friz Freleng were consulting producers for the series.

Voodoo Man

Voodoo Man became a major supporting star of the 1990s Pink Panther Show. His wild personality made him a fan favorite. In *Pink Kong* the Panther opposes Voodoo Man when he helps Queen Kong become a nightclub singer. In *Lights, Camera, Voodoo*, studio guard Panther tries to keep the obsessive, starstruck fan (Voodoo Man) off his movie lot. And in *Pink Thumb* they work together to try to stop a non-stop eating plant!

Dan Castellaneta (Homer Simpson) provided a voice for Voodoo Man.

In *The Ghost And Mr. Panther*, The Dogfather's gang tries to scare the Panther out of a haunted house filled with "jewels." It turns out that "Jules" is the name of an abusive parrot (voiced by Charles Nelson Reilly) who lives there.

John Byner once again voiced The Ant and The Aardvark.

Down On The Ant Farm

The Pink Panther, hoping to win a science prize with his ant farm, tries to rescue his research from The Aardvark, who was sent the package by mistake and thinks it's his lunch.

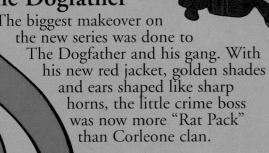

The Dogfather and Pug were now voiced by comedian Joe Piscapo.

The Dogfather

The biggest makeover on the new series was done to The Dogfather and his gang. With his new red jacket, golden shades and ears shaped like sharp horns, the little crime boss was now more "Rat Pack" than Corleone clan.

Other Characters

The series featured several hilarious supporting players. Panther adversaries included The Little Man, with the voice of actor Wallace Shawn, and The Witch, voiced by comedienne Jo Anne Worley. The Inspector also returned, partnering the Panther in several shorts and solving crimes in their usual conflicting ways.

Pink Episodes

Comedy, adventure, and cool were the chief ingredients of the 1993 series. Sixty episodes were produced, each with two, 11-minute cartoons. Here are just a few of the highlights:

Big Top Pink

The Pink Panther, a popcorn vendor, tries to join the circus and become a star—but the circus ringmaster (The Little Man) won't let him in the ring. Disguised as a clown, the Panther beats the ringmaster at his own game.

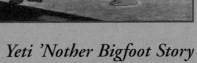

Cleopanthra

In ancient Egypt, The Pink Panther, an aspiring pyramid builder, clashes with the King's architect, Salami Ben Baloney, over the erecting of a monument to the princess.

Yeti 'Nother Bigfoot Story

The Pink Panther travels to Alaska in search of the Abominable Snowman. With accident-prone Mukluk as his guide, and a game warden as his adversary, the Panther almost becomes an endangered species himself.

The Pinky 500

The Panther challenges manly-man Clutch to an auto race. He purchases a strange pink vehicle with a mind of its own—the amorous auto is in love with a lady car!

PINK PANTHER FOOD

I T'S ALL PART OF the price of fame: your face on a cereal box, your name on a chocolate bar. The Pink Panther's appetite for fun made him a natural for food product endorsements—particularly on candy and fruit flavored drinks. If you've a sweet tooth and a taste for adventure, you may want to hunt down these snacks from around the world and give them a try. But be warned: some items shown here are exceedingly rare and highly prized.

Collectible Wrappers

As candy wrappers or soft drink bottles are usually thrown away after use, and the Pink Panther's endorsement is for a limited time only, Pink Panther food packaging is highly sought-after by collectors. Wrappers from countries other than the U.S. are especially uncommon.

The Panther is considered a sweetie all over the world, as these candies from Italy clearly demonstrate.

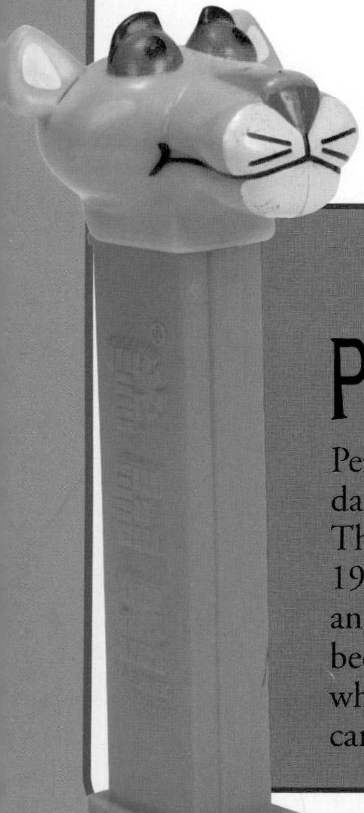

Lemonade box drinks from Natural Choice Industries (1984).

Pez

Pez candies date back to 1920s Germany. They came to the U.S. in the 1950s. The Pink Panther and his animated co-stars have since become popular among "pez-heads" who collect the colorful plastic candy dispensers.

Pez also featured The Ant & The Aardvark and The Inspector.

PINK PANTHER
Orange Punch
10% FRUIT JUICE

104

Fast Food

In 1999, Burger King featured the Pink Panther on packaging and drinking cups. With a "Kid's Club" meal they offered plastic toys, including a bendable Panther figure and an Inspector car.

Burger King toy: Panther's head as a clip-to-your-belt change holder (left).

Soda from Sweden (1984).

Lemon Sherbet and "Rinky Dink" Wafers by Rivington Foods (1998).

These Pink Panther Flakes turned the milk pink in the 1970s.

Food for thought: gumball machine and bank by Tarrson, dating from 1974.

MEMORABILIA 1990s

THE PINK PANTHER'S sophisticated image endowed all manner of toys, apparel, and decorative objects with class. In the cat's fourth decade, "The Color of Cool" became a key merchandising theme, and the range of items bearing The Pink Panther's likeness continued to soar.

Lunch Boxes and Handbags

Nostalgia for tin lunch boxes and 1960s television gave rise to this highly collectible item from Vandor (above). Panther carryalls, as a fashion accessory or a snack-time necessity, became the stylish solution for hip cats on campus.

The Panther adorns a tin lunchbox.

The car is cool enough, but The Pink Panther's shades are even cooler.

This Pink Panther tin tote is not for squares.

Fast Food Car

This 1997 Pink Panther toy was given free with a kids' meal, from a chain of "Quick" restaurants in Belgium.

Perhaps the only piece of memorabilia to feature The Dogfather.

Pugg

Mrs. Chubalingo

Collectors' Item

This plastic crockery set from Peter Pan Industries, based on the 1993 Pink Panther TV series, uses all the supporting characters on the plate, bowl, and cup.

Thelma

Manly Man

PINK PANTHER

PINK PANTHER

Soft Toys

The makers of Pink Panther plush dolls sell as many to adults who keep them for themselves as they do to parents who buy them for their children.

1999 Plush toy by Kuddle Me Toys has pink eyebrows and highlights in eyes.

1995 Cal Toys plush toy has lighter pink fur and open mouth.

1991 Plush hand puppet from 24 K Company.

Cigar Bands

These four paper bands, from a series of 12, were produced by the Dutch cigar maker Derk de Vries. They feature scenes from various Pink Panther cartoons, and are highly collectible.

Cool Cards

Happy Birthday! Get Well Soon! Having A Wonderful Time! The Panther sent you his warmest wishes in these stylish retro promotional postcards from MGM's The Color of Cool collection.

Ceramics

Vandor took the lead with Pink Panther ceramics during the 1990s. The Pink beatnik bongo drummer (left) is a salt and pepper set. So are the pair of Panther loafers (above). The Kit Kat Club bartender (right) is called a "bar bobber." It's a decoration for the kitchen or liquor cabinet.

The kitten on the keys (below) and the Panther at the bar (right) are not only clever sculptures, but imaginative salt and pepper shakers as well.

The Panther reclines atop a dice-shaped cookie jar (below). Vandor ceramics were designed to appeal to adult fans.

KIT KAT CLUB

The 2000s

FORTY YEARS OF FUN—and the Pink Panther still knows how to party. It's a new century for Pink Panthermania: the international artist Shag masterminds a new sophisticated look for the Coolest Cat; and The Pink Panther movie franchise is refreshed with a new comedy, starring Steve Martin as Inspector Clouseau. Life certainly begins at 40 for The Pink Panther!

THE 40TH ANNIVERSARY

LIGHTS! CAMERA! ACTION! The Pink Panther entered his 5th decade with a Martini-splashed celebration, a posh pink redesign, and a return to an adult sensibility. The chief architect behind the 40th Anniversary stylized visuals was modern pop artist "Shag" (a.k.a. Josh Agle), whose cocktail lounge-inspired, retro-60s designs recalled the graphics used to promote the original 1964 feature film and Friz Freleng's animated opening titles.

What was your favorite version of the Pink Panther?

SHAG: I liked that half-cat, half anthropomorphic character from the first movie credits, where he'd walk around on four legs sometimes. I sort of imagined him half way between being an actual panther and a walkin'-around-on-two-legs cartoon character. I loved the pantomime aspect of The Pink Panther, it goes back to the tradition of silent comedy.

Your version of the Pink Panther was quite sophisticated......

SHAG: I think in the minds of most people, for the last 30 years The Pink Panther has existed as a Saturday morning cartoon character—something for kids. What he originally was, however, was not a kids thing.

Your paintings evoked a cool early bachelor pad lifestyle. What inspired that? The Mancini music?

SHAG: The Henry Mancini music was perfect for it. His music of the 1950s and 1960s evoked that era a bit the same way my art did, I guess. I think a lot of people loved The Pink Panther for the music.

What kind of cartoon animation do you like?

SHAG: I like the really spare animation of the 1950s era—not that I don't like the high-quality Warner Bros. stuff, too—but I have a fondness for those studios that came up with creative ways of making the animation look good—and often ended up with some really fresh things.

How much Pink Panther merchandising with your artwork was there?

SHAG: The merchandise, I have no idea. People kept telling me about seeing my art on different items. Initially MGM wanted my art for an adult line of merchandise. On most of the pieces I did, the Panther was smoking or drinking. MGM loved it—then reality hit them. They also wanted the same poses without the cigarettes and alcohol, so they could use them on kids' stuff, too.

What was your favorite piece of merchandising?

SHAG: I loved the really high end stuff, like a limited edition line of clothing. They did a shirt, some cufflinks and a tie. They were subtle. If you look at them at first you wouldn't even know that they were Pink Panther. The cufflinks were little silver Panthers jumping through the button holes on the cuff, which was pretty cool. The tie was pink-striped with the Panther image on the reverse side. My favorite piece of art was the one with the woman holding a Pink Panther eye mask, with the Panther himself lounging on the floor.

How many pieces of art did you do for The Pink Panther's 40th Anniversary and how did you create it?

SHAG: Normally I work with Acrylic paints on a wood panel canvas. For the Pink Panther, however, I drew by hand and completed the piece on the computer. I did 80 pieces of art for The Pink Panther Anniversary—some of which was used to create animation for the website.

www.pinkpanther.com

More of Shag's artwork is featured on The Pink Panther's official website, as well as Henry Mancini's theme music, screen savers, instant message icons, and information about new Panther products and film productions.

PINK PANTHER LIFESTYLE

MORE THAN EVER, The Pink Panther has found his way into all aspects of our everyday lives. The kids who grew up with the character on Saturday morning have embraced the Panther on merchandise created by top designers and labels. The Pink Panther's not just a cartoon, he's a lifestyle!

Thomas Pink created an eye-catching window display with Shag artwork for The Pink Panther's 40th birthday.

Discreet styling was the hallmark of Thomas Pink's ties and cufflinks.

Thomas Pink

Luxury clothing label Thomas Pink celebrated the 40th Anniversary of The Pink Panther with a line of limited-edition clothing and accessories. Inspired by Shag, this rose-hued wardrobe included men and women's shirts, men's ties, and boxer shorts.

The Pink Panther Shop

Now you can wrap yourself in (simulated) panther fur and walk a mile in his shoes! The first-ever retail establishment devoted to the Pink Panther opened in Shanghai, China in 2004.

Nirve Bike

The Panther rides in style, and only on the coolest set of wheels. Nirve Sports created a distinctive Pink Panther 40th Anniversary bicycle with graphics by Shag.

"Cowhorn" handlebars give the bike a distinctive, retro look.

Watches

Inspired by Shag's revision c The Pink Panther collection were these classy watches fo ladies and gentlemen.

Pink Panther Party

The Pink Panther has inspired several dozen luscious libations—including some that are actually pink thanks to ingredients like pink lemonade and grapefruit juice. The cocktail recipe book (right) by Adam Rocke, features drinks with names like "The Clouseau" and "The Phantom, a.k.a. The Sir Charles Cocktail." Virgin Records' *Pink Panther's Penthouse Party* (left) keeps the affair fine and mellow with classic lounge music such as "The Girl From Ipanema," and Henry Mancini's "The Pink Panther Theme."

This CD features three remixes of "The Pink Panther Theme" as well as the original by Henry Mancini.

PINK PANTHER'S PENTHOUSE PARTY

PINK PANTHER Cocktail Party

Pink-a-licious drinks to seduce and entertain

Adam Rocke   Pink Panther™ 40th

The Pink Panther

$3/4$ oz. gin
$3/4$ oz. dry vermouth
$1/2$ oz. crème de cassis
$1/2$ oz. orange juice
1 egg white

Use a cocktail glass: shake with ice, strain.

Keychains for cool cats about town.

The Panther Scooter

Vespa, the famed Italian creator of the motor scooter, designed a special line of Pink Panther scooters in black, pink, and purple. Vespa decorated these limited-edition vehicles with Shag's Pink Panther designs.

AN INTERVIEW WITH STEVE MARTIN

What led to you reviving Clouseau?

Well it wasn't my idea; it was someone else's. I resisted a long time, and then I found a creative partner on the team I had just worked with, Shawn Levy and Bob Simonds, who had produced *Cheaper By The Dozen*. I had a really nice experience and I love Shawn's eagerness and sense of comedy. I met him in a parking lot one day and said I was being offered this... I was lost as to whether I could actually play the role or not. I tried out a couple of things on him, just standing in a parking lot. And he responded very very well to it. I got a little encouraged, took it a little further—and I was in. Once I started writing down a few ideas, then I felt more at ease with doing it—and feeling I could be funny in it.

There was a script in place, but you became its co-writer. Did you rewrite the story? Change the plot?

The plot was pretty much in place—though I added a few plot elements to it. But mostly it was jokes. Jokes, scenes, and bits. The original writer Len Blum did a good job, but I added my own sense of comedy.

What did you think of the original Pink Panther films?

Well, I grew up on them so I had great affection for them. We hadn't seen anything like it in my youth, so they were highly prized. Of course Peter Sellers proved himself to be a great performing artist, a great comedian as well as a dramatic actor. He was at the top of our list—and we'd constantly quote lines from the movie. Even the tiniest things we'd remember. In one bit the phone rings, and it was answered, "It's for Inspector Clouseau"—and Sellers just said, "That would be me!" In our college days that got us through a lot of stuff. I don't know what it means... but it was funny.

Did you ever have a chance to meet Peter Sellers?

Yes I did. I met him in Hawaii. I was promoting *The Jerk* and he was promoting something else, about 1980. Nice man. Never got to work with him.

You and Sellers have an affection for physical comedy. Were you inspired by the great comedians of the golden age? Laurel & Hardy?

I was inspired by Laurel & Hardy when I was growing up. I loved them because they were funny and they were touching. But mainly "the funny" we cared about—but we didn't realize how much the "touching" part was affecting us as kids.

Do you consider yourself part of the legacy of slapstick comedy?

I don't really consider it "slapstick." That refers to a very specific kind of vaudeville style—where comedians hit each other with baseball bats. You really mean physical comedy, and I love being part of that group. I realize that although it's 2005, I'm still part of early comic history—recorded comic history. 500 years from now we'll all be bunched as a group.

How would you describe the character that you are playing in this film?

It's different from Peter Sellers, why I can't quite tell you. Both Shawn and I like the inner workings of Clouseau—where he can only ascribe evil to the bad guys but not any sinister motives to his friends. For example, he never views Dreyfus as a bad egg, or out to get him. He's always trying help Dreyfus to do the best job. I don't know if that's different from the original or not. But we learned things about the character, and certainly as defined by Peter Sellers, that we either kept within those bounds—or changed slightly because I'm a different actor than he is.

Did you watch the old Pink Panther films to research the role?

I didn't. I saw them actually by accident later. I looked at them a little bit. I didn't go study them, I know that. I was a little afraid to do that.

What are some traits that are pure Clouseau?

There are certain mannerisms that are Clouseau. Certainly overconfidence, a little bit of arrogance. The way he likes to push around the small guy. He thinks he's some kind of mastermind. He also has a great affection for women.

Henry Mancini is as much a part of these films as Sellers and Edwards...

The music is fantastic. It really makes you interested in what's going on. I knew Henry Mancini a little bit. A very sweet, nice, unassuming guy for having written all those hits.

Your opinion of Blake Edwards?

Blake Edwards was a breakthrough comedy director. He modernized the entire pace of comedies up till then. There was something he had that created a new way of looking at comedy. He loved physical comedy.

Do your films reflect your personality?

Of course. They can't help it. If they express anything, it's my love of comedy. An attempt to pay my respects, and do something that people you admire do. Sometimes the theme of a movie is not as important as, "Is it funny?" So you might end up doing something you don't quite believe in morally, but it's funny so you do it anyway.

THE PINK PANTHER (2005)

Steve Martin revived and reinvented the role of Inspector Clouseau for 2005's *The Pink Panther*. "This new Pink Panther inherits the great tradition of physical and absurdist comedy," said director Shawn Levy. "But due to Steve Martin's unique writing tone, it has a level of wit and verbal cleverness that feels very fresh and unique."

The Plot

A murder at a soccer match and the disappearance of the famed Pink Panther diamond has Chief Inspector Charles Dreyfus plotting to solve the crimes and achieve his lifelong ambition: to win the National Medal of Honor. His plan is to put an incompetent officer—Clouseau—on the case, who will distract the public and the press from his own intense investigation to hunt down the killer. Clouseau, however, has a knack for being in the right place at the wrong time, a way with the ladies, and a nose (and mustache) for sniffing out criminals. His investigation leads him into the arms of the case's chief suspect, singing superstar Xania, and to confronting musclebound soccer players, and confounding his assistant, Ponton. Just when it looks as if all is lost, Clouseau solves the crime and becomes forever known as "The Pink Panther Detective."

First Impressions

Gendarme third class Clouseau is honored to be plucked from obscurity by Chief Inspector Dreyfus. As soon as they meet, Dreyfus is discomfited when Clouseau's badge flies out of his wallet and sticks in Dreyfus' chest.

Clouseau impresses Nicole, Dreyfus' stylish secretary. She offers the Inspector her services—day or night.

"It's nice weather we're having!"

Facing the Press

Dreyfus presents his chosen bungler, "A man brought in specially for this case— Inspector Clouseau." A reporter asks Clouseau: "Do you know if the killer was a man or a woman?" Clouseau replies, supremely confident: "Of course I know that! What else is there? A kitten?" And Dreyfus starts to wonder if he has chosen the right man after all...

Game Over

Soccer star Bizu is a chief suspect in the Pink Panther mystery. Bizu was jealous of his teammate Glaunt, who stole his thunder on the field and was also the owner of the Pink Panther gem. Bizu was seen arguing with Glaunt; a few minutes later, Glaunt was found dead.

Murder in the changing room: Ponton and Clouseau inspect the scene of the crime.

A Born Loser

To interview a suspect named Raymond Larocque, Clouseau heads for the casino and uses his eagle eyes to spot criminal activity. "You should only gamble what you can afford to lose," says Clouseau, airily giving advice to his assistant Ponton. Of course, Clouseau doesn't practice what he preaches—and winds up out of luck and out of cash.

Luckily Clouseau has his trench coat—he's about to lose his shirt!

Clouseau & Dreyfus

Dreyfus' fears that Clouseau is not as stupid as he appears to be begin to grow. For how could *anyone* be as clumsy, bumbling and absurd as Clouseau appears to be? Furthermore, Clouseau rapidly begins to get on Dreyfus' nerves, wreaking havoc in his office and causing him minor injuries.

Sheer Torture!

Clouseau uses the old "good cop, bad cop" routine to make Bizu confess, with himself as both cops. He threatens to hook Bizu up to an electrical gizmo, but instead ends up with his own pants on fire!

THE PLOT THICKENS...

THE HUNT FOR a murderer and the Pink Panther jewel leads Inspector Clouseau and his assistant Ponton to various cities around the world. The trail also leads to one of the world's most beautiful women, the pop superstar Xania. Could the glamorous chanteuse be the killer? Ponton is *sure* she is guilty! "Oh, you poor, sick little sidekick," declares love-struck Clouseau.

Cherchez la Femme

In New York, Clouseau tracks Xania to a black-market diamond cutter. Suspicions aroused, he accepts her invitation to dinner at the Waldorf. "It might be a trap," warns Ponton. "But what a trap," says Clouseau.

Apparently without a care in the world, Xania leaves her Waldorf Hotel suite and heads downtown to a street of seedy warehouses. Close behind, watching her every move, are Clouseau and Ponton. Where can she be going?

The Gem Man

Sykorian is a notorious underworld jewel cutter, whom Inspector Clouseau suspects of being involved in the crime. Clouseau catches him with a pink diamond—could it be the Pink Panther?

Room Service

Clouseau checks for bugs in Xania's hotel room. He finds a metal plate with wires attached to it under a rug. A moment later he has unwittingly dismantled the fixings of a massive chandelier hanging in the hotel lobby below.

Xania Mania

Strange as it may seem, the beautiful talented Xania is susceptible to Inspector Clouseau's peculiar brand of Gallic charm. Less surprisingly, the Inspector is totally bowled over by the alluring Xania. "You like to make a girl wait," she purrs when he visits her in her hotel room. "All part of the game," he suavely replies.

Caught Short

On the flight back to Paris, Clouseau gets food poisoning. The restrooms are either occupied or out of order. "I'm going to explode," cries Clouseau. In-flight security assume he has a bomb and jump on him. Upon landing, the police take him into custody, to Dreyfus' delight.

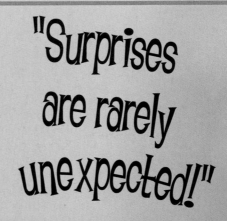

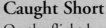

"*Surprises are rarely unexpected!*"

The Invisible Men

Gazing at a photo of Xania, Clouseau spots a clue. He and Ponton rush to the Presidential Palace and infiltrate a party by wearing unitards that blend with the palace curtains on one side, and the palace walls on the other. They then don cat-burglar suits to close in on the murderer.

The Accidental Genius

Realizing the game is up, the murderer flees. Dreyfus looks on in astonishment as Inspector Clouseau tumbles over a balustrade and lands smack dab on top of the fleeing murderer. Incredibly, it appears that there was method in Clouseau's madness, after all!

Medals of Honor

Following their brave deeds, Clouseau and Ponton are hailed as heroes. Barely able to keep from wringing their necks, Inspector Dreyfus presents Ponton with the Star of Valor and Clouseau with the Medal of Honor— the very award Dreyfus longed to win for himself!

Hero of France

"For exceptional bravery and outstanding service to the people of France, we award the Medal of Honor to a man whose name will forever be synonymous with this case— the Pink Panther Detective—Inspector Jacques Clouseau!"

At the time of printing, the film was being edited. Some scenes may have changed.

CLOUSEAU COLLAPSO

AFTER YEARS of acclaim as an actor, playwright, and author, the role of Inspector Clouseau marked a return to zany slapstick comedy for Steve Martin. The director Shawn Levy commented: "It is a return to what he does uniquely and with greatness: that is, a deep comedic character, with a thoroughness of applied persona that he hasn't done in decades."

The Great Defective

Clouseau rarely pulls a gun and it's probably just as well: the cylinder falls open, and the bullets drop out! But little setbacks like this don't deter Clouseau. "Crime is like a jigsaw puzzle," he informs Ponton. "You have to have the jig, and you have to have the saw."

Burning Love

The Inspector's date with Xania fans the flames of his desire. His cocktail of choice, a flaming Mojito, ignites not only his passions, but also his hair!

Vase Vexation

"One must always handle a ceramic from the inside," declares Clouseau, valiantly attempting to conceal his embarrassment as he gets his hands stuck in two priceless Chinese vases. The antiques belong to casino boss Raymond Larocque, one of many suspects in the case.

If there's a screw loose anywhere, you can be sure Clouseau will find it. A couple of twiddles during a visit to a soccer training ground is all it takes to send the Inspector on the slide!

Window Wrecker

Using a glass cutter and suction cup, Clouseau breaks into a drug store. He carefully cuts a circle in the window—and all the outside glass falls away!

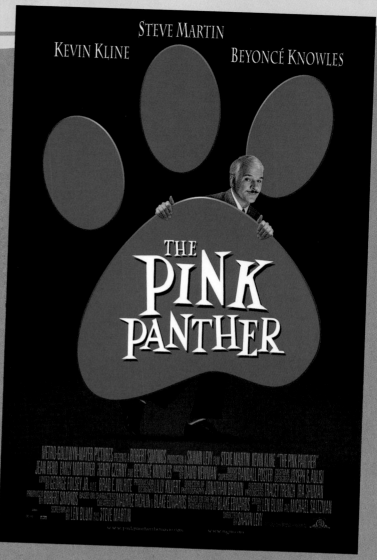

A Bridge Too Far

In a final insult to his pride, Chief Inspector Dreyfus pulls a "Clouseau" by leaping out of a police van without looking—and going right off the bridge.

Film Credits

DIRECTOR . . . Shawn Levy

PRODUCER . . . Robert Simonds

EXECUTIVE PRODUCERS . . . Tracey Trench, Ira Shuman

STORY . . . Len Blum, Michael Saltzman

SCREENPLAY . . . Len Blum and Steve Martin, based on characters created by Maurice Richlin and Blake Edwards; based on The Pink Panther Films of Blake Edwards

DIRECTOR OF PHOTOGRAPHY . . . Jonathan Brown

PRODUCTION DESIGNER . . . Lilly Kilvert

MUSIC . . . David Newman

MUSIC SUPERVISOR . . . Randall Poster

FILM EDITOR . . . George Folsey Jr. A.C.E., Brad E. Wilhite

COSTUME DESIGNER . . . Joseph G. Aulisi

CAST

Steve Martin . . . . Inspector Jacques Clouseau

Kevin Kline. . . . . Chief Inspector Dreyfus

Beyoncé Knowles. . . . . Xania

Jean Reno . . . . Ponton

Kristin Chenoweth. . . . . Chérie

Henry Czerny. . . . . Yuri

Boris McGiver. . . . . Vainqueur

Emily Mortimer. . . . . Nicole

Clouseau and Ponton, those masters of disguise, pose proudly in their presidential palace curtain and wallpaper outfits.

"Randy Raspberry" Cocktail Candy (produced for Planet Sugar, Inc. by Twang, Inc.) was a promotional item for the 40th Anniversary.

Sleek, slick, pink and proud—the proper place for your Panther parasol!

MEMORABILIA 2000

THE PINK PANTHER continues to make his mark in collectibles and merchandising, achieving a status reserved only for Hollywood's greatest stars. With his mischievous manner, suave style, and playful personality, he has secured his place as an icon of cool and a cartoon classic.

Umbrella Fella

Made of resin, this umbrella stand is 4 feet tall and 17 inches wide. Manufactured in the Philippines in the year 2000, this is one of the largest Panther statues ever created for sale.

The Pink Panther Film Collection

Shown here is the international DVD box set containing five of Blake Edwards' Pink Panther movies. The special features include Pink Panther cartoons and an all-new documentary entitled "The Pink Panther Story."

This bikini swimsuit is sure to attract attention at the beach!

Cap-sleeve T-shirt by Jerry Leigh.

Clothing

Outer wear... underwear... anywhere! The Pink Panther on your person provides a laugh and a half of high style and fashion fun. T-shirts, camisoles, lingerie, swimsuits—this cat is cute on any attire, and on any occasion. Dress up or dress down, but dress pink!

Furry Panther slippers from SG footwear keep your feet warm on the coldest night.

Cocktail Time

3E Trading created this spectacular "Pink Drink" Neon Wall Clock featuring Shag's 40th Anniversary Pink Panther. The clock is 11.75 inches in diameter with a black metal face and pink neon tubing surround.

A Touch of Class

Accessorize your outfit with this selection of 40th Anniversary buttons and patches, produced by C&D Visionary Inc.

Panther Rings

The Pink Panther and The Inspector make popular subjects for novelty key rings.

Switched On Panther

The Pink Panther, in his signature tip-toe pose, holds an exposed light bulb. This 2-foot-tall, resin lamp has a quirky, Bohemian touch guaranteed to brighten up any dark corner.

Special Watches

Pink Panther watches are always highly sought after. This Pink Panther watch was designed by Accutime for Avon.

Proclaim your class, taste, and love of the Panther with these silk ties by MJC.

A PINK CAREER

THE SHEER VOLUME OF FILM created by The Pink Panther's worldwide success has left an indelible mark—a pink one, naturally—on our collective consciousness. The Pink Panther has appeared in a hugely successful series of feature films, in theatrical animated shorts, made-for-TV cartoons, prime-time specials, numerous commercials, as well as featuring in decades of memorabilia. His first short, *The Pink Phink,* won an Academy Award®, and his theme tune by Henry Mancini won a Grammy®. Like the spectacular diamond that inspired the character's first ever screen appearance, each sighting of the Pink Panther is a gem.

THE CARTOONS

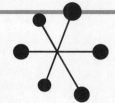

The following is a complete list of all DePatie-Freleng cartoons originally released by United Artists to theaters between 1964 and 1982. They are listed in order of their release dates. Please note that *The Pink Phink* won the Academy Award® for Best Animated Short of 1964 and *The Pink Blue Print* was nominated in the same category in 1966. This list is followed by a listing of Pink Panther Saturday Morning TV Shows, live-action features, and TV specials.

1964

The Pink Phink
December 18—The Pink Panther
Director: Friz Freleng **Co-director:** Hawley Pratt **Story:** John Dunn **Music:** William Lava **Animation:** Don Williams, Bob Matz, Norm McCabe, LaVerne Harding
A painter tries to paint a house blue, but the Pink Panther has pink in mind.

Pink Pajamas
December 25—The Pink Panther
Director: Friz Freleng **Co-director::** Hawley Pratt **Story:** John Dunn **Music:** William Lava **Animation:** Bob Matz, Norm McCabe, LaVerne Harding, Don Williams
The Pink Panther sneaks into a drunk's house for a night's sleep.

1965

We Give Pink Stamps
February 12—The Pink Panther
Director: Friz Freleng **Co-director:** Hawley Pratt **Story:** John Dunn **Music:** William Lava **Animation:** Norm McCabe, LaVerne Harding, Don Williams, Manny Perez, Warren Batchelder, Bob Matz
The Pink Panther spends a night in a department store.

Dial "P" for Pink
March 17—The Pink Panther
Director: Friz Freleng **Co-director:** Hawley Pratt **Story:** Bob Kurtz **Music:** William Lava **Animation:** LaVerne Harding, Don Williams, Manny Perez, Warren Batchelder, Bob Matz, Norm McCabe
The Pink Panther matches wits with a safe cracker.

Pink Panther Oscar

Sink Pink
April 12—The Pink Panther
Director: Friz Freleng (uncredited) **Co-director:** Hawley Pratt **Story:** John Dunn **Music:** William Lava **Animation:** Don Williams, Manny Perez, Warren Batchelder, Bob Matz, Norm McCabe, LaVerne Harding **Voices:** Paul Frees, Rich Little.
Tex, a hunter from Texas, builds a "Nora's Ark" to trap a Pink Panther.
One of two Pink Panther theatrical cartoons where the Panther talks. He says: "Why can't man be more like animals?" at the end.

Pickled Pink
May 12—The Pink Panther
Director: Friz Freleng **Co-director:** Hawley Pratt **Story:** Bob Kurtz **Music:** William Lava **Animation:** Manny Perez, Warren Batchelder, Bob Matz, Norm McCabe, LaVerne Harding, Don William **Voices:** Mel Blanc
The Pink Panther is brought home by a drunken little man—to the dismay of his overbearing wife.

Pinkfinger
May 13—The Pink Panther
Director: Friz Freleng **Co-director:** Hawley Pratt **Story:** Bob Kurtz **Music:** William Lava **Animation:** LaVerne Harding, Don Williams, Norm McCabe
The Pink Panther becomes a secret agent.

Shocking Pink
May 13—The Pink Panther
Director: Friz Freleng **Co-director:** Hawley Pratt **Story:** Bob Kurtz **Layout:** Dick Ung **Music:** William Lava **Animation:** Norm McCabe, La Verne Harding, Don Williams **Narrator:** Larry Storch.
The Pink Panther gets a lesson on how to use his free time.

Pink Ice
June 10—The Pink Panther
Director: Friz Freleng **Co-director:** Hawley Pratt **Story:** John Dunn **Music:** William Lava **Animation:** Warren Batchelder, Bob Matz, Norm McCabe, LaVerne Harding, Don Williams, Manny Perez **Voice:** Rich Little.
The Pink Panther's rivals steal from a diamond mine.
The only Pink Panther cartoon, until a 1993 series, where he had extensive dialogue.

The Pink Tail Fly
August 25—The Pink Panther
Director: Friz Freleng **Co-director:** Hawley Pratt **Story:** Bob Kurtz **Music:** William Lava **Animation:** Don Williams, Norm McCabe, LaVerne Harding
A bothersome fly bugs the Panther.
The last Pink panther cartoon directed by Friz Freleng.

Pink Panzer
September 15—The Pink Panther
Director: Hawley Pratt **Story:** David Detiege **Music:** William Lava **Animation:** Norm McCabe, LaVerne Harding, Don Williams
The Pink Panther gets into battle with his next-door neighbor.

An Ounce of Pink
October 20—The Pink Panther
Director: Hawley Pratt **Story:** Bob Kurtz **Music:** William Lava **Animation:** LaVerne Harding, Don Williams, Norm McCabe
A speak-your-weight machine tells more than The Pink Panther's weight.

A safecracker's explosive plans go awry in Dial "P" for Pink (1965)

Reel Pink
November 16—The Pink Panther
Director: Hawley Pratt **Music:** William Lava **Animation:** Don Williams, Norm McCabe, LaVerne Harding, Manny Perez
An uncooperative worm gets in the way of The Pink Panther's fishing.

Bully for Pink
December 14—The Pink Panther
Director: Hawley Pratt **Story:** John Dunn **Music:** William Lava **Animation:** Norm McCabe, Warren Batchelder, Don Williams
The Pink Panther becomes a matador.

The Great DeGaulle Stone Operation
December 21—The Inspector
Director Friz Freleng **Co-director:** Gerry Chiniquy **Story:** John Dunn **Theme:** Henry Mancini **Music:** William Lava **Animation:** Manny Perez, Don Williams, Bob Matz, Warren Batchelder, Norm McCabe, George Grandpre **Voices:** Pat Harrington, Paul Frees, Larry Storch.
The Inspector guards the DeGaulle jewel from the sinister Matzoriley Brothers.

1966

Reaux, Reaux, Reaux Your Boat
February 1—The Inspector
Director: Gerry Chiniquy **Story:** John W. Dunn **Music:** William Lava **Animation:** Warren Batchelder, Norm McCabe, Manny Perez, Don Williams, Bob Matz, George Grandpre
The Inspector and Sgt. Deux-Deux are assigned to catch pearl smuggler Captain Calamity and his henchman Crab Louie.

Napoleon Blown-Aparte
February 2—The Inspector
Director: Gerry Chiniquy **Story:** John Dunn **Music:** William Lava **Animation:** Manny Perez, Don Williams, Bob Matz, Warren Batchelder, Norm McCabe, George Grandpre
The Inspector tries to stop a mad bomber intent on getting even with The Commissioner.

Pink Punch
February 21—The Pink Panther
Director: Hawley Pratt **Story:** Michael O'Connor **Music:** William Lava **Animation:** Warren Batchelder, Don Williams, Norm McCabe, Bob Matz, LaVerne Harding
The Pink Panther tries to promote his new drink, Pink Punch, but becomes annoyed by a pesky green asterisk.

Cirrhosis Of The Louvre
March 9—The Inspector
Director: Gerry Chiniquy **Story:** John Dunn **Music:** William Lava **Animation:** Bob Matz, Warren Batchelder, Norm McCabe, George Grandpre, Manny Perez, Don Williams
A shape-shifting criminal known as The Blotch threatens to steal paintings from the Louvre museum.

Pink Pistons
March 16—The Pink Panther
Director: Hawley Pratt **Story:** Michael O'Connor **Music:** William Lava **Animation:** Don Williams, Norm McCabe, LaVerne Harding, Warren Batchelder
A car with a mind of its own takes The Pink Panther hostage.

Plastered in Paris
April 5—The Inspector
Director: Gerry Chiniquy **Story:** John Dunn **Music:** William Lava **Animation:** Norm McCabe, Manny Perez, Don Williams, Warren Batchelder, Ted Bonnicksen
The Inspector travels from France to Egypt and onto Nairobi in pursuit of the elusive villain "X."

Vitamin Pink
April 6—The Pink Panther
Director: Hawley Pratt **Story:** Michael O'Connor **Music:** William Lava **Animation:** Norm McCabe, LaVerne Harding, Warren Batchelder, Don Williams
The Pink Panther turns a wild west convict on to his super-vitamins.

The Pink Blue Print
May 25—The Pink Panther
Director: Hawley Pratt **Story:** John Dunn **Music:** William Lava **Animation:** Warren Batchelder, Don Williams, Norm McCabe, Dale Case, LaVerne Harding
The Pink Panther battles with a contractor in order to build his dream house.
Nominated for Academy Award®— Best Short Subject [animated]

Pink-A-Boo (1966)

Pink, Plunk, Plink
May 25—The Pink Panther
Director: Hawley Pratt **Story:** Michael O'Connor **Music:** William Lava **Animation:** Norm McCabe, Dale Case, LaVerne Harding, Warren Batchelder, George Grandpre, Don Williams
The Pink Panther vies with a musical conductor over who shall conduct a concert orchestra.
The composer Henry Mancini makes a cameo appearance at the end.

Smile Pretty, Say Pink
May 29—The Pink Panther
Director: Hawley Pratt **Story:** John Dunn **Music:** William Lava **Animation:** LaVerne Harding, Warren Batchelder, Don Williams, Norm McCabe, Bob Matz
The Pink Panther decides to try his hand at becoming a photographer.

Cock-A-Doodle Deux-Deux
June 15—The Inspector
Director: Robert McKimson **Story:** Michael O'Connor **Music:** William Lava **Animation:** Manny Perez, Don Williams, Warren Batchelder, Ted Bonnicksen, Norm McCabe, George Grandpre, Bob Matz
Assigned to guard the world's largest diamond necklace, The Inspector disguises himself as a chicken to uncover a fowl plot.
The last DePatie-Freleng cartoon to credit William lava for music score.

Ape Suzette
June 24—The Inspector
Director: Gerry Chiniquy **Story:** John Dunn **Music:** Walter Greene **Animation:** Don Williams, Warren Batchelder, Ted Bonnicksen, George Grandpre
The Inspector tracks a gang of banana hijackers to an old English sailor and his pet ape.

The Pink Blue Print (1966)

Pink-A-Boo

June 26—The Pink Panther
Director: Hawley Pratt **Story:** John Dunn
Music: Walter Greene **Animation:** Don
Williams, Norm McCabe, Dale Case, LaVerne
Harding, Warren Batchelder
The Pink Panther tries to get rid of a
troublesome mouse.

The Pique Poquette Of Paris

August 25—The Inspector
Director: George Singer **Story:** John Dunn
Music: Walter Greene **Animation:** Warren
Batchelder, George Grandpre, Bob Matz,
Norm McCabe, Manny Perez
The Inspector tracks down the wall-crawling
menace, Spider Pierre.

Genie With The Light Pink Fur

September 14—Pink Panther
Director: Hawley Pratt **Story:** John Dunn
Music: Walter Greene **Animation:** Dale Case,
LaVerne Harding, George Grandpre, Don
Williams, Virgil Raddatz
The Pink Panther becomes a
genie in a magic
lamp.

1960s character sketches: The
Inspector (far right) appears with
the drunk from *Pickled Pink* (1964),
the villain from *Pinkfinger* (1964),
and the muscle man from *Come On
In! The Water's Pink* (1968).

Sicque! Sicque! Sicque!

September 23—The Inspector
Director: George Singer **Story:** John Dunn
Music: Walter Greene **Animation:** Norm
McCabe, Manny Perez, Warren Batchelder,
Don Williams, Bob Matz
Sgt. Deux-Deux becomes a Mr. Hyde as The
Inspector searches the home of a mad scientist.

Super Pink

October 12—The Pink Panther
Director: Hawley Pratt **Story:** John Dunn
Music: Walter Greene **Animation:** LaVerne
Harding, Don Williams, Bob Matz, Warren
Batchelder, John Gibbs
The Pink Panther becomes a super hero.

That's No Lady—That's Notre Dame

October 26—The Inspector
Director: George Singer **Story:** John Dunn
Music: Walter Greene **Animation:** Warren
Batchelder, Don Williams, Bob Matz, Ted
Bonnicksen, John Gibbs, LaVerne Harding
The Inspector, disguised as a lady to track a purse
thief, catches the amorous eye of The
Commissioner.

Unsafe and Seine

November 9—The Inspector
Director: George Singer **Story:** John Dunn
Music: Walter Greene **Animation:** Manny Perez,
Warren Batchelder, Don Williams, Bob Matz,
Dale Case
The Inspector tracks a mysterious secret agent to
various points around the world.

The Panther goes green in *Jet Pink* (1967)

Rock-A-Bye Pinky

December 23—The Pink Panther
Director: Hawley Pratt **Story:** John Dunn
Music: Walter Greene **Animation:** Bob Matz,
Warren Batchelder, John Gibbs, LaVerne
Harding, Manny Perez, Manny Gould,
Ted Bonnicksen
A snoring neighbor keeps The Pink Panther
awake through the night.

Toulouse La Trick

December 30—The Inspector
Director: Robert McKimson **Story:** John
Dunn **Music:** Walter Greene **Animation:**
Don Williams, Bob Matz, Ted
Bonnicksen, Warren Batchelder,
Manny Perez
The Inspector handcuffs himself to a
huge prisoner, who escapes captivity,
dragging The Inspector along
with him.

1967

Pinknic

**January 6—The Pink
Panther**
Director: Hawley Pratt **Story:** John Dunn
Music: Walter Greene **Animation:** Don
Williams, Warren Batchelder, John Gibbs,
Manny Perez, LaVerne Harding
The Pink Panther finds himself snowbound in a
mountain cabin.

Pink Panic

January 11—The Pink Panther
Director: Hawley Pratt **Story:** John Dunn
Music: Walter Greene **Animation:** Warren
Batchelder, John Gibbs, LaVerne Harding,
Manny Perez, Manny Gould, Don Williams,
Bob Matz
Ghosts and spooky skeletons chase The Pink
Panther through a haunted hotel.

Sacré Bleu Cross

February 1—The Inspector
Director: Gerry Chiniquy **Story:** John Dunn
Music: Walter Greene **Animation:** Bob Matz,
Ted Bonnicksen, Manny Perez, Norm McCabe,
Art Leonardi, Don Williams
On the trail of a dangerous criminal, Sgt. Deux-
Deux fnds that his lucky rabbit's foot has become
a magnet for disaster.

Pink Posies

April 26—The Pink Panther
Director: Hawley Pratt **Story:** Jim Ryan
Music: Walter Greene **Animation:** Bob
Matz, Warren Batchelder, Art Leonardi,
Don Williams, Manny Gould
A shared garden causes problems between The
Pink Panther and his neighbor.

Le Quiet Squad

May 17—The Inspector
Director: Robert McKimson **Story:** Jim Ryan
Music: Walter Greene **Animation:** Ted
Bonnicksen, Manny Perez, Norm McCabe, Don
Williams, Manny Gould, Bob Matz
The stressed-out Commissioner is advised
to stay in bed in absolute quiet by his doctor.
Unfortunately, The Inspector is dispatched
to keep the peace.
*Bugs Bunny makes a cameo
appearance.*

Pink Of The Litter

May 17—The Pink Panther
Director: Hawley Pratt **Story:** John Dunn
Music: Walter Greene **Animation:** Warren
Batchelder, Don Williams, Manny Gould,
Bob Matz, Manny Perez
The Pink Panther literally cleans up a dirty town.

In The Pink

May 18—The Pink Panther
Director: Hawley Pratt **Story:** John Dunn
Music: Walter Greene **Animation:** Manny Perez,
Norm McCabe, Don Williams, Manny Gould,
Warren Batchelder, Ted Bonnicksen, Art
Leonardi
The Pink Panther enrolls in a health club.

Bomb Voyage

May 22—The Inspector
Director: Robert McKimson **Story:** Tony
Benedict **Music:** Walter Greene **Animation:**
Manny Perez, Don Williams, Manny Gould,
Bob Matz, Ted Bonnicksen, Warren Batchelder
The Inspector attempts to rescue The
Commissioner, who has been captured by aliens
from outer space.

Le Pig-Al Patrol

May 24—The Inspector
Director: Gerry Chiniquy **Story:** Jim Ryan
Music: Walter Greene **Animation:** Manny
Gould, Bob Matz, Warren Batchelder, Manny
Perez, Art Leonardi, Don Williams
The Inspector tries to apprehend a vicious
motorcycle gang.

Le Bowser Bagger

May 30—The Inspector
Director: Gerry Chiniquy **Story:** Jim Ryan
Music: Walter Greene **Animation:** Bob Matz,
Warren Batchelder, Manny Perez, Don Williams,
Manny Gould
The Inspector and his police dog track down
a robber.

The Panther singes his tail in *Jet Pink* (1967)

Jet Pink

June 13—The Pink Panther
Director: Gerry Chiniquy **Story:** Tony Benedict
Music: Walter Greene **Animation:** Don
Williams, Bob Matz, Warren Batchelder, Manny
Perez, Art Leonardi
The Pink Panther flies a jet.

Pink Paradise

June 24—The Pink Panther
Director: Gerry Chiniquy **Story:** John Dunn
Music: Walter Greene **Animation:** Manny
Gould, Bob Matz, Warren Batchelder
The Pink Panther is marooned on a
tropical island with The
Little Man.

Le Escape Goat

June 29—The Inspector
Director: Gerry Chiniquy **Story:** Jim Ryan
Music: Walter Greene **Animation:** Don
Williams, Manny Gould, Bob Matz, Warren
Batchelder, Manny Perez
Fired for letting a prisoner to escape,
The Inspector tries to get his job
back by protecting The
Commissioner from a vengeful
convict named
Louie Le Fink.

Le Cop On Le Rocks

June 3—The Inspector
Director: George Singer **Story:** Jim Ryan
Music: Walter Greene **Animation:** Manny Perez,
Don Williams
The Inspector is sent to prison by mistake.

Pinto Pink

July 19—The Pink Panther
Director: Hawley Pratt **Story:** John Dunn
Music: Walter Greene **Animation:** Don
Williams, Manny Gould, Bob Matz, Manny
Perez, Warren Batchelder, Chuck Downs
The Pink Panther tries to ride a horse.

Crow DeGuerre

August 16—The Inspector
Director: Gerry Chiniquy **Story:** John Dunn
Music: Walter Greene **Animation:** Don
Williams, Chuck Downs, John Gibbs, Bob Matz,
Warren Batchelder, Manny Perez
The Inspector tangles with a crow who is an
expert jewel thief.

Canadian Can-Can

September 20—The Inspector
Director: Gerry Chiniquy **Story:** John Dunn
Music: Walter Greene **Animation:** Bob Matz,
Manny Perez, Don Williams, Manny Gould,
Chuck Downs
The Inspector is transferred to the Northwest
Mounted Police where he must track down the
outlaw Two-Faced Harry.

Tour De Farce

October 25—The Inspector
Director: Gerry Chiniquy **Story:** Jim Ryan
Music: Walter Greene **Animation:** Chuck
Downs, Bob Matz, Warren Batchelder, Manny
Perez, Don Williams, Manny Gould
The Inspector findsd himself trapped on a desert
island with a notorious criminal known as
Mack Latrukk.

Congratulations! It's Pink

October 27—The Pink Panther
Director: Hawley Pratt **Story:** John Dunn
Music Score: Walter Greene **Animation:** Manny
Gould, Bob Matz, Manny Perez, Warren
Batchelder, Chuck Downs, Don Williams
The Pink Panther experiences the dubious joys of
parenthood.

*The Hand Is Pinker Than
The Eye* (1967)

The Hand Is Pinker Than The Eye (1967).

Prefabricated Pink

November 22—The Pink Panther
Director: Hawley Pratt **Story:** Jim Ryan
Music: Walter Greene **Animation:** Warren
Batchelder, Chuck Downs, Don Williams,
Manny Gould, Manny Perez, Bob Matz
The Pink Panther takes a job as a construction
worker, with hilariously destructive results.

The Hand Is Pinker Than The Eye

December 20—The Pink Panther
Director: Hawley Pratt **Story:** Jim Ryan
Music: Walter Greene **Animation:** Bob Matz,
Warren Batchelder, Chuck Downs,
Don Williams, Manny Gould
The Pink Panther takes refuge in the trick house
of a magician.

The Shooting of the Caribou Lou

December 20—The Inspector
Director: Gerry Chiniquy **Story:** John Dunn
Music: Walter Greene **Animation:** Manny Perez,
Don Williams, Manny Gould, Chuck Downs,
Bob Matz
The Inspector is held hostage by evil Caribou
Lou in the Canadian northwoods.

Pink Outs

December 27—The Pink Panther
Director: Gerry Chiniquy **Story:** Art Leonardi
Music: Walter Greene **Animation:** Manny Perez,
Bob Matz, Warren Batchelder, Don Williams,
Manny Gould
This cartoon contains an unrelated series of
funny skits or "blackout" gags.

1968

Sky Blue Pink

January 3—The Pink Panther
Director: Hawley Pratt **Story:** John Dunn
Music: Walter Greene **Animation:** Don
Williams, Manny Gould, Manny Perez, Bob
Matz, Warren Batchelder
The Pink Panther creates chaos when he tries
to fly a kite.

London Derrière

February 7—The Inspector
Director: Gerry Chiniquy **Story:** Jim Ryan **Music:** Walter Greene **Animation:** Don Williams, Manny Gould, Chuck Downs, Bob Matz, Manny Perez
In England, where policeman are unarmed, The Inspector has a hard time catching a jewel thief without the use of his gun.

Pinkadilly Circus

February 21—The Pink Panther
Director: Hawley Pratt **Story:** John Dunn **Music:** Walter Greene **Animation:** Manny Gould, Manny Perez, Bob Matz, Warren Batchelder, Don Williams
The Pink Panther becomes devoted to a man who helps him remove a tack from his foot.

Psychedelic Pink

March 13—The Pink Panther
Director: Hawley Pratt **Story:** Jim Ryan **Music:** Walter Greene **Animation:** Bob Matz, Warren Batchelder, Don Williams, Manny Gould, Manny Perez
The Pink Panther enters a hippie book shop and has a psychedelic experience.

Les Miserobots

March 21—The Inspector
Director: Gerry Chiniquy **Story:** Jim Ryan **Music:** Walter Greene **Animation:** Warren Batchelder, Tom Ray, Manny Perez, Don Williams, Manny Gould
The Inspector tries to destroy a robot which has taken his job.

Transylvania Mania

March 26—The Inspector
Director: Gerry Chiniquy **Story:** John Dunn **Music:** Walter Greene **Animation:** Don Williams, Manny Gould, Warren Batchelder, Tom Ray, Manny Perez
A vampire and his monstrous assistant need The Inspector's brain for a transplant experiment.

Little Beaux Pink (1968).

Come On In!

The Water's Pink

April 10—The Pink Panther
Director: Hawley Pratt **Story:** Jim Ryan **Music:** Walter Greene **Animation:** Manny Perez, Warren Batchelder, Don Williams, Tom Ray, Manny Gould
The Panther spends a day at Bicep Beach, where he meets a jealous body builder.

Put-Put Pink

April 14—The Pink Panther
Director: Gerry Chiniquy **Story:** Jim Ryan **Music:** Walter Greene **Animation:** Warren Batchelder, Don Williams, Tom Ray, Manny Gould, Manny Perez
The Pink Panther builds a motorcycle—and quickly confronts a motorcycle cop.

Bear De Guerre

April 26—The Inspector
Director: Gerry Chiniquy **Story:** Jim Ryan **Music Score:** Walter Greene **Animation:** Manny

---

The Inspector as a Canadian Mountie.

Gould, Warren Batchelder, Tom Ray, Manny Perez, Don Williams
On vacation, The Inspector goes quail hunting and disturbs a sleeping bear.

G.I. Pink

May 1—The Pink Panther
Director: Hawley Pratt **Story:** John Dunn **Music:** Walter Greene **Animation:** Warren Batchelder, Don Williams, Tom Ray, Manny Gould, Manny Perez
The Pink Panther is drafted into the army and drives his sergeant crazy.

Lucky Pink

May 7—The Pink Panther
Director: Hawley Pratt **Story:** Bob Ogle **Music:** Walter Greene **Animation:** Tom Ray, Manny Gould, Manny Perez, Warren Batchelder, Don Williams
The Pink Panther tries to return a lucky horseshoe to a bank robber.

The Pink Quarterback

May 22—Pink Panther
Director: Hawley Pratt **Story:** John Dunn **Music:** Walter Greene **Animation:** Don Williams, Tom Ray, Manny Gould, Manny Perez, Warren Batchelder
The Pink Panther tries to retrieve a quarter he dropped into the subway.

Cherche Le Phantom

June 13—The Inspector
Director: Gerry Chiniquy **Story:** Tony Benedict **Music:** Walter Greene **Animation:** Manny Perez, Don Williams, Manny Gould, Warren Batchelder, Tom Ray
The Inspector has to capture an opera-loving gorilla.

Twinkle, Twinkle Little Pink

June 30—The Pink Panther
Director: Hawley Pratt **Story:** John Dunn **Music:** Walter Greene **Animation:** Manny Gould, Manny Perez, Warren Batchelder, Don Williams, Tom Ray, John Gibbs
The Panther's new house is directly in the path of an observatory telescope and a peeping astronomer.

Le Great Dane Robbery

July 7—The Inspector
Director: Gerry Chiniquy **Story:** Jim Ryan **Music:** Walter Greene **Animation:** Manny Gould, Chuck Downs, Bob Matz, Manny Perez, Don Williams
To gain entry to a foreign embassy, The Inspector has to sneak past a guard dog.

Pink Valiant

July 10—The Pink Panther
Director: Hawley Pratt **Story:** John Dunn **Music:** Walter Greene **Animation:** Tom Ray, Manny Gould, Manny Perez, Warren Batchelder, Don Williams
The Pink Panther is dubbed "Sir Pink of the Round Table" and sets off to rescue a princess from the Black Knight.

La Feet's Defeat

July 24—The Inspector
Director: Gerry Chiniquy **Story:** Jim Ryan **Music:** Walter Greene **Animation:** Manny Gould, Warren Batchelder, Tom Ray, Manny Perez, Don Williams
Muddy La Feet, the dirtiest crook in France, escapes from Le Hoozgow Prison.

Le Ball And Le Chain Gag

July 24—The Inspector
Director: Gerry Chiniquy **Story:** Jim Ryan **Music:** Walter Greene **Animation:** Don Williams, Manny Gould, Warren Batchelder, Manny Perez
The Inspector pursues a man and wife who have no idea why the police are after them.

The Pink Pill

July 31—The Pink Panther
Director: Gerry Chiniquy **Story:** John Dunn **Music:** Walter Greene **Animation:** Don Williams, Manny Gould, Manny Perez, Warren Batchelder
The Pink Panther has a series of accidents during a hospital stay.

Prehistoric Pink

August 7—The Pink Panther
Director: Hawley Pratt **Story:** John Dunn **Music:** Walter Greene **Animation:** Warren Batchelder, Don Williams, Manny Gould, Manny Perez, Art Leonardi
In prehistoric times, The Pink Panther and a caveman create the wheel.

Pink In The Clink

September 18—The Pink Panther
Director: Gerry Chiniquy **Story:** John Dunn **Music:** Walter Greene **Animation:** Art Leonardi, Warren Batchelder, Don Williams, Manny Gould, Manny Perez
A burglar forces the Panther to help him.

Little Beaux Pink

October 2—The Pink Panther
Director: Hawley Pratt **Story:** John Dunn **Music:** Walter Greene **Animation:** Warren Batchelder, Manny Perez, Don Williams
Out west, The Pink Panther is a shepherd in "Cattle Country, Texas," who encounters a short-tempered cattle baron.

Tickled Pink

October 6—The Pink Panther
Director: Gerry Chiniquy **Story:** John Dunn **Music:** Walter Greene **Animation:** Don Williams, Manny Perez, Art Leonardi, Warren Batchelder
The Pink Panther uses a magic wish to get roller skates. Unfortunately, the skates have minds of their own.

A flying Panther: Think Before You Pink (1969).

The Pink Sphinx

October 23—The Pink Panther
Director: Hawley Pratt **Story:** Jim Ryan **Music:** Walter Greene **Animation:** Tom Ray, Don Williams, Manny Gould, Manny Perez, Art Leonardi
The Pink Panther has trouble with his camel en route to the pharaoh's tomb.

Pink Is A Many Splintered Thing

November 20—Pink Panther
Director: Gerry Chiniquy **Story:** Don Jurwich **Music:** Walter Greene **Animation:** Art Leonardi, Warren Batchelder, Ed DeMattia, Don Williams
The Panther tries to become a lumberjack.

The Pink Package Plot

December 11—Pink Panther
Director: Art Davis **Story:** Chuck Couch **Music:** Walter Greene **Animation:** Herman Cohen, Warren Batchelder, Ed Love, Ed DeMattia
The Pink Panther is forced to deliver a bomb to the Slobovainian Embassy.

Hawks And Doves

December 18—Roland and Rattfink
Director: Hawley Pratt **Story:** John Dunn **Music:** Doug Goodwin **Animation:** Don Williams, Manny Perez, Art Leonardi, Warren Batchelder, Ed DeMattia
Roland, the flying ace of Doveland, and Rattfink, the evil baron of Hawkland, go to war with each other in the skies.
The first Roland and Rattfink cartoon.

A Roland and Ratfink storyboard.

Pinkcome Tax

December 20—The Pink Panther
Director: Art Davis **Story:** David Detiege **Music:** Walter Greene **Animation:** Warren Batchelder, Ed DeMattia, Don Williams, Manny Perez
A tax collector tries to collect from The Pink Panther.

1969

Pink-A-Rella

January 8—Pink Panther
Director: Hawley Pratt **Story:** John Dunn **Music:** Walter Greene **Animation:** Manny Perez, Herman Cohen, Warren Batchelder, Manny Gould, Ed DeMattia
The Pink Panther uses a magic wand to transform a poor girl into a princess.

French Freud

January 22—The Inspector
Director: Gerry Chiniquy **Story:** Jack Miller **Music:** Walter Greene **Animation:** Manny Perez, Ed Love, Ed DeMattia, Don Williams
The Inspector is wooed by temptress Melody Mercurochrome who secretly plots to steal the DuBarry emerald.

Hurts And Flowers

February 11—Roland and Rattfink
Director: Hawley Pratt **Story:** John Dunn **Music:** Doug Goodwin **Animation:** Manny Gould, Manny Perez, Warren Batchelder, Don Williams
No matter what evil "weed" Rattfink does to hippie flower child Roland, he is rewarded with a flower.

Pink Pest Control

February 12—The Pink Panther
Director: Gerry Chiniquy **Story:** John Dunn **Music:** Walter Greene **Animation:** Ed DeMattia, Don Williams, Manny Perez, Warren Batchelder
The Pink Panther has a tricky time trying to get the better of a troublesome termite.

Pierre And Cottage Cheese

February 26—The Inspector
Director: Gerry Chiniquy **Story:** Jim Ryan **Music:** Walter Greene **Animation:** Manny Gould, Don Williams, Warren Batchelder, Manny Perez
The notorious Pierre Le Punk escapes from prison and cunningly disguises himself as a robot aid to The Inspector.

The Ant and The Aardvark

March 5—The Ant and The Aardvark
Director: Friz Freleng **Story:** John Dunn **Music:** Doug Goodwin **Animation:** Manny Perez, Warren Batchelder, Manny Gould, Don Williams **Voices:** John Byner
The Ant's picnic lunch is disturbed by The Aardvark's attacks.

Hasty But Tasty

March 6—The Ant and The Aardvark
Director: Gerry Chiniquy **Story:** John Dunn **Music:** Doug Goodwin **Animation:** Don Williams, Bob Taylor, Manny Gould, Manny Perez
The Aardvark employs hot-air balloons, boulders, an "instant hole" and other gimmicks in his efforts to catch The Ant.

Think Before You Pink

March 19—The Pink Panther
Director: Gerry Chiniquy **Story:** Sid Marcus **Music:** Walter Greene **Animation:** Don Williams, Manny Gould, Manny Perez, Herman Cohen, Warren Batchelder
The Pink Panther has trouble crossing a busy road.

An intrusive cuckoo clock spoils the Panther's rest: *In The Pink Of The Night* (1969)

The Ant From Uncle

April 2—The Ant and The Aardvark
Director: George Gordon **Story:** John Dunn
Music: Doug Goodwin **Animation:** Art Leonardi, Warren Batchelder, Don Williams
Attempting to catch The Ant, The Aardvark corks up all the anthills.

Slink Pink

April 2—The Pink Panther
Director: Hawley Pratt **Story:** John Dunn
Music: Walter Greene **Animation:** Ed DeMattia, Manny Perez, Herman Cohen, Art Leonardi, Warren Batchelder
A frozen Pink Panther takes refuge in the warm house of a big game hunter.

Flying Feet

April 10—Roland and Rattfink
Director: Gerry Chiniquy **Story:** Irv Spector
Music: Doug Goodwin **Animation:** Warren Batchelder, Don Williams, Manny Gould, Manny Perez, Bob Richardson
Roland goes off to college and joins the track team. His first race is with Rattfink.

Carte Blanched

May 14—The Inspector
Director: Gerry Chiniquy **Story:** David Detiege
Music: Walter Greene **Animation:** Don Williams, Manny Perez, Don Towsley
The Inspector has a hard time trying to return a supermarket trolley cart.
The last Inspector cartoon.

I've Got Ants In My Plans

May 14—The Ant and The Aardvark
Director: Gerry Chiniquy **Story:** John Dunn
Music: Doug Goodwin **Animation:** Warren Batchelder, Don Williams, Manny Gould, Manny Perez
A strong green Aardvark competes with the blue Aardvark to catch The Ant.

In The Pink Of The Night

May 18—The Pink Panther
Director: Art Davis **Story:** Lee Mishkin **Music:** Walter Greene **Animation:** Warren Batchelder, Don Williams, Manny Perez, Herman Cohen
The Pink Panther has a hard time waking up for work, so he buys an annoying cuckoo clock.

Pink On The Cob

May 29—The Pink Panther
Director: Hawley Pratt **Story:** Jack Miller
Music: Walter Greene **Animation:** Manny Perez, Don Williams, Don Towsley, Manny Gould
The Pink Panther is thwarted in his efforts to farm a cornfield by two clever crows.

The Deadwood Thunderball

June 6—Roland and Rattfink
Director: Hawley Pratt **Story:** John Dunn
Music: Doug Goodwin **Animation:** Manny Gould, Manny Perez, Art Leonardi, Warren Batchelder, Don Williams
Engineer Roland must outrun the bandit Rattfink, who is out to destroy the railroad.

Extinct Pink

June 20—The Pink Panther
Director: Hawley Pratt **Story:** John Dunn
Music: Doug Goodwin **Animation:** Manny Gould, Manny Perez, Warren Batchelder, Don Williams
During the Stone Age, The Pink Panther competes with a caveman and a couple of dinosaurs for a bone.

Sweet And Sourdough

May 18—Roland and Rattfink
Direction: Art Davis **Story:** John Dunn
Music: Manny Perez, Warren Batchelder, Don Williams, Arthur Leonardi
Roland the mountie is tracking down Rattfink the desperado, in the snowy woods of Canada.

Technology, Phooey

June 25—The Ant and The Aardvark
Director: Gerry Chiniquy **Story:** Irv Spector
Music: Doug Goodwin **Animation:** Art Leonardi, Manny Gould, Manny Perez, Warren Batchelder, Don Williams
The Aardvark buys a computer to catch The Ant.

Tijuana Toads

August 6—The Tijuana Toads
Director: Hawley Pratt **Story:** John Dunn
Music: Doug Goodwin **Animation:** Don Williams, Manny Perez, Manny Gould, Bob Richardson, Warren Batchelder **Voices:** Don Diamond, Tom Holland.
The Toads try to catch a tough Texas grasshopper.
The first Tijuana Toads cartoon.

Never Bug An Ant

September—The Ant and the Aardvark
Director: Gerry Chiniquy **Story:** David Detiege
Music: Doug Goodwin **Animation:** Warren Batchelder, Don Williams, Manny Gould, Manny Perez
The Aardvark uses a vacuum cleaner to suck The Ant out of his home.

A Pair Of Sneakers

September 17—Roland and Rattfink
Director: Art Davis **Story:** John Dunn

Music: Doug Goodwin **Animation:** Manny Perez, Manny Gould, Bob Richardson, Warren Batchelder, Don Williams
Secret agent Roland uses every gadget at his disposal to keep the secret papers from enemy agent Rattfink.

Dune Bug

October 27—The Ant and The Aardvark
Director: Art Davis **Story:** John Dunn **Music:** Doug Goodwin **Animation:** Manny Gould, Bob Goe, Tom Ray, Lloyd Vaughan
On a beach, a nearsighted lifeguard mistakes The Aardvark for a dog.

A Pair Of Greenbacks

December 16—The Tijuana Toads
Director: Art Davis **Story:** John Dunn
Music: Doug Goodwin **Animation:** Manny Gould, Warren Batchelder, Don Williams, Bob Taylor, Manny Perez
The Toads catch a red ant—but have trouble keeping him caught.

Isle Of Caprice

December 18—The Ant and The Aardvark
Director: Gerry Chiniquy **Story:** Dave Detiege
Music: Doug Goodwin **Animation:** Manny Perez, Don Williams, Bob Bentley, Bob Taylor, Manny Gould
The hungry Aardvark is stranded on a desert island, near another island swarming with ants.

Go For Croak

December 25—The Tijuana Toads
Director: Hawley Pratt **Story:** John Dunn
Music: Doug Goodwin **Animation:** Manny Perez, Manny Gould, Warren Batchelder, Don Williams
The Tijuana Toads are chased by a large, hungry, yellow crane.

A fine selection of *The Pink Panther Show*'s supporting stars.

A Texas Toad from
A Leap In The Deep (1971).

1970

Scratch A Tiger

January 28—The Ant and The Aardvark
Director: Hawley Pratt **Story:** Irv Spector
Music: Doug Goodwin **Animation:** Art
Leonardi, Manny Gould, Manny Perez, Warren
Batchelder, Don Williams
After the Ant pulls a thorn from a tiger's paw,
the tiger protects the ant colony from the
ever-hungry Aardvark.

The Froggy Froggy Duo

March 15—The Tijuana Toads
Director: Hawley Pratt **Story:** John Dunn
Music: Doug Goodwin **Animation:** Warren
Batchelder, Don Williams, Bob Taylor,
Manny Perez, Manny Gould
The Toads are chased around a hotel by a chef
who wants to put frogs' legs on the menu.

Odd Ant Out

April 20—The Ant and The Aardvark
Director: Gerry Chiniquy **Story:** Sid Marcus
Music: Doug Goodwin **Animation:** Warren
Batchelder, Don Williams, Bob Taylor,
Manny Perez
The Aardvark feuds with a green anteater.

An inked and painted Pink
Panther cel (left), with the
original penciled production art.

Say Cheese, Please

June 7—Roland and Rattfink
Director: Art Davis **Story:** John Dunn **Music:**
Doug Goodwin **Animation:** Don Williams,
Bob Taylor, Ken Muse, Warren Batchelder
Rattfink demands to be cast as "the hero" in a
Hollywood movie—with Roland as his stand-in.

Ants In The Pantry

June 10—The Ant and The Aardvark
Director: Hawley Pratt **Story:** John Dunn
Music: Doug Goodwin **Animation:** Manny
Perez, Don Williams, Manny Gould, John Gibbs
The Aardvark tries to rid a house of its
troublesome ant problem.

Hop And Chop

June 17—The Tijuana Toads
Director: Grant Simmons **Story:** Dale Hale
Music: Doug Goodwin **Animation:** Ken Muse,
Bob Richardson, Art Leonardi
The Toads try to catch a Japanese Beetle who has
a black belt in karate.

A Taste Of Money

June 24—Roland and Rattfink
Director: Art Davis **Music:** Doug Goodwin,
Animation: Warren Batchelder, Don Williams,
Art Leonardi, Bob Taylor, Manny Perez, John Gibbs
Rattfink marries a rich widow but must take care
of her oversized son.
Roland does not appear in this cartoon.

Science Friction

June 28—The Ant and The Aardvark
Director: Gerry Chiniquy **Story:** Larz Bourne
Music: Doug Goodwin **Animation:** Warren
Batchelder, Robert Taylor, Bob Richardson, John
Gibbs, Manny Perez
The Aardvark chases an ant being tested by a
scientist in his laboratory

The Foul Kin

August 5—Roland and Rattfink
Director: Grant Simmons **Story:** Sid Marcus
Music: Doug Goodwin **Animation:** Ken Muse,
Warren Batchelder, Robert Taylor
Rattfink tries to flatter his old uncle in hopes of
being mentioned in his will.

Never On Thirsty

August 5—The Tijuana Toads
Director: Hawley Pratt **Story:** John Dunn
Music: Doug Goodwin **Animation:** Manny
Gould, Don Williams, Robert Taylor,
Manny Perez, Ken Muse
The thirsty Toads try to get to a pool of water on
a private estate guarded by a vicious dog.

Bridgework

August 26—Roland and Rattfink
Director: Art Davis **Story:** Dale Hale **Music:**
Doug Goodwin **Animation:** Manny Perez, Irv
Spence, Robert Taylor, Ken Muse, Warren
Batchelder, Don Williams
Rattfink does his best to sabotage a bridge-
building construction site.

Robin Goodhood

**September 9—Roland and
Rattfink**
Director: Gerry Chiniquy **Story:**
John W. Dunn **Music:** Doug
Goodwin **Animation:** Robert
Taylor, Manny Gould, Manny
Perez, Don Williams, Irv Spence
Robin Hood Roland robs from the
rich to give to the poor—Rattfink
just robs for himself.

War And Pieces

September 20—Roland and Rattfink
Director: Art Davis **Story:** Sid Marcus **Music:**
Doug Goodwin **Animation:** Robert Taylor, Ken
Muse, Warren Batchelder, Manny Gould, Manny
Perez, Don Williams
Captain Roland versus Pirate Rattfink, the
"Scourge of the Spanish Main."

Mumbo Jumbo

September 27—The Ant and The Aardvark
Director: Art Davis **Story:** John Dunn **Music:**
Doug Goodwin **Animation:** Phil Roman, Bob
Bentley, Don Williams, Manny Gould, Irv
Spence, Ken Muse, Warren Batchelder
The Aardvark tries to get The Ant at his lodge,
where all the members stick together.
Roland from Roland and Rattfink has a cameo.

Roland and
Rattfink in
Flying Feet
(1969).

Gem Dandy

October 25—Roland and Rattfink
Director: Gerry Chiniquy **Story:** Dale Hale
Music: Doug Goodwin **Animation:** Ken Muse,
Warren Batchelder, Manny Perez, Robert Taylor
Brave security guard Roland guards a diamond
from that sneaky jewel thief Rattfink.

The Froze Nose Knows

November 18—The Ant and The Aardvark
Director: Gerry Chiniquy **Story:** Dale Hale
Music: Doug Goodwin **Animation:** Manny
Perez, Robert Taylor, Bob Bentley, Ken Muse,
Manny Gould
The Ant gives the Aardvark the runaround in the
frozen Antartic.

A Dopey Hacienda

December 6—The Tijuana Toads
Director: Hawley Pratt **Story:** John Dunn
Music: Doug Goodwin **Animation:** Irv Spence,
Ken Muse, Manny Gould, Don Williams,
Bob Bentley
A fat cat has designs on the Toads and
chases them into a house.

Pancho prepares for a siesta
in *Frog Jog* (1972).

Don't Hustle An Ant
With Muscle

December 27—The Ant and The Aardvark
Director: Art Davis **Story:** Dale Hale **Music:**
Doug Goodwin **Animation:** Bob Bentley,
Manny Gould, Ken Muse, Phil Roman, Warren
Batchelder, Manny Perez
The Ant attains super-strength through a bottle
of vitamins.

1971

Rough Brunch

January 3—The Ant and The Aardvark
Director: Art Davis **Story:** Sid Marcus
Music: Doug Goodwin
Animation: Manny Gould,
Ken Muse, Don Williams, Irv
Spence, Robert Taylor, Manny Perez
The Ant is protected from The Aardvark
by his cousin—The Termite.

Snake In The Gracias

January 24—The Tijuana Toads
Director: Hawley Pratt **Story:** John Dunn
Music: Doug Goodwin **Animation:** Don
Williams, George Nicholas, Phil Roman, Warren
Batchelder, Ken Muse
The Toads convince an amnesiac Crane that he's
a frog in order to gain his protection from The
Blue Racer, the fastest snake alive.
This cartoon introduced The Blue Racer.

Trick Or Retreat

March 3—Roland and Rattfink
Director: Art Davis **Story:** Sid Marcus
Music: Doug Goodwin **Animation:** Manny
Perez, Robert Taylor, Ken Muse, Don Williams
Out west, Roland protects a fort against an
Indian attack led by Rattfink.

Two Jumps And
a Chump

March 28—The Tijuana Toads
Director: Gerry Chiniquy **Story:** John Dunn
Music: Doug Goodwin **Animation:** Warren
Batchelder, Ken Muse, Don Williams
The Toads look for lunch at the city dump.

Mud Squad

April 28—The Tijuana Toads
Director: Art Davis **Story:** John Dunn **Music:**
Doug Goodwin **Animation:** Warren Batchelder,
Ken Muse, Don Williams
The Toads get tangled up with a baby alligator
and his mother.

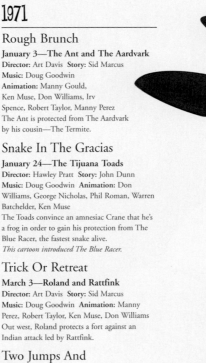

From Bed To Worse

May 16—The Ant and The Aardvark
Director: Art Davis **Story:** John Dunn
Music: Doug Goodwin **Animation:** Robert
Taylor, Ken Muse, Manny Gould, Don Williams,
Warren Batchelder, Manny Perez
The Ant and The Aardvark land in an animal
hospital, where a Gorilla gives the anteater
new problems.

The Great Continental Over-
land Cross-Country Race

May 23—Roland and Rattfink
Director: Art Davis **Story:** John Dunn
Music: Doug Goodwin **Animation:** Robert
Taylor, Don Williams, Warren Batchelder,
Manny Gould, Bob Richardson, Manny Perez
Roland and Rattfink compete in a road race.

The Egg And Ay-Yi-Yi!

June 6—The Tijuana Toads
Director: Gerry Chiniquy **Story:** Dale Hale
Music: Doug Goodwin **Animation:** Don
Williams, Manny Gould, Robert Taylor,
Manny Perez
The Toads adopt a baby bird.

Fastest Tongue In The West

June 20—The Tijuana Toads
Director: Gerry Chiniquy **Story:** Larz Bourne
Music: Doug Goodwin **Animation:** Don
Williams, Manny Gould, Manny Perez, Robert
Taylor, Warren Batchelder
El Toro tries to run the Cactus Kid out of town.

A Leap In The Deep

June 20—The Tijuana Toads
Director: Hawley Pratt **Story:** John Dunn
Music: Doug Goodwin **Animation:** Don
Williams, Manny Gould, Manny Perez, Robert
Taylor, Warren Batchelder
Driven from their pond by a tough frog, The
Toads decide to go to sea.

A Fly In The Pink

June 23—The Pink Panther
Director: Hawley Pratt **Music:** Walter Greene
Animation: Manny Gould, Manny Perez, Warren
Batchelder, Bob Richardson,
Don Williams
The Pink Panther comes up against a surprisingly
strong fruit fly.

A Fink In The Rink

July 4—Roland and Rattfink
Director: Art Davis **Story:** John Dunn
Music: Doug Goodwin **Animation:** Don
Williams, Manny Gould, Manny Perez, Robert
Taylor, Warren Batchelder
Rattfink attempts to out-perform Roland on a
skating rink.

A Hoot Kloot model sheet captures the sheriff's bossy side.

Pink Blue Plate

July 18—The Pink Panther
Director: Gerry Chiniquy **Story:** Dale Hale
Music: Walter Greene **Animation:** Don
Williams, Manny Gould, Manny Perez,
Warren Batchelder, Robert Taylor
The Pink Panther tries his hand at becoming a
short-order cook.

Cattle Battle

August 4 – Roland and Rattfink
Director: Art Davis **Story:** John Dunn
Music: Doug Goodwin **Voices:** Leonard Weinrib
Animation: Don Williams, Warren Batchelder,
Manny Perez, Bob Richardson, Robert Taylor
Rattfink tries to steal some cows from under the
watchful eye of the bull, and cowboy Roland.
The last Roland and Rattfink cartoon.

Pink Tuba-Dore

August 4—The Pink Panther
Director: Art Davis **Story:** John Dunn
Music: Walter Greene **Animation:** Manny Perez,
Warren Batchelder, Don Williams, Manny Gould
The Pink Panther's precious slumber is rudely
disturbed by a tuba player.

Pink Pranks

August 28—The Pink Panther
Director: Gerry Chiniquy **Story:** John Dunn
Music: Walter Greene **Animation:** Robert
Taylor, Manny Gould, Manny Perez, Warren
Batchelder, Don Williams
The Pink Panther lands in Nome, Alaska,
where he tries to help a seal escape from a bear
and an Eskimo hunter.

Pink Flea

September 15—The Pink Panther
Director: Gerry Chiniquy **Story:** John Dunn
Music: Walter Greene **Animation:** Robert
Taylor, Don Williams, Manny Gould, Warren
Batchelder
The Pink Panther can't get rid of a pesky flea.

Psst Pink

September 15—The Pink Panther
Director: Art Davis **Story:** Larz Bourne
Music: Walter Greene **Animation:** Don
Williams, Manny Gould, Warren Batchelder
The Pink Panther's car has tire troubles.

This artwork of The Ant and The Aardvark was used as a "bumper" between cartoons on *The Pink Panther Show.*

Gong With The Pink

October 20—The Pink Panther
Direction: Hawley Pratt **Story:** Irv Spector
Music: Walter Greene **Animation:** Manny
Gould, Bob Richardson, Don Williams
Working as a waiter, The Pink Panther places his
food orders by using a gong—which shatters the
glassware on sale at the shop next door.

Pink-In

October 20—The Pink Panther
Director: Art Davis **Story:** Art Leonardi **Music:**
Walter Greene **Animation:** Warren Batchelder,
Robert Taylor, Don Williams, Manny Gould
The Panther investigates a trunk in his attic with
old movie props in it.
*This cartoon uses clips from previous Pink Panther
cartoons: G.I. Pink (1968), Pink in the Clink
(1968), Pink Pajamas (1964), Pickled Pink
(1965), The Pink Package Plot (1968).*

The song-loving Japanese Beetle made his debut in a Tijuana Toads cartoon and went on to plague The Blue Racer.

Croakus Pocus

December 26—The Tijuana Toads
Director: Art Davis **Story:** John Dunn
Music: Doug Goodwin **Animation:** Warren
Batchelder, Don Williams, Bob Richardson,
Manny Gould
A witch needs the hair of a frog for her potion.
Enter The Tijuana Toads.

Serape Happy

December 26—The Tijuana Toads
Director: Gerry Chiniquy **Story:** John Dunn
Music: Doug Goodwin **Animation:** Manny
Gould, Warren Batchelder, Arthur Leonardi,
Don Williams
The Toads try to catch a slippery grasshopper.

1972

Pink 8 Ball

February 6—The Pink Panther
Director: Gerry Chiniquy **Story:** John Dunn
Music: Walter Greene **Animation:** Don
Williams, Manny Gould, Art Leonardi, John
Gibbs, Bob Matz
The Pink Panther chases a gift basketball all
over town.

The Blue Racer in *Fowl Play* (1973).

Frog Jog

April 23—The Tijuana Toads
Director: Gerry Chiniquy **Story:** John Dunn
Music: Doug Goodwin **Animation:** John Gibbs,
Bob Matz, Don Williams
El Toro tries to lose weight for his date with
Flora.

Flight To The Finish

April 30—The Tijuana Toads
Director: Art Davis **Story:** John Dunn
Music: Doug Goodwin **Animation:** Bob
Richardson, Don Williams, John Gibbs,
Doug Goodwin
The Toads disguise themselves as "Rosarita," a
female bird, to escape a hungry crane.

Hiss And Hers

July 3—The Blue Racer
Director: Gerry Chiniquy
Music: Doug Goodwin
The Blue Racer tries to feed his family by
chasing a Japanese Beetle.

Nippon Tuck

July—The Blue Racer
Director: Gerry Chiniquy **Story:**
John Dunn **Music:** Doug Goodwin
Animation: Don Williams, Warren
Batchelder, Bob Richardson,
Bob Taylor
The Japanese Beetle gets lost in the desert.

Support Your Local Serpent

July 9—The Blue Racer
Director: Art Davis **Story:** John Dunn
Music: Doug Goodwin **Animation:** Don
Williams, Dick Thompson, Bob Matz, John
Gibbs.
In Japan, The Blue Racer matches wits with the
Japanese Beetle.

Punch And Judo

July 23—The Blue Racer
Director: Art Davis **Music:** Doug Goodwin
Story: John Dunn. **Animation:**
Manny Gould, Warren Batchelder,
Don Williams
The Blue Racer tries to take on the judo expert
Japanese Beetle.

Love And Hisses

August 3—The Blue Racer
Director: Gerry Chiniquy **Music::**
Doug Goodwin **Story:** John
Dunn **Animation:** Robert
Taylor, Manny Gould,
Warren Batchelder, Don
Williams
The Beetle befriends an
elephant, whose trunk the
Racer mistakes for a female snake.

Camera Bug

August 6—The Blue Racer
Director: Art Davis **Story:** John Dunn
Music: Doug Goodwin **Animation:** Bob
Richardson, Manny Gould, Warren Batchelder,
Don Williams
The Japanese Beetle tricks The Blue Racer into
posing for some snapshots.

Yokohama Mama

December 24—The Blue Racer
Director: Gerry Chiniquy **Story:** John Dunn.
Music: Doug Goodwin **Animation:** Bob
Richardson, Jim Davis, Manny Gould,
Don Williams.
In China, The Blue Racer tries to get some eggs
from an oriental chicken.

Blue Racer Blues

December 31—The Blue Racer
Director: Gerry Chiniquy **Story:** John Dunn.
Music: Doug Goodwin **Animation:** Bob
Richardson, Jim Davis, Manny Gould,
Don Williams
The Blue Racer heads for the city in search of love.

1973

Kloot's Kounty

January 19—Hoot Kloot
Director: Hawley Pratt **Writer:** John Dunn
Music: Doug Goodwin **Animation:** Bob
Richardson, Don Williams, Bob Bemiller, John
Freeman, Reuben Timmins
Kloot tries to bring in Crazywolf, an insane
desperado.
The first Hoot Kloot cartoon.

The Boa Friend

February 11—The Blue Racer
Director: Gerry Chiniquy **Story:** John Dunn
Music: Doug Goodwin **Animation:** Lloyd
Vaughn, Bob Matz, Bob Bransford, Reuben
Timmens, Norm McCabe.
The Blue Racer tries to win his girl from a rival
boa constrictor.

Wham And Eggs

February 18—The Blue Racer
Director: Art Davis **Story:** John Dunn
Music: Doug Goodwin **Animation:** Norm
McCabe, Manny Gould, John Gibbs, Bob
Richardson
The Blue Racer hatches a Chinese egg. Out pops
a dragon who thinks The Blue Racer is his
mother.

Blue Aces Wild

May 16—The Blue Racer
Director: Art Davis **Story:** John Dunn **Music:**
Doug Goodwin **Animation:** Bob Matz, Manny
Gould, Don Williams, John Gibbs
A wizard grants The Blue Racer three wishes.

Hoot Kloot, mounted on his trusty steed Fester.

Killarney Blarney

May 16—The Blue Racer
Director: Gerry Chiniquy **Story:** John Dunn
Music: Doug Goodwin **Animation:** John Gibbs,
Norm McCabe, Manny Gould
The Blue Racer is plagued by two scheming
leprechauns.

Fowl Play

June 1—The Blue Racer
Director: Robert McKimson **Story:** John Dunn
Music: Doug Goodwin **Animation:** Don
Williams, Ken Muse, John Freeman.
A baby chick mistakes The Blue Racer for a
worm.

Rattfink has a visit from the taxman: drawings for *Hawks And Doves* (1968).

Freeze A Jolly Good Fellow

June 1—The Blue Racer
Director: Sid Marcus **Story:** John Dunn
Music: Doug Goodwin **Animation:** Fred
Madison, Bob Richardson, Bob Bransford,
Ken Muse
The Blue Racer battles a bear for a winter cabin.

Apache On The County Seat

June 16—Hoot Kloot
Director: Hawley Pratt **Writer:** John Dunn
Music: Doug Goodwin **Animation:** Bob
Richardson, Manny Gould, Warren Batchelder,
Don Williams
Kloot tries to bring in the Jolly Red Giant, an
Indian with a criminal record.

The Shoe Must Go On

June 16—Hoot Kloot
Director: Gerry Chiniquy **Writer:** John Dunn
Music: Doug Goodwin **Animation:** Bob Matz,
Manny Gould, Norm McCabe, Fred Madison,
Ken Muse
Kloot needs his horse to chase bandits, but has a
tough time getting the horseshoes on.

Aches And Snakes

August 10—The Blue Racer
Director: David Deneen **Story:** John Dunn
Music: Doug Goodwin **Animation:** Kenny Uset,
Phil Normle, Warren Peace Jr., Dick Fitz
The Blue Racer competes with Crazy Legs Crane
for a bee.
Made at Filmgraphics in Australia.

Snake Preview

August 10—The Blue Racer
Director: Cullen Houghtaling **Story:** John
Dunn **Music:** Doug Goodwin **Animation:** Bob
Matz, Bob Bransford, Don Williams, John
Gibbs, Ken Muse
Trying to steal an egg for breakfast, the Racer
competes with Crazy Legs Crane and a bee.

A Self-Winding Sidewinder

October 9—Hoot Kloot
Director: Roy Morita **Writer:** John Dunn
Music: Doug Goodwin **Animation:** Bob Matz,
Bob Bransford, Frank Gonzales, Ken Muse
Title: Arthur Leonardi
Kloot is trying to get re-elected as sheriff, but his
opponent is the popular Crazywolf.

Pay Your Buffalo Bill

October 9—Hoot Kloot
Director: Gerry Chiniquy **Writer:** John Dunn
Music: Doug Goodwin **Animation:**
John Gibbs, Ken Muse, Bob Richardson,
Don Williams, Norm McCabe **Title:** Arthur
Leonardi
Crazywolf sells a tonic that makes
Hoot Kloot super-strong.

The Blue Racer in *Nippon Tuck* (1972).

Stirrups And Hiccups

October 15—Hoot Kloot
Director: Gerry Chiniquy **Writer:** John Dunn
Music: Doug Goodwin **Animation:** Don
Williams, Bob Matz, Norm McCabe, Ken Muse,
John Gibbs **Titles:** Arthur Leonardi
Kloot hires hillbilly "Mild Bill" Hiccup, as his
deputy—but he turns out to be "Wild Bill"
Hiccup, a notorious bandit.

Ten Miles To The Gallop

October 15—Hoot Kloot
Director: Arthur Leonardi **Writer:** John Dunn
Music: Doug Goodwin **Animation:** Don
Williams, Bob Matz, John Freeman, Bob
Richardson, Bob Bemiller **Titles:** Art Leonardi
Kloot pursues Crazywolf on a motorcycle.

1974

Phony Express

January 4—Hoot Kloot
Director: Gerry Chiniquy **Writer:** John Dunn
Music: Doug Goodwin **Voices:** Bob Holt
Animation: Bob Matz, Don Williams, Norm
McCabe, Bob Richardson, John Gibbs **Titles:**
Arthur Leonardi
Kloot risks everything to make sure that the mail
gets through.

Giddy Up Woe

January 9—Hoot Kloot
Director: Sid Marcus **Writer:** John Dunn
Music: Doug Goodwin **Voices:** Bob Holt
Animation: Bob Bemiller, Ken Muse, Norm
McCabe, Don Williams, Bob Bransford
Titles: Arthur Leonardi
Kloot trades his old horse for a younger model.

Gold Struck

January 9—Hoot Kloot
Director: Roy Morita **Writer:** John Dunn
Music: Doug Goodwin **Animation:** Bob
Bransford, Don Williams, Norm McCabe, Ken
Muse, John Freeman **Titles:** Arthur Leonardi
Kloot stops at a haunted house.

Little Boa Peep

January 16—The Blue Racer
Director: Bob Balsar **Story:** John Dunn
Animation: Dick Nicksen, Harry Paper,
Phil Herup
A psychiatrist convinces the Racer that he is a
sheepdog.
*The last Blue Racer cartoon; made at Halas and
Batchelor in England.*

As The Tumbleweed Turns

April 8—Hoot Kloot
Director: Gerry Chiniquy **Writer:** John Dunn
Music: Doug Goodwin **Voices:** Bob Holt, Hazel
Shermet **Animation:** Bob Bransford, Norm
McCabe, Ken Muse, Reuben Timmins, Bob
Bemiller **Titles:** Arthur Leonardi
Kloot vainly attempts to evict an old lady and
her guard dog.

Taking things easy: *Pink Aye* (1974)

The Badge And The Beautiful

April 17—Hoot Kloot
Director: Bob Balsar **Writer:** John Dunn
Music: Doug Goodwin **Voices:** Bob Holt,
Larry Mann, Joan Gerber **Animation:** Tim
Miller, John Ward, Richard Rudler **Titles:**
Arthur Leonardi
Cowgirl Calamitous Jane has her eye on
marrying Hoot Kloot.
Made at Halas and Batchelor in England.

Big Beef At The O.K. Corral

April 17—Hoot Kloot
Director: Bob Balsar **Writer:** John Dunn
Music: Doug Goodwin **Animation:** John Ward,
Richard Rudler, Tim Miller **Titles:** Arthur
Leonardi
Kloot takes on cattle rustler Billy The Kidder.
Made at Halas and Batchelor in England.

By Hoot Or By Crook

April 17—Hoot Kloot
Director: Bob Balsar **Writer:** John Dunn
Music: Doug Goodwin **Animation:** Tim Miller,
John Ward, Richard Rudler **Titles:** Arthur
Leonardi
Kloot tries to protect a strongbox from a bandit
known as "The Fox."
Made at Halas and Batchelor in England.

Strange On The Range

April 17—Hoot Kloot
Director: Durward Bonaye **Writer:** John Dunn
Music: Doug Goodwin **Animation:** Richard
Rudler, Tim Miller, John Ward **Titles:** Arthur
Leonardi
Billy The Kidder escapes from jail.
Made at Halas and Batchelor in England.

Pink Aye

May 16—The Pink Panther
Director: Gerry Chiniquy **Story:** John Dunn
Music: Walter Greene **Animation:** Norm
Timmins, Norm McCabe, Ken Muse, John
Freeman
The Pink Panther, a stowaway on an ocean liner,
tries to evade a steward on his trail.

The Dogfather

Mesa Trouble

May 16—Hoot Kloot
Director: Sid Marcus **Writer:** John W. Dunn
Music: Doug Goodwin **Animation:** John
Freeman, Don Williams, Bob Bransford, Ken
Muse **Titles:** Arthur Leonardi
Kloot tries to get help to capture outlaw Big Red.

Saddle Soap Opera

May 16 - Hoot Kloot
Director: Gerry Chiniquy **Writer:** John Dunn
Music: Doug Goodwin **Animation:** Bob
Bransford, Norm McCabe, Bob Matz, Ken
Muse, Bob Bemiller **Titles:** Arthur Leonardi
The last Hoot Kloot cartoon.
Kloot is assigned to protect Judge Soy Bean,
The Hanging Judge.

The Dogfather

June 27—The Dogfather
Director: Hawley Pratt **Story:** Bob Ogle
Music: Dean Elliott **Lyrics:** John Bradford
Voices: Bob Holt, Daws Butler, Frank Welker
Animation: Bob Richardson, John V. Gibbs,
Bob Matz, Norm McCabe **Titles:** Arthur
Leonardi **Layouts:** Dick Ung **Backgrounds:**
Richard H. Thomas
When The Dogfather puts a contract out on an
alley cat, Pug and Louie get tangled up with an
escaped lion.
The first Dogfather cartoon.

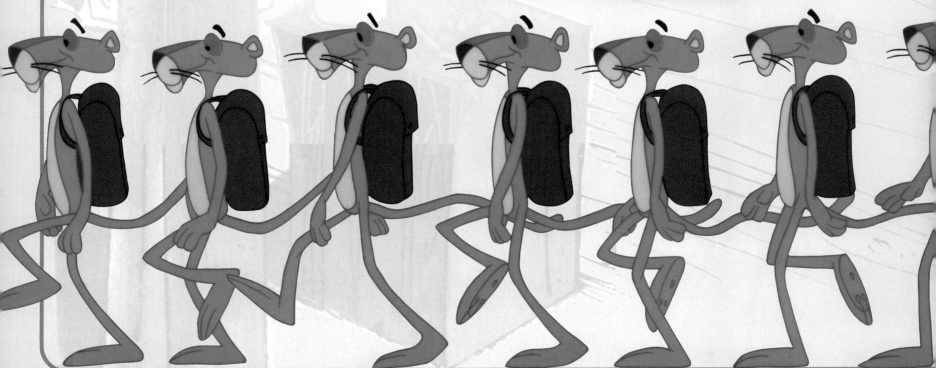

The Dogfather in *Saltwater Tuffy* (1975)

Trail Of The Lonesome Pink

June 27—The Pink Panther
Director: Gerry Chiniquy
Story: John Dunn
Music: Walter Greene
Animation: Ken Walker, John Gibbs, Bob Bemiller, Norm McCabe
The Panther gets caught by trappers in the Canadian northwoods.

The Goose That Laid A Golden Egg

October 4—The Dogfather
Director: Hawley Pratt **Story:** Friz Freleng
Music: Dean Elliott **Voices:** Bob Holt, Daws Butler, Hazel Shermet **Animation:** Bob Richardson, John V. Gibbs, Nelson Shin, Bob Bransford **Titles:** Arthur Leonardi. **Layouts:** Dick Ung **Backgrounds:** Richard H. Thomas.
The Dogfather mob kidnaps a chicken and forces him to lay a golden egg.

Heist & Seek

October 4—The Dogfather
Director: Gerry Chiniquy **Story:** Don Christenson **Music:** Dean Elliott **Voices:** Bob Holt, Daws Butler **Animation:** Bob Bransford John V. Gibbs, Bob Matz, Nelson Shin **Titles:** Arthur Leonardi **Layouts:** Dick Ung **Backgrounds:** Richard H. Thomas
Pug and Rocky hide out in an old house – where private eye Sam Spaniel tricks them into the paddy wagon.

The Big House Ain't A Home

October 31—The Dogfather
Director: Gerry Chiniquy **Story:** David Detiege **Music:** Dean Elliott **Voices:** Bob Holt, Daws Butler **Animation:** Bob Richardson, Nelson Shin, Bob Bransford, John V. Gibbs **Titles:** Arthur Leonardi **Layouts:** Dick Ung **Backgrounds:** Richard H. Thomas
Pug and Louie attempt to break Benny the Boom-Boom out of prison, but wind up trapped inside themselves.

Mother Dogfather

October 31—The Dogfather
Director: Arthur Leonardi **Story:** Dave Detiege **Music:** Dean Elliott **Voices:** Bob Holt, Larry D. Mann **Lyrics:** John Bradford **Animation:** Bob Richardson, Nelson Shin, Bob Bransford, Norm McCabe
Crazy Legs Crane, as a stork, tries to deliver a baby to the Dogfather. Pug sets up booby traps to keep him out—until they learn the little bundle is some lost loot.

Bows & Errors

December 29—The Dogfather
Director: Gerry Chiniquy **Story:** John Dunn **Music:** Dean Elliott **Voices:** Bob Holt, Daws Butler **Animation:** Nelson Shin, Bob Bransford Norm McCabe **Film Editor:** Rick Steward.
Layout: Dick Ung **Backgrounds:** Richard H. Thomas.
Pug and Louie try to emulate Robin Hood, by taking from the rich and giving to the poor—but first must retrieve their loot from rival Al E. Catt.

The Croaker, a drawing for *Devilled Yeggs* (1974).

Devilled Yeggs

December 29—The Dogfather
Director: Gerry Chiniquy **Story:** John Dunn **Music:** Dean Elliott **Voices:** Bob Holt, Frank Welker **Animation:** Bob Richardson, Nelson Shin, Bob Bransford, Norm McCabe **Film Editor:** Rick Steward. **Layout:** Dick Ung **Backgrounds:** Richard H. Thomas
Dogfather assigns Croaker McClaw (a cat) to rub out Charlie The Singer (a bird). Croaker's attempts end up costing him his nine lives.

1975

Watch the Birdie

March 20—The Dogfather
Director: Gerry Chiniquy **Story:** John Dunn **Music:** Dean Elliott **Voices:** Bob Holt, Frank Welker **Lyrics:** John Bradford **Animation:** Nelson Shin, Bob Bransford, Warren Batchelder **Titles:** Arthur Leonardi
The Dogfather and Pug chase Charlie the Singer (a bird) into Dr. Jeckel's lab, where Charlie drinks a Mr. Hyde potion.

Saltwater Tuffy

March 20—The Dogfather
Director: Art Leonardi **Story:** John Dunn **Music:** Dean Elliott **Voices:** Bob Holt, Daws Butler. **Animation:** Nelson Shin, Bob Bransford **Editor:** Rick Steward **Layouts:** Dick Ung **Backgrounds:** Richard H. Thomas.
The Dogfather sends Pug & Louie to get rival mobster Bucky McClaw off his yacht.

M-O-N-E-Y Spells Love

April 23—The Dogfather
Director: Art Leonardi **Story:** Dave Detiege **Music:** Dean Elliott **Voices:** Bob Holt, Joan Gerber **Animation:** Nelson Shin, Bob Bransford, Warren Batchelder **Editor:** Rick Steward **Layouts:** Dick Ung **Backgrounds:** Richard H. Thomas
The Dogfather competes with mobster Rocky to woo a widow who inherited $20 million dollars.

Rock-a-Bye...Maybe

April 23—The Dogfather
Director: Gerry Chiniquy **Story:** John Dunn **Music:** Dean Elliott **Voices:** Bob Holt **Animation:** Bob Richardson, Don Williams, Norm McCabe Nelson Shin **Editor:** Rick Steward **Layout:** Dick Ung **Backgrounds:** Richard H. Thomas
The Dogfather tries to get peace and quiet in his mountain cabin, but is disturbed by two noisy squirrels.

Haunting Dog

May 2—The Dogfather
Director: Gerry Chiniquy **Story:** John Dunn **Music:** Dean Elliott **Voices:** Bob Holt **Animation:** Bob Richardson, Don Williams, Nelson Shin **Editor:** Rick Steward **Layouts:** Dick Ung **Backgrounds:** Richard H. Thomas
The Dogfather inherits a haunted getaway car from a rival, the late Machine Gun Kolly.

Eagle Beagles

May 5—The Dogfather
Director: Gerry Chiniquy **Story:** John Dunn **Music:** Dean Elliott **Voices:** Bob Holt **Animation:** Bob Richardson, Warren Batchelder, Don Williams, Nelson Shin, Bob Bransford **Editor** Rick Steward **Layouts:** Dick Ung **Backgrounds:** Richard H. Thomas
After robbing a bank, Pug and Dogfather escape the police in an airplane, which neither of them knows how to fly.

From Nags to Riches

May 5—The Dogfather
Director Gerry Chiniquy **Story** John Dunn **Music** Dean Elliott **Voices** Bob Holt, daws Butler **Animation** Bob Richardson, Don Williams, Nelson Shin, Norm McCabe, Warren Batchelder **Editor** Rick Steward **Layout** Dick Ung **Backgrounds** Richard H. Thomas
The Dogfather trades in his old nag for a race horse named Lightning—but first they have to catch him.

Pink Panther frames from *Pink Plasma* (1975)

The Panther's umbrella goes up in smoke in *Olym-Pinks* (1980).

Pink Da Vinci

June 23—Pink Panther
Director: Robert McKimson **Story:** John W. Dunn **Music:** Walter Greene **Animation:** Warren Batchelder, Virgil Ross, Bob Richardson, Nelson Shin, Bob Bemiller
The Pink Panther Gets into a dispute with Leonardo da Vinci over Mona Lisa's smile.

Pink Streaker

June 27—Pink Panther
Director: Gerry Chiniquy **Story:** John Dunn **Music:** Walter Greene **Animation:** Bob Matz, Don Williams, Nelson Shin, Norm McCabe
The Pink Panther kindly helps a novice skier become a champion.

The Pink Panther police force

Salmon Pink

July 25—Pink Panther
Director: Gerry Chiniquy **Story:** John Dunn **Music:** Walter Greene **Animation:** Nelson Shin, Bob Richardson, Bob Matz, John Gibbs
The Panther takes his new pet, a salmon, for a stroll.

Forty Pink Winks

August 8—The Pink Panther
Director: Gerry Chiniquy **Story:** John Dunn **Music:** Walter Greene **Animation:** Bob Richardson, Don Williams, Bob Matz, Norm McCabe
Trying to get some sleep, the Panther blends in with a convention at a luxury hotel and evades the hotel detective.

Pink Plasma

August 8—The Pink Panther
Director: Art Leonardi **Story:** John W. Dunn **Music:** Walter Greene **Animation:** Don Williams, Bob Richardson, Virgil Ross, John Gibbs
In Transylvania, the Pink Panther eludes a vampire.

Goldilox & The Three Hoods

August 28—The Dogfather
Director: Gerry Chiniquy **Story:** John Dunn **Music:** Dean Elliott **Voices:** Bob Holt, Daws Butler, Joan Gerber **Animation:** Bob Richardson, Don Williams, Norm McCabe, Nelson Shin
Dogfather tells his nephew the bedtime story, about three mobsters trying to catch Goldilox, a moll wanted by the police for a $5000. reward.

Pink Elephant

October 20—The Pink Panther
Director: Gerry Chiniquy **Story:** John Dunn **Music:** Walter Greene **Animation:** John Gibbs, Nelson Shin, Jim Davis, Virgil Ross
An elephant follows The Pink Panther home.

Keep Our Forests Pink

November 20—The Pink Panther
Director: Gerry Chiniquy **Story:** John Dunn **Music:** Walter Greene **Animation:** Bob Richardson, Nelson Shin, Norm McCabe, Bob Matz
As a forest ranger, The Panther tries to show a careless camper the error of his littering ways.

Rock Hounds

November 20—The Dogfather
Director: Arthur Leonardi **Story:** John Dunn **Music:** Dean Elliott **Voices:** Bob Holt **Animation:** Bob Richardson, Warren Batchelder, Nelson Shin, Don Williams **Editor:** Rick Steward. **Layout:** Dick Ung **Backgrounds:** Richard H. Thomas
Pug poses as a butler to steal the Van Waggers Pedigree Diamond.

Bobolink Pink

December 30—The Pink Panther
Director: Gerry Chiniquy **Story:** John Dunn **Music:** Walter Greene **Animation:** John Gibbs, Virgil Ross, Don Williams, Nelson Shin
The Pink Panther tries to help a bird fly south for the winter.

It's Pink But Is It Mink?

December 30—The Pink Panther
Director: Robert McKimson **Story:** Tom Yakutis **Music:** Walter Greene **Animation:** Don Williams, Bob Richardson, John Gibbs, Nelson Shin
The Panther tries to elude a jungle man who wants his pink fur for his "Jane."

Pink Campaign

December 30—The Pink Panther
Director: Art Leonardi **Story:** John Dunn
Music: Walter Greene **Animation:** Bob
Richardson, Don Williams, Norm McCabe,
Warren Batchelder
The Panther exacts revenge on a lumberjack who
cut down his home. He takes the man's
townhouse apart piece by piece.

The Scarlet Pinkernel

December 30—The Pink Panther
Director: Gerry Chiniquy **Story:** John Dunn
Music: Walter Greene **Animation:** Nelson Shin,
John Gibbs, Bob Richardson, Don Williams
The Pink Panther becomes "The Scarlet
Pinkernel" and sets out to save the canine world
from a menacing dogcatcher.

The Commissioner
from The Inspector
cartoons.

1976

Mystic Pink

January 6—The Pink Panther
Director: Robert McKimson **Story:** John Dunn
Music: Walter Greene **Animation:** Norm
McCabe, Don Williams, Bob Richardson,
John Gibbs
A magic hat causes trouble for The Pink Panther.

The Pink of Arabee

March 13—The Pink Panther
Director: Gerry Chiniquy **Story:** Bob Ogle
Music: Walter Greene **Animation:** Don
Williams, Bob Richardson, John Gibbs
In the Middle East, The Pink Panther's tail
becomes an object of affection.

The Pink Pro

April 12—The Pink Panther
Director: Robert McKimson **Story:** Lee Mishkin
Music: Walter Greene **Animation:** Bob
Richardson, John Gibbs, Don Williams,
Norm McCabe
The Pink Panther is a sports pro who trains an
athletic novice.

Medicur

April 30—The Dogfather
Director: Gerry Chiniquy **Story:** John Dunn
Voices: Bob Holt **Animation:** Bob Richardson,
Warren Batchelder, Norm McCabe, Don
Williams. **Layouts:** Roy Morita **Backgrounds:**
Richard H. Thomas.
When his revenge-seeking nemesis Rocky
McSnarl escapes from prison, the Dogfather
hides out as a patient in a hospital. But McSnarl
is also there, disguised as a nurse.
The last Dogfather cartoon.

Pink Piper

April 30—Pink Panther
Director: Cullen Houghtaling **Story:** John
Dunn **Music:** Walter Greene **Animation:** Warren
Batchelder, Virgil Ross, John Gibbs, Bob Matz
The Panther, a pied piper in medieval times, tries
to rid an inn of a mouse pest.

Pinky Doodle

May 28—The Pink Panther
Director: Sid Marcus **Story:** John Dunn **Music:**
Walter Greene **Animation:** Bob Richardson,
Don Williams, Norm McCabe, John Gibbs
The Pink Panther, as Paul Revere, must warn the
colonists that the British are coming—
unfortunately his horse won't cooperate.

Sherlock Pink

June 29—The Pink Panther
Director: Robert McKimson **Story:** John Dunn
Music: Walter Greene **Animation:** Nelson Shin,
Jim Davis, Bob Bemiller, Bob Bransford
The Pink Panther investigates the disappearance
of a delicious cake.

Rocky Pink

July 9—The Pink Panther
Director: Art Leonardi **Story:** John Dunn
Music: Walter Greene **Animation:** Nelson Shin,
Don Williams, John Gibbs, Bob Richardson
In tune with the craze sweeping the land, The
Pink Panther adopts a "pet rock."

1977

Therapeutic Pink

April 1—Pink Panther
Director: Gerry Chiniquy **Story:** Tom Yakutis
Music: Walter Greene **Animation:** Warren
Batchelder, Bob Matz, Norm McCabe, Don
Williams
On a cold night, the hungry Panther has
problems with his empty stomach—and a tail-
loving dog.

1978

*The following 32 Pink Panther cartoons were
produced for the "All New Pink Panther Show,"
which aired on ABC from 1978-1979. They were
also theatrically released by UA on dates indicated.
Music, not credited, is primarily by Steve DePatie,
with some cues by Doug Goodwin.*

Pink Arcade

September 1—The Pink Panther
Director: Sid Marcus - **Story:** Dave Detiege -
Animation: Warren Batchelder, Bob Richardson,
Bob Kirk, Bill Hutten.
The Pink Panther has trouble with a series of
arcade games.

Pink Lightning

October 1—The Pink Panther
Director: Brad Case - **Story:** John Dunn -
Animation: Nelson Shin, Bob Bemiller, Virgil
Ross, Walter Kubiak.
The Pink Panther buys a new automobile, a
demon car with an evil mind of it own.

Pink In The Drink

November 1—The Pink Panther
Director: Sid Marcus - **Story:** John Dunn -
Animation: Bob Matz, John Gibbs, Tiger West,
Tony Love.
The Pink Panther take a cruise on a pirate ship,
and runs afoul of the captain.

Pink S.W.A.T.

December 1—The Pink Panther
Director: Sid Marcus - **Story:** John W. Dunn -
Animation: Don Williams, Lee Halpern, Bernard
Posner, Joan Case.
The Pink Panther tries to get rid of a particularly
pesky fly.

Looking for clues
in *Sherlock Pink*
(1976).

1979

String Along In Pink

January 1—The Pink Panther
Director: Gerry Chiniquy **Story:** Tony Benedict
Animation: Norm McCabe, Bob Bransford,
Art Vitello, Malcolm Draper
The Pink Panther follows a piece of string.

Pink Bananas

February 1—The Pink Panther
Director: Art Davis- **Story:** John Dunn
Animation: Warren Batchelder, Bob Richardson,
Bob Kirk, Bill Hutten.
The Pink Panther swings through the jungle,
aping Tarzan. *First shown on TV in 1978*

Pink-Tails For Two

March 1—The Pink Panther
Director: Art Davis **Story:** Tony Benedict
Animation: Nelson Shin, Bob Bemiller, Virgil
Ross, Walter Kubiak
The Pink Panther has problems with his enlarged tail.
First shown on TV in 1978

Pink Quackers

April 1—The Pink Panther
Director: Brad Case- **Story:** Dave Detiege
Animation: Bob Matz, John Gibbs, Tiger West,
Tony Love.
The Pink Panther befriends a little duck.

The Inspector grabs the loot.

Pink and Shovel

May 1—The Pink Panther
Director: Gerry Chiniquy **Story:** John Dunn
Animation: Don Williams, Lee Halpern, Bernard
Posner, Joan Case.
The Pink Panther tries to dig up his money from
a secret burial place. *First shown on TV in 1978*

Pink Breakfast

June 1—The Pink Panther
Director: Brad Case **Story:** Cliff Roberts
Animation: Norm McCabe, Bob Bransford, Art
Vitello, Malcolm Draper.
A typical morning for the Pink Panther as he
tries to get breakfast – the hard way.

Toro Pink

July 1—The Pink Panther
Director: Sid Marcus **Story:** Dave Detiege
Animation: Warren Batchelder, Bob Richardson,
Bob Kirk, Bill Hutten.
The Pink Panther takes bull fighting out of the
arena and all over town.

Pink in the Woods

August 1—The Pink Panther
Director: Brad Case **Story:** Cullen Houghtaling
Animation: Nelson Shin, Bob Bemiller, Virgil
Ross, Walter Kubiak
Lumberjack Pink Panther goes into battle with a
power saw.

Pink Pull

September 1—The Pink Panther
Director: Sid Marcus **Story:** Cliff Roberts
Animation: Bob Matz, John Gibbs, Tiger West,
Tony Love
The Pink Panther tries to retrieve a lost coin with
a powerful magnet.

Spark Plug Pink

October 1—The Pink Panther
Director: Brad Case **Story:** Cullen Houghtaling
Animation: Don Williams, Lee Halpern, Bernard
Posner, Joan Case
The Pink Panther tries to retrieve a sparkplug
from a yard guarded by a vicious dog.

Pink Lemonade

November 2—The Pink Panther
Director: Gerry Chiniquy **Story:** John Dunn
Animation: Norm McCabe, Bob Bransford, Art
Vitello, Malcolm Draper
The Pink Panther hides out from a vicious dog
in the home of two children, who think he's a
toy! *First shown on TV in 1978*

Supermarket Pink

December 1—The Pink Panther
Director: Brad Case **Story:** Cliff Roberts -
Animation: Warren Batchelder, Bob Richardson,
Bob Kirk, Bill Hutten.
The Pink Panther causes problems in a
supermarket. *First shown on TV in 1980*

1980

Pink Daddy

January 1—The Pink Panther
Director: Gerry Chiniquy **Story:** Dave Detiege
Animation: Nelson Shin, Bob Bemiller, Virgil
Ross, Walter Kubiak
The Pink Panther becomes the parent of a baby
crocodile. *First shown on TV in 1978*

Title card from *Pink Daddy* (1980).

Pink Pictures

February 2—The Pink Panther
Director: Gerry Chiniquy **Story:** Cliff Roberts
Animation: Nelson Shin, Bob Bemiller, Virgil
Ross, Walter Kubiak
The Pink Panther tries to photograph wildlife.
First shown on TV in 1978

Pink Suds

March 1—The Pink Panther
Director: Art Davis **Story:** Cullen Houghtaling -
Animation: Don Williams, Lee Halpern, Bernard
Posner, Joan Case.
The Pink Panther creates havoc at a laundrette.
[First shown on TV in 1979]

Pink Trumpet

April 1—The Pink Panther
Director: Art Davis **Story:** Dave Detiege -
Animation: Norm McCabe, Bob Bransford, Art
Vitello, Malcolm Draper
At a hotel, The Pink Panther has a feud with the
noisy man in the next room.
[First shown on TV in 1978]

Sprinkle Me Pink

May 1—The Pink Panther
Director: Bob Richardson **Story:** Cliff Roberts
Animation: Warren Batchelder, Bob Richardson,
Bob Kirk, Bill Hutten. A rain cloud spoils the
Panther's picnic. *[First shown on TV in 1978]*

A rough ride for
the Panther:
Pinto Pink
(1967).

Cat And The Pinkstalk

June 1—The Pink Panther
Director: Dave Detiege **Story:** Tony Benedict -
Animation: Nelson Shin, Bob Bemiller, Virgil
Ross, Walter Kubiak
Jack and the Beanstalk with the Panther as Jack.
First shown on TV in 1978

Doctor Pink

July 1—The Pink Panther
Director: Sid Marcus **Story:** Dave Detiege -
Animation: Bob Matz, John Gibbs, Tiger West,
Tony Love
The Pink Panther is a hospital janitor who
infuriates a doctor. *First shown on TV in 1979*

Dietetic Pink

August 1—The Pink Panther
Director: Sid Marcus **Story:** Cliff Roberts
Animation: Don Williams, Lee Halpern, Bernard
Posner, Joan Case. The Panther tries to stay on a
diet. *First shown on TV in 1978*

Pink Z-Z-Z

September 1—The Pink Panther
Director: Sid Marcus **Story:** Tony Benedict
Animation: Bob Matz, John Gibbs,
Tiger West, Tony Love
The Panther can't
sleep due to an
annoying cat.
First shown on TV in 1978

Pink U.F.O.

October 1—The Pink Panther
Director: Dave Detiege **Story:** Dave Detiege
Animation: Warren Batchelder, Bob Richardson,
Bob Kirk, Bill Hutten
The Pink Panther tries to catch a rare butterfly,
but captures space aliens instead.
First shown on TV in 1978

Star Pink

November 1—The Pink Panther
Director: Art Davis **Story:** John Dunn
Animation: Bob Matz, John Gibbs, Tiger West,
Tony Love. In a galaxy far, far away, the Panther
is a gas station attendant being chased by a
robot. *First shown on TV in 1978*

Pink Press

December 1—The Pink Panther
Director: Art Davis **Story:** John Dunn
Animation: Nelson Shin, Bob Bemiller, Virgil Ross, Walter Kubiak.
The Pink Panther is a reporter trying to get an interview with industrial giant, Howard Huge.
First shown on TV in 1978.

1981

Yankee Doodle Pink

January 1—The Pink Panther
Director: Sid Marcus **Story:** John Dunn
Animation: Norm McCabe, Bob Bransford, Art Vitello, Malcolm Draper
Resoundtrack of Pinky Doodle; first shown on TV in 1978.

Pet Pink Pebbles

February 1—The Pink Panther
Director: Gerry Chiniquy (uncredited: Art Leonardi) **Story:** John Dunn **Animation:** Warren Batchelder, Bob Richardson, Bob Kirk, Bill Hutten. *[Resoundtrack of Rocky Pink; first shown on TV in 1978]*

The Pink Panther in *Rocky Pink* (1976).

The Pink Of Bagdad

March 1—Pink Panther
Director: Art Davis (uncredited: Gerry Chiniquy) **Story:** John Dunn (uncredited: Bob Ogle) **Animation:** Nelson Shin, Bob Bemiller, Virgil Ross, Walter Kubiak (uncredited: Don Williams, Bob Richardson, John Gibbs).
Resoundtrack of The Pink Of Arabee; first shown on TV in 1978]

Pinkologist

April 1—Pink Panther
Director: Gerry Chiniquy **Story:** John Dunn **Animation:** Don Williams, Lee Halpern, Bernard Posner, Joan Case.
The Little Man goes to a psychiatrist and recalls his past problems with the Pink Panther.
Footage reused from previous cartoons; first shown on TV in 1978

Misterjaw the shark.

1995

Driving Mr. Pink

April 12—The Pink Panther
Director: Paul Sabella.
The Panther goes on a wild taxi-cab ride when his cabby turns out to be Voodoo Man.
Released theatrically with the feature film The Pebble and the Penguin.

TV Series

THE PINK PANTHER SHOW (1969) NBC
Pink Panther shorts and Inspector cartoons.

THE PINK PANTHER MEETS THE ANT AND THE AARDVARK (1970) NBC

THE NEW PINK PANTHER SHOW (1971) NBC
The Pink Panther, The Ant and The Aardvark, and The Inspector cartoons

THE PINK PANTHER LAUGH AND A HALF HOUR AND A HALF SHOW (1976) NBC
The Pink Panther Show combined with The Inspector, The Ant and The Aardvark, The Texas Toads (originally "Tijuana Toads" for theatrical release. All voices re-dubbed), and Misterjaw cartoons

The Pique Poquette Of Paris (1966).

Misterjaw Episode Guide

Misterjaw cartoons do not have individual credits. All were made in 1976.

To Catch a Halibut
Misterjaw tries an electro-magnet to catch Harry Halibut.

Shopping Spree
Misterjaw goes on land to get fish from a supermarket.

Flying Fool
Misterjaw tries flying, so he can catch fish like a pelican.

Beach Resort
Misterjaw matches wits with shark hunter Fearless Freddie at a beach resort.

Monster Of The Deep
Misterjaw encounters a ghost.

Showbiz Shark
Misterjaw competes with a porpoise for a spot in the Marina water show.

Moulin Rogues
Misterjaw terrorizes Paris.

The Codfather
Misterjaw strays into the turf of a mob boss when he follows a treasure map to a sunken ship.

Little Red Riding Halibut
Misterjaw disguises as Grandma to trick Harry Halibut out of his basket full of food.

Aladdin's Lump
Misterjaw finds a magic lamp and finds trouble in Monte Carlo, the Sahara and the North Pole.

Davey Jones' Locker
Misterjaw challenges a swordfish to a game of pool.

Flying Saucer
Misterjaw and Catfish are abducted by aliens from outer space.

The Shape Of Things
Misterjaw goes to a gym to lose weight.

Mary Sharkman, Mary Sharkman
Misterjaw versus Fearless Freddie at an oil rig.

Caught In The Act
Misterjaw tries to get past Granny Neptune who has food in her home.

Sea Chase
Fearless Freddie disguises a giant fish in his pursuit of Misterjaw.

Aloha, Hah, Hah!
Misterjaw heckles an old pirate.

Stand-In Room Only
Misterjaw gets to star in his own movie.

Never Shake Hands With a Piranha
Misterjaw tries to elude a piranha in the waters off South America.

The $6.95 Bionic Shark
Misterjaw and Catfish reprogram a robot shark that lands in their backyard.

Transistorized Shark
After Misterjaw swallows a radio, Fearless Freddie tunes into his frequency.

The Fishy Time Machine
Misterjaw and Catfish take a trip back in time to ancient Egypt and Rome.

Shark and the Beanstalk
Climbing a beanstalk in search of a huge meal, Misterjaw tries to escape a Giant's dinner plate.

Holiday in Venice
In Italy, Catfish is kidnapped and Misterjaw comes to the rescue.

The Aquanuts
Misterjaw is captured and becomes an exhibit at Sea World.

Fish Anonymous
Misterjaw goes on a diet.

Cannery Caper
Misterjaw impersonates the president of a fish canning factory.

Deep Sea Rodeo
Misterjaw challenges Seaweed the Seahorse to a duel, wild west style.

Cool Shark
Misterjaw versus a little octopus.

Mama
A baby sea monster mistakes Misterjaw for his mother.

Easy Come, Easy Go
Misterjaw tries to become a house pet.

No Man's Halibut
Misterjaw competes with a man stranded on a deserted island for a halibut meal.

Sweat Hog Shark
Misterjaw and Catfish become motorcycle bikers.

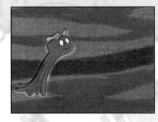

A scene from *Cool Shark* (1976).

THINK PINK PANTHER
Spring 1978 NBC
Old Pink Panther shorts.

ALL NEW PINK PANTHER SHOW
(Fall 1978) NBC
New Pink Panther cartoons (released theatrically between 1978-1981) combined with Crazy Legs Crane.

Crazy Legs Crane Episode Guide

Life With Feather
Crane Brained
King Of The Swamp
Sonic Broom
Winter Blunderland
Storky And Hatch
Fly-by-Knight
Sneaker Snack
Barnacle Bird

Animal Crackups
Jet Feathers
Nest Quest

Bug Off!
Beach Bummer
Flower Power
Trail Of The Lonesome Mine

PINK PANTHER & SONS (1984) CBS Episode Guide

Anney's Invention
Anney accidentally switches briefcases containing her invention plans for science class with Prof. Dilfod's.

Arabian Frights
Panky dreams of crossing a desert to a cave filled with candy. .

Brothers Are Special
Finko and Howl use a tape recorder to cheat their musical abilities in the talent contest.

The Fixup Fowlup
The Pink Panthers try to retrieve a valuable painting they threw out while renovating an old house.

The Great Bumpo
The Pink Panthers give shelter to a runaway Elephant.

A Hard Day's Knight
Panky gets lost in Medieval Manor, where he is chased by robotic knights.

Haunted Howlers
The Pink Panthers solve the mystery of a haunted house.

Insanity Claus
On Christmas Eve, Panky tries to help a Santa Claus who arrives a bit early.

Joking Genie
The Pink Panthers fight over a magic lamp.

Millionaire Murfel
Murfel switches places with a young millionaire.

Mister Money
Pink and Panky try to earn money to buy a gold watch for their father's birthday.

Panky and the Angels
Feeling unwanted, Panky joins the Howl's Angels.

Panky's Pet
While on a tropical cruise, the Panthers find a dinosaur egg.

Pink Encounters of the Panky Kind
Spacemen abduct Panky and replace him with a super-strong robot duplicate.

The Pink Link
The Pink Panthers mistake an escaped "missing link" for their expected cousin Punky.

Pink Shrink
Anney's invention shrinks Rinky to mouse size.

Howl's Angels.

Pinky At The Bat
A baseball game between the Pink Panthers and the How's Angels gang.

Pinky Enemy #1
Pinky, Panky and their friends find a robber who has framed their father by disguising himself as The Pink Panther.

Punkin's Home Companion
Anney invents a pet rock for Punkin.

The Pursuit Of Panky
A secret military invention falls into Panky's diaper.

Rocko's Last Round
The Panther's mistakenly believe Rocko is dying.

Sitter Jitters
Panky tries to join his brothers at the movies.

Sleep Talking Chatta
Sleepwalking Chatta holds a winning contest ticket.

Spinning Wheels
Pinky and Finko race each other in an effort to win a new bike.

Take A Hike
On a hike, the Pink Panthers lose Panky and spend their time looking for him.

Traders Of The Lost Bark
Panky's puppy is lost— and Finko and Howl are after the reward.

THE NEW PINK PANTHER (1993) Episode Guide

60 episodes—two cartoons per episode

1. Pink Pink And Away; Down On The Ant Farm
2. Pink & Quiet; The Pinky 500
3. The Ghost & Mr. Panther; Cleopanthera
4. Big Top Pinky; Yeti 'Nother Big Foot Story
5. Pinky In Paradise; Department Store Pink-erton
6. Moby Pink; The Pink Stuff
7. Pink Pizza; The Pink Painter
8. Pink Paparazzi; Werewolf In Panther's Clothing
9. Rock Me Pink; Pinkis Pantherus
10. Pilgrim Panther; That Old Pink Magic
11. Pink-anthertal Man; Pink Kong
12. The Magnificent Pink One; Downhill Panther
13. 14 Karat Pink; Robo Pink
14. Pink Encounters; Junkyard Pink Blues
15. Patherobics; Pinkenstein

16. Pinky Rider; Midnight Ride of Pink Revere
17. Pinky… He Delivers; Super-Pink's Egg-cellent Adventure
18. Cowboy Pinky; Stealth Panther
19. Pinkazuma's Revenge; Pinky Down Under
20. Pinkadoon; A Comp-Pink We Will Go
21. Icy Pink; The End Of Superpink
22. All For Pink And Pink For All; Service With A Pink Smile
23. Trains, Pains, And Panthers; Wet and Wild Pinky

A scene from The Pinky 500 (1993).

24. From Hair To Eternity; Strike Flea You're Out
25. Cinderpink; It's A Bird! It's A Pain! It's Superfan
26. Who's Smiling Now? (The Inspector); Rob'n Hoodwinked
27. Hook Line & Pinker; Valentine Pink
28. Dino Sour Head; The Lucky of the Pinkish
29. The Inspector...Not (The Inspector); Pink Links
30. Stool Parrot (The Inspector); Pinky And Slusho
31. Panthergeist; Pinky's Pending Pink Slip
32. The Three Pink Porker; The Heart of Pinkness
33. The Inspector's Most Wanted (The Inspector); Pinky Appleseed

THE FEATURE FILMS

THE PINK PANTHER (1964)

Director: Blake Edwards **Screenplay:** Maurice Richlin, Blake Edwards **Producer:** Martin Jurow **Music:** Henry Mancini ("The Pink Panther Theme") **Cinematography:** Philip H. Lathrop **Editor:** Ralph E. Winters **Art Direction:** Fernando Carrere **Costume Design:** Yves Saint-Laurent **Special Effects:** Lee Zavitz **Song:** "It Had Better Be Tonight" (lyrics: Johnny Mercer, Franco Migliacci; music: Henry Mancini) **Animators (title animation):** David H. DePatie, Friz Freleng **Running time:** 113 minutes. **Cast:** David Niven (Sir Charles Litton); Peter Sellers (Inspector Jacques Clouseau); Claudia Cardinale (Princess Dala); Robert Wagner (George Litton); Capucine (Simone Clouseau; Brenda De Banzie (Angela Dunning); Colin Gordon (Tucker) John Le Mesurier (Defense attorney); James Lanphier (Saloud); Guy Thomajan (Artoff); Michael Trubshawe (Novelist); Riccardo Billi (Greek shipowner); Meri Welles (Hollywood starlet); Martin Miller (Photographer); Fran Jeffries (Greek "cousin").
See pp. 16–19 for more information.

A SHOT IN THE DARK (1964)

Director/producer: Blake Edwards **Screenplay:** Blake Edwards, William Peter Blatty, based on the play by Harry Kurnitz and the play l'Idiot by Marcel Achard **Music:** Henry Mancini **Cinematography:** Christopher Challis **Editors:** Bert Bates, Ralph E. Winters **Production Design:** Michael Stringer **Costume Design:** Margaret Furse **Song:** "Shadows of Paris" (lyrics: Robert Wells; music: Henry Mancini) **Animators (title animation):** David H. DePatie, Friz Freleng **Running time:** 101 minutes.
Cast: Peter Sellers (Inspector Jacques Clouseau); Elke Sommer (Maria Gambrelli); George Sanders (Benjamin Ballon); Herbert Lom (Charles Dreyfus); Tracy Reed (Dominique Ballon); Graham Stark (Hercule Lajoy); Moira Redmond (Simone); Vanda Godsell (Madame LaFarge); Maurice Kaufmann (Pierre); Ann Lynn (Dudu); David Lodge (Georges); André Maranne (François); Martin Benson (Maurice); Burt Kwouk (Cato); Reginald Beckwith (Receptionist at Camp); Douglas Wilmer (Henri LaFarge); Bryan Forbes, as Turk Thrust (Camp Attendant), Andre Charisse (Game Warden); Howard Greene (Gendarme); John Herrington (Doctor); Jack Melford (Psychoanalyst); Victor Baring (Taxi Driver); Victor Beaumont (Gendarme); Tutte Lemkow; (Cossack Dancer).
See pp. 26–31 for more information.

INSPECTOR CLOUSEAU (1968)

Director: Bud Yorkin **Screenplay:** Frank Waldman, Tom Waldman, Blake Edwards **Producer:** Lewis J. Rachmil **Music:** Ken Thorne **Cinematography:** Arthur Ibbetson **Editor:** John Victor-Smith **Art Direction:** Norman Dorme **Costume Design:** Ivy Baker, Dinah Greet **Production Design:** Michael Stringer **Animators (title cartoon):** David H. DePatie, Friz Freleng.
Running time: 96 minutes.
Cast: Alan Arkin (Insp. Jacques Clouseau), Frank Finlay (Supt. Weaver), Delia Boccardo (Lisa Morrel), Beryl Reid (Mrs. Weaver), Patrick Cargill (Commissioner Braithwaite), John Bindon (Bull Parker), Susan Engel (Policewoman Carmichael), Barry Foster (Addison Steele), Clive Francis (Clyde Hargreaves), Anthony Ainley (Bomber LeBec), Tutte Lemkow (Frenchie LeBec).
See pages 36-37 for more information.

THE RETURN OF THE PINK PANTHER (1975)

Unfortunately, at the time of this book's publication, rights to show images and material from this movie were not available.
Director/producer: Blake Edwards **Screenplay:** Frank Waldman, Blake Edwards **Music:** Henry Mancini **Lyricist:** Hal David **Associate Producer:** Tony Adams **Cinematography:** Geoffrey Unsworth **Editor:** Tom Priestley **Production Design:** Peter Mullins **Special Effects:** John Gant **Animator (title animation):** Ken Harris **Production Supervisor:** Derek Kavanagh **Running time:** 113 mins.
Cast: Peter Sellers (Clouseau), Christopher Plummer (Sir Charles Litton), Catherine Schell (Lady Claudine Litton), Herbert Lom (Chief Insp. Dreyfus), Peter Arne (Col. Sharky), Peter Jeffrey (Gen. Wadafi), Grégoire Aslan (Chief of Lugash Police), David Lodge (Mac), Burt Kwouk (Cato), Graham Stark (Pepi).

A scene from *Cleopanthra* (1993).

Voodoo Man

TV SPECIALS

A PINK CHRISTMAS -

December 7th, 1978—ABC
Director: Bill Perez **Written by:** Friz Freleng, John Dunn, adapted from O'Henry's *The Cop and The Anthem* **Producers:** David H. DePatie, Friz Freleng **Music:** Doug Goodwin **Lyrics:** Johnny Bradford **Backgrounds:** Paul Julian, Consuelo Julian **Animators:** Warren Batchelder, Art Davis, Malcolm Draper, John Gibbs, Art Leonardi, Bob Matz, Tom Ray, Nelson Shim, Don Williams, Art Vitello.
The homeless Pink Panther has many misadventures in an attempt to gain food and shelter on Christmas night.

A scene from *Pink Christmas* (1978).

OLYM-PINKS

February 22nd, 1980—ABC
Director: Friz Freleng **Producers:** David H. DePatie, Friz Freleng **Story:** Friz Freleng, John Dunn, Dave Detiege **Sequence Directors:** Gerry Chiniquy, Art Davis, Art Leonardi.
Animators: Warren Batchelder, Bob Bransford, Malcolm Draper, John Gibbs, Art Bob Bemiller, Bob Matz, Tom Ray, Nelson Shim, Don Williams, Art Vitello. **Backgrounds:** Richard H. Thomas **Music:** Rob Walsh
The Pink Panther challenges The Little Man in the Olympic winter games.

A scene from *Olym-Pinks* (1980).

PINK AT FIRST SIGHT

May 10th, 1981—ABC
Director: Bob Richardson **Producer:** David DePatie **Written by:** Owen Crump, D.W. Owen **Sequence Directors:** Nelson Shin, Art Vitello. **Music:** Stephen DePatie **Animators:** Lee Halperin, Bob Bransford, Malcolm Draper, John Gibbs, Art Bob Bemiller, Tom Ray, Nelson Shin, Norm McCabe, Jim Davis, Al Wilzbach, Joe Roman, Norton Virgien, Lloyd Vaughn, Ruth Kissane, Bill Hutten **Voices:** Frank Welker, Weaver Copeland, Brian Cummings, Marilyn Schreffler, Hal Smith
A Marvel Production.
A lovelorn Pink Panther fantasizes about meeting the perfect lady panther while working as a singing messenger.

THE PINK PANTHER STRIKES AGAIN (1976)

Director/producer: Blake Edwards **Screenplay:** Blake Edwards, Frank Waldman **Music:** Henry Mancini **Lyricist:** Don Black **Associate Producer:** Tony Adams **Cinematography:** Harry Waxman **Editor:** Alan Jones **Art Direction:** John Siddall **Production Design:** Peter Mullins **Production Supervisor:** Derek Kavanagh **Costume Design:** Tiny Nicholls, Bridget Sellers **Special Effects:** Kit West **Singers:** Tom Jones ("Come to Me"); Julie Andrews ("Until You Love Me") **Titles designer/producer:** Richard Williams
Running time: 103 mins.
Cast: Peter Sellers (Clouseau), Herbert Lom (Dreyfus), Lesley-Anne Down (Olga Bariosova), Burt Kwouk (Cato), Colin Blakely (Alec Drummond), Leonard Rossiter (Insp. Quinlan), André Maranne (François), Byron Kane (Kissinger), Dick Crockett (President), Richard Vernon (Professor Hugo Fassbender), Briony McRoberts (Margo Fassbender).
See pages 66–71 for more information.

REVENGE OF THE PINK PANTHER (1978)

Director: Blake Edwards **Screenplay:** Blake Edwards, Frank Waldman, Ron Clark **Producers:** Blake Edwards, Peter Sellers **Music:** Henry Mancini **Executive Producer:** Tony Adams **Associate Producers:** Derek Kavanagh, Ken Wales **Cinematography:** Ernest Day **Editor:** Alan Jones **Art Direction:** Benjamin Fernandez, John Siddall **Production Design:** Peter Mullins **Production Manager:** John Comfort **Costume Design:** Tiny Nicholls **Special Effects:** Brian Johnson, Dennis Lowe **Animators (title animation):** David H. DePatie, Friz Freleng **Designers (title sequence):** Art Leonardi, John Dunn **Running time:** 104 mins
Cast: Peter Sellers (Clouseau), Herbert Lom (Dreyfus), Burt Kwouk (Cato), Dyan Cannon (Simone Legree), Robert Webber (Philippe Douvier), Tony Beckley (Guy Algo), Robert Loggia (Al Marchione), Paul Stewart (Julio Scallini), André Maranne (François), Graham Stark (Professor Auguste Balls).
See pages 76–79 for more information.

TRAIL OF THE PINK PANTHER (1982)

Director: Blake Edwards **Screenplay:** Frank Waldman, Tom Waldman, Blake Edwards, Geoffrey Edwards **Producers:** Tony Adams, Blake Edwards **Music:** Henry Mancini **Cinematography:** Dick Bush **Film Editing:** Alan Jones **Production Design:** Peter Mullins **Art Direction:** Tim Hutchinson, John Siddall, Alan Tomkins **Set Decoration:** Jack Stephens **Costume Design:** Patricia Edwards **Title animation:** Art Leonardi, Marvel Productions **Running time:** 96 minutes
Cast: Peter Sellers (Clouseau), David Niven (Sir Charles Litton), Herbert Lom (Chief Insp. Charles Dreyfus) Richard Mulligan (Clouseau's Father), Joanna Lumley (Marie Jouvet), Capucine (Lady Simone Litton), Robert Loggia (Bruno Langois), Harvey Korman (Prof. Auguste Balls), Burt Kwouk (Cato Fong), Graham Stark (Hercule Lajoy).
See pages 82–85 for more information.

CURSE OF THE PINK PANTHER (1983)

Director: Blake Edwards **Screenplay:** Blake Edwards, Geoffrey Edwards **Producers:** Tony Adams, Blake Edwards **Music:** Henry Mancini **Cinematography:** Dick Bush **Film Editing:** Robert Hathaway, Ralph E. Winters **Production Designer:** Peter Mullins **Art Directors:** Tim Hutchinson, John Siddall, Alan Tomkins **Costume Designer:** Patricia Edwards **Stunt coordinator:** Joe Dunne **Animated title designer:** Arthur Leonardi
Running time: 109 minutes
Cast: Ted Wass (Sergeant Clifton Sleigh), David Niven (Sir Charles Litton), Robert Wagner (George Litton), Herbert Lom (Chief Insp. Dreyfus), Capucine (Lady Simone Litton), Joanna Lumley (Countess Chandra), Robert Loggia (Bruno Langois), Harvey Korman (Prof. Auguste Balls), Burt Kwouk (Cato Fong), Roger Moore (Clouseau), Leslie Ash (Juleta Shane), Denise Crosby (Bruno's Moll), Graham Stark (bored waiter).
See pages 90–91 for more information.

SON OF THE PINK PANTHER (1993)

Director Blake Edwards **Screenplay** Blake Edwards, Madeline Sunshine, Steven Sunshine **Producer** Tony Adams **Music** Henry Mancini **Cinematography** Dick Bush **Film Editor** Robert Pergament **Casting** Nancy Klopper **Production Designer** Peter Mullins **Art Direction** David Minty, John Siddall, Leslie Tomkins **Set Decoration** Peter Howitt **Animation** Bill Kroyer **Running time:** 93 minutes
Cast: Roberto Benigni (Jacques Gambrelli), Herbert Lom (Commissioner Charles Dreyfus), Claudia Cardinale (Maria Gambrelli), Shabana Azmi (Queen), Debrah Farentino (Princess Yasmin), Jennifer Edwards (Yussa), Robert Davi (Hans), Burt Kwouk (Cato Fong), Graham Stark (Professor Auguste Balls), Mark Schneider (Arnon), Anton Rodgers (Police Chief Charles Lazar).
See pages 98–101 for more information.

THE PINK PANTHER (2005)

Director: Shawn Levy **Story:** Len Blum, Michael Saltzman **Screenplay:** Len Blum and Steve Martin; based on characters created by Maurice Richlin and Blake Edwards; based on the Pink Panther films of Blake Edwards **Producer:** Robert Simonds **Executive Producers:** Tracey Trench, Ira Shuman **Music:** David Newman **Music Supervisor:** Randall Poster **Costume Design:** Joseph G. Aulisi **Editors:** George Folsey Jr. A.C.E., Brad E. Wilhite **Production Design:** Lilly Kilvert **Photography:** Jonathan Brown **Cast:** Steve Martin (Inspector Jacques Clouseau), Beyoncé Knowles (Xania), Kevin Kline (Dreyfus), Jean Reno (Ponton), Emily Mortimer (Nicole), Kristin Chenoweth (Chérie), William Abadie (Bizu), Scott Adkins (Jacquard), Henry Czerny (Yuri), Roger Rees (Larocque).
See pages 116–121 for more information.

The 40th Anniversary Pink Panther features DVD box set; artwork by Shag.

FRIZ FRELENG REMEMBERED

ISADORE "FRIZ" FRELENG remains a legendary figure in the field of animation. One of the architects of Warner Bros.' Looney Tunes studio, he created the characters Porky Pig, Sylvester the cat, and Yosemite Sam (he was also the inspiration for Sam's fiery personality!), directed Oscar®-winning cartoons starring Tweety and Speedy Gonzales, and was one of several fathers to the most popular of all Looney Tunes' characters, Bugs Bunny. Friz Freleng had a rare talent for animating characters to a musical theme, and this specialty gave rise to his greatest-ever triumph, the one-and-only Pink Panther.

As a Young Man

Born in Kansas City on August 21, 1905, Freleng dreamed of becoming a newspaper cartoonist. His first art job out of high school was for the Kansas City Film Ad Co., working alongside fledgling animators Hugh Harman and Ub Iwerks. They soon joined their former colleague Walt Disney in California and urged Freleng to follow suit. Friz went out west in 1927 but the job didn't work out. Friz had his own, decidedly un-Disney-like ideas. Freleng then spent several years animating in Kansas City and in New York, returning to California two years later to work for Leon Schlesinger, who had just begun a new series of animated shorts for Warner Bros. called *Looney Tunes*.

Achievements

Fifteen cartoons directed by Freleng have been nominated for Academy Awards®, with five winning. He won three Emmy Awards® (one pictured at right), two for producing Dr. Seuss specials and one for directing an ABC After School movie. He was honored by The American Film Institute and the British Film Institute with major retrospectives of his work and in 1985, the Museum of Modern Art honored Freleng as part of their golden anniversary salute to Warner Bros. Animation. In August 1992, Friz was honored with his own star on the Hollywood Walk of Fame.

DePatie-Freleng

Freleng's greatest career move came with his partnership with David DePatie. It began in 1963 and gave Friz more control over his work. The company had unique success in theatrical shorts, television programming, commercials, and movies.

The Pink Panther

Everything Friz pioneered, perfected and practiced during his 32-year career at Warner Bros. culminated with the creation of the Pink Panther: the cool design, the jazzy musical score, the character's actions set to a musical beat, and the hilarious gags. An instant classic born in a single, three-and-a-half-minute sequence and a cartoon star that summed up a lifetime desire to entertain, The Pink Panther earned Freleng his final and most satisfying Academy Award®.

This full page ad appeared in the Hollywood trade papers as a tribute to Friz within days of his passing on May 26, 1995.

Highlights of Friz's career include Rhapsody In Rivets *(1941), in which characters build a skyscraper to the tune of Liszt's* Hungarian Rhapsody; Life With Feathers *(1945) the debut of Sylvester the cat;* The Three Little Bops *(1957), a jazzy take-off of* The Three Little Pigs; *and* Knighty Knight Bugs *(1958) the only Bugs Bunny cartoon to win an Oscar®.*

AFTERWORD BY ART LEONARDI

THE PINK PANTHER has played a pivotal part in my life. I first met the Panther when I rejoined my animation colleagues at a new studio called DePatie-Freleng Enterprises in 1964. I had previously worked for producer David DePatie and director Friz Freleng at Warner Bros., where we made made Looney Tunes, featuring Bugs Bunny, Daffy Duck, Tweety and Sylvester.

"In 1964 this new studio was bursting with great ideas, fresh designs and new characters. My role was initially as a trouble-shooter—to fix scenes, design title cards, clean up and correct animation, and touch up background paintings. I was soon writing, directing, designing and doing just about anything else David and Friz could think up. I've been with the Panther now for over 40 years.

"I have to admire the hard work Friz, Hawley Pratt, Bob McKimson, John Dunn, Gerry Chiniquy, Art Davis and the rest of the crew did in those early days. We had a lot of crazy fun at the studio, but the final result was always top-notch, Academy-Award® level, quality cartoons. Friz was a character, a living legend and a great friend. He could spot talent and knew how to use it. Without him, The Pink Panther's personality and charm would be a different animal.

"Hawley Pratt styled the original Pink Panther, under Friz's guidance, and was a master of animation

Friz Freleng thanks Art for his contribution to The Pink Panther series.

ART
BEST WISHES
AND THANKS FOR
YOUR CONTRIBUTIONS
TO THE FIRST SUCCESSES
FROM
FRIZ

design and direction. I learned a lot from him and he should be remembered as one of the true greats.

"My colleague Gerry Chiniquy directed The Inspector and Deux-Deux cartoons and gave them a unique style. One of the things that made The Inspector cartoons soar was the beautiful background paintings of Tom Yakutis.

"John Dunn was a good friend whom I admired for his wonderful and wacky writing. He wrote the funniest, most original, cartoon shorts we did.

"John Burton Jr. also deserves special mention. He was, in my estimation, the finest animation cameraman in the business. He figured out all the techniques and mechanics. That optical 'jewel' effect at the start of every Pink Panther cartoon was his invention.

"As for me, to have been there when the Panther was

Art and Shirley's children Dawn and Lisa standing behind an Aardvark cut out in the mid 1970s.

born in '64, and to help shape his character in various capacities through theatrical shorts, TV shows, specials, and commercials—and my proudest moment: writing, boarding, designing and directing the opening titles for *Revenge of the Pink Panther*—has been a blast. Kids sometimes ask me if The Pink Panther is real. He is real to me. I work with the Panther every day, drawing the best pictures of him that I can. His theme song is always playing in my head. We had a great time putting him on the screen and I'm delighted that I played a part in creating an animation classic."

Art drew this spectacular Pink Panther horoscope chart in the mid 1980s.

New Fans

I was asked to go to my grandson Alex's grade school class and talk about what I do. On the blackboard I drew a picture of The Pink Panther and told the kids how we make cartoons. I drew a Pink Panther cartoon for each student and in return, the kids each sent me a thank-you letter and their own drawing of the Panther. These drawings are now prized possessions—and a testament to the popularity of this great character.

The teacher later told Art that the kids wouldn't let her erase a picture of The Pink Panther he had drawn on the blackboard. It stayed there the entire semester, and the teacher had to work around it.

Art with author Jerry Beck, who is holding a mocked up copy of this book!

INDEX

ACKNOWLEDGMENTS

The Author would especially like to thank the following people: Art Leonardi; David DePatie; Charles Brubaker—http://dfe.toonzone.net/; Dave Mackey—http://www.davemackey.com/animation/; Mike Kazaleh; Elaine Piechowski; Julia Tapia; Shawn Levy; Steve Martin; Josh Agle (Shag); Hope Freleng; Amid Amidi; Mark Kausler; Leonard Maltin Marea Boylan–http://www.cartoonbrew.com/; http://www.cartoonresearch.com/

Dorling Kindersley would like to thank the following people: Elaine Piechowski at MGM for all her help; Art Leonardi for his fabulous artwork; Paul Gilbert for loan of his Pink Panther collection; Howard Sidebottom for Pink Panther DVDs; Julia March for editorial assistance; Ann Barrett for the index.

MGM would like to thank the following people: Hope and Sybil Freleng and Ginny Mancini for availing to us their personal archives; David DePatie, Steve Martin, Shawn Levy, Shag and Art Leonardi for their time and insight; the Tapias for their collection; Jerry Beck for his wealth of knowledge, Alastair, Guy, Jill and Alex at DK for their talent and vision, AJ, Kristen, Jennifer and Travis at MGM who made this book a priority; the Niven and Sellers' estates, Walter Mirisch, Dyan Cannon, Roberto Benigni, Lesley-Anne Down, Graham Stark, Burt Kwouk, Elke Sommer, Joanna Lumley, Sol Rosenthal, John Byner, Doug Goodwin and the gentleman who started it all, Blake Edwards—thank you.

The Publisher would like to thank the following for their kind permission to reproduce their photographs. Key: a=above; b=below; c=center; l=left; r=right; t=top
Corbis: Tania Midgley 81tl; Gail Mooney 81cl; DK Images: 36br; Kim Sayer 92br.
Image of PINK PANTHER PENCIL BY NUMBERS [74c] and THE PINK PANTHER GAME [75tr] © 2005 Hasbro, Inc. Used with permission.
Image of MATTEL CHATTER CHUM [74l] used with permission from Mattel, Inc. All Rights Reserved.
Image of inflatable Pink Panther [95r] reproduced with the permission of Ringling Bros.-Barnum & Bailey Combined Shows, Inc. RINGLING BROS. AND BARNUM & BAILEY® and THE GREATEST SHOW ON EARTH® are federally registered trademarks and service marks of Ringling Bros.–Barnum & Bailey Combined Shows, Inc.
Image of The BURGER KING® Big Kids meal [105tr] is used with permission from Burger King Brands, Inc.
Special photography of Pink Panther memorabilia by Jack Foley.